MW00929828

The Laura Black Scottsdale Mystery Series

The Laura Black
Scottsdale Mystery Series
by B A Trimmer

~~~~

Scottsdale Shadow

Scottsdale Shadow

B A Trimmer

Saguaro Sky Media Co.
Scottsdale, Arizona, USA

Editors: 'Andi' Anderson and Kimberly Mathews
Cover Design: Tammy Malunas
ISBN-13: 978-1093720228
Saguaro Sky Media Co., Scottsdale, Arizona, USA
050119

E-mail the author at:
LauraBlackScottsdale@gmail.com

For my baby sister Stacey.
Gone too soon.

Thanks to:
Katie Hilbert, Kendall Cusick,
Bonnie Costilow, Jeanette Ellmer,
Barbara Hackel, Cari Gray,
and Tony Tumminello

Scottsdale Shadow

Introduction

If you've never read a Laura Black Scottsdale mystery, you can start with *Scottsdale Heat*, the first book in the series. If you'd rather start with this book, here are a few of the people you'll need to know:

Laura Black – Works as an investigator in a Scottsdale Arizona law firm. She'd love to make the world a better place, but she also has bills to pay.

Sophia Rodriguez – Laura's best friend who works in the law office as the receptionist and paralegal. She sometimes gets to help Laura in her investigations. Sophie's a former California surfer chick and a free spirit who enjoys dating multiple men at the same time.

Gina Rondinelli – Laura's other best friend. She's a former Scottsdale police detective and the law firm's senior investigator. She has a strict moral code and likes playing by the rules.

Leonard Shapiro – Head of the law firm. He has no people skills, but with the help of Laura, Sophie, and Gina, he usually wins his cases.

Anthony "Tough Tony" DiCenzo – Head of the local crime family. He likes Laura and almost thinks of her as a daughter. Through various adventures over the past several months, he owes Laura several favors.

Maximilian – Laura's boyfriend and number two man in the local crime family. Before coming to Scottsdale, he was a secret operative for the U.S. government, mainly working in Eastern Europe. For Laura's safety, they need to keep their relationship a secret.

Gabriella – A former government operative from somewhere in Eastern Europe. She currently works as a bodyguard for Tony and Max. She takes pleasure in hurting men.

Danielle Ortega – Laura's friend and the head of a rival local crime organization. Her father is Escobar Salazar, the ruthless head of an international drug cartel called the *Muerte Negro* or Black Death.

Milo and Snake – Sophie's main boyfriends. Milo works as a mid-level minion for Tough Tony DiCenzo and Snake is the third-string quarterback for the Arizona Cardinals.

Grandma Peckham – Laura's longtime neighbor. She recently became engaged to a man named Grandpa Bob.

Chapter One

November is a time of change in Scottsdale. The slow and measured pace of the hot summer months changes to a high-pitched frenzy as paradise weather returns to the Valley of the Sun. The Beeline Highway becomes clogged with thousands of winter visitors, or Snowbirds as the locals call them, streaming down in their RV's from parts of the country that have already been hit by a blizzard or two.

Thanksgiving is known as the official start of Snowbird season. In anticipation of this, the trickle of northerners in October becomes a flood in November. Once the Snowbirds arrive, they all want to eat at the best restaurants, play at the best golf courses, and shop at the best stores. This is great for the Scottsdale economy, but plays havoc on us working girls who are only trying to get along. Snowbirds don't know how to drive, how to call ahead for a reservation, or how to stand in line. Good luck trying to get a doctor or dentist appointment when the winter visitors are in town. By the time Thanksgiving rolls around each year, I start wishing for Easter, the official end of Snowbird season.

~~~~

"Why am I doing this?" Sophie asked, for about the fifth time.

"I keep telling you," I said as we stood in the living room of a beautiful sixth-floor condo, located a little north of the Scottsdale Fashion Square. "My spy cameras normally broadcast the video with radio waves. But there's something about this building that won't let the signals through. I've already wasted three days trying to make them work. I needed to switch to the type of camera that stores the video on memory cards. But with these cameras, I need to come here every day to change out the memory cards and put fresh batteries in all the cameras."

"I get that part," she said. "I mean, why am I here with you? Why can't you do this by yourself?"

"I told you, the husband, Chet, works from home. He's the bookkeeper for the business he owns with his wife. Every day he goes out for cigarettes and lunch at around eleven thirty. He's only out of the apartment for twenty-five or thirty minutes. I almost got caught yesterday when he came home early. I need a faster way to change everything out. I'll show you where the cameras are and tomorrow you can do half of them. I'll do the other half and we'll both get out of here with plenty of time to spare. Besides, I thought you liked getting out of the office."

"I do like getting out, but how long are we going to have to do this?"

"Until we get videos of him together with his girlfriend. The wife thinks she's an instructor named Angie who works at the Pilates studio they own. The wife thinks Angie comes over to the apartment during the day while she's at work. Once we get proof of Chet having the affair, we're done. Why are you so grouchy? You know how this works."

"Yeah, I know how it works. But you're the one who likes to go out and do the spy stuff. I like it when we can do something fun and exciting, like the time we went to Sedona with Suzie Lu. Remember? We found that rock to stand on where everything was so pretty. Then there was the time we went on that road trip to Mexico to find Jackie. That was great."

"The only reason you thought it was fun was because you spent the entire time drinking margaritas and sangria."

"Well, yeah, that helped. But sneaking around somebody's house isn't a lot of fun. I can see why you're always grumbling about it."

We walked into the den and I showed Sophie where I'd hidden the camera, next to a Boston fern on a shelf facing the desk.

"After you replace the memory card and the battery, make sure the camera's facing the couch, or the bed, or wherever looks like the most likely place for sex."

"I can do that. How many of these camera things are in the apartment?"

"Seven. I put one in every room."

Sophie picked up the camera and looked at it. "Hey, this camera's cute. It looks like a little cat statue. He'll never know it's a camera, even if he happens to see it on the shelf."

"That's the idea. I have cameras that look like statues, picture frames, and tissue boxes. He'll assume the wife bought everything and put them on the shelves."

For the next five minutes, I showed Sophie how to change out the batteries and where to insert the fresh memory cards.

"Okay," Sophie said as we finished up the camera in the bathroom. "Where next?"

"One in the master and one in the living room. After that, let's get out of here. We're going too slow as it is."

We both froze at the distinctive sound of a key sliding into the lock of the main door in the living room. Sophie heard it at the same time as I did.

"Thirty minutes?" she asked in an annoyed whisper. "That couldn't have been more than fifteen minutes, tops."

"Maybe he forgot something. Let's hide and wait for him to leave again."

We slipped into the guest bedroom and I slowly closed the door. Sophie was giving me a look that said she still wasn't happy about being a spy.

We heard someone making noise in the living room. I silently hoped he didn't need to come into the guest bedroom to get whatever he'd forgotten. We then heard a woman's voice. A man's voice I assumed to be Chet answered her and their voices grew louder as they walked back towards the bedrooms. Sophie's eyes grew big as we waited to see which room they'd end up in.

We heard more noises as they moved into the master and I breathed a sigh of relief. We then sat on the bed and waited a few minutes, hoping they'd leave. Instead, we began to hear the unmistakable sounds of a woman's needs being attended to.

"Wow," Sophie whispered. "She's really loud. At least they didn't come in here."

"But we haven't changed out the battery or the memory card of the camera in the master bedroom. I doubt we're recording a thing."

"You mean they're in there right now having sex and just because you don't have a working camera in the room, we're going to have to keep coming back over here every day until you do happen to catch them?"

"Yeah," I whispered. "There's nothing else we can do."

We sat on the bed for a little while longer. If anything, the woman's moans were getting louder. In addition to the moaning, she'd started slapping her hand on the bed and doing the "Oh my God, Oh my God," thing.

"You know," Sophie said. "Listening to her in there is sorta getting me worked up."

"Yeah," I said. "It happens to me too. I start having fantasies of Max whenever I hear it."

"Damn. I'm thinking I might have to call one of my honeys

tonight for a quickie."

We continued to sit on the bed, listening to the woman pound on the bed and moan.

"You end up doing this a lot, don't you?" Sophie asked.

"Yup," I said. "But this time isn't so bad. The last time, I was stuck in a closet and it was really hot."

"What about the camera in your cell phone? Why don't you just walk in and catch 'em in the act."

"We can't do that in a condominium. It wouldn't be safe."

"Hey, didn't you and Gina do the exact same thing, like a month ago, with Timothy and Crystal in the gym?"

"That was different. It was a public place. I don't want this guy to pull a gun out of the nightstand and shoot us as home invaders."

"I think you're worrying too much," Sophie said as she pulled her phone out of her purse. "I don't know about you, but I don't want to have to keep coming over here every day. It's going to mess up my lunch hour."

I saw her setting the camera to video mode and knew what she was about to do.

Shit.

"Fine," I said. "If you don't mind getting shot at, let's get this over with."

I pushed open the guest bedroom door and we walked out into the hallway. The door to the master was open, so we crept down the hall until we had an unobstructed view of the two of them on the bed. We then stood there for almost five minutes shooting video.

After the initial shock of watching two naked people having sex, I was able to get a handle on what I was seeing. The woman was about our age, maybe a few years older, had straight blonde hair, and a body that was incredibly toned. She was riding him cowgirl and was still making a lot of noise. Chet was older, pale, and a little pudgy. Clearly, he was someone who didn't get out of his condominium a lot.

After about five minutes, I knew we had more than enough for what we needed. I motioned to Sophie that it was time to go, while they were still distracted. We'd started to slowly back up the hallway when Chet noticed we were filming them.

"What the hell!" Chet yelled as he pushed the woman off him. She got off the bed and looked back and forth between him and us, visibly confused.

Why do I keep having arguments with angry naked people?

Chet sat up on the bed and seemed stunned. His eyes were darting around the room, like he was trying to process what was happening. I knew I should say something before his jumbled thoughts turned violent and things got out of hand.

"We're here with the permission of your wife," I said. "We work for her attorney at Halftown, Oeding, Shapiro, and Hopkins."

"Why are you taking pictures of us?" the blonde girl, who I assumed was Angie, asked.

"Before they got married," Sophie said, "Chet and his wife signed a pre-nup that would give his wife jack squat when they divorced. Unfortunately, the agreement also had a clause that voided it if Chet wasn't faithful. You'd be surprised how many guys let the woman slip that one in. We get 'em all the time."

Angie looked over at Chet. Her hands were on her hips and she was starting to get angry. "You said you were going to keep everything after the divorce."

"Oh, that was with the pre-nup," Sophie said. "Now he's blown that and everything goes back to plain old Arizona family court."

"What does that mean?" Angie asked.

"It means they split everything fifty-fifty and the wife will likely get all the good stuff, seeing how the husband's such a low-life cheating scumbag and all."

"What about Chet's company, the Pilates studio? Who'll get that?"

"Well," I said. "The business amounts to about eighty percent of the marital assets. There's no way one side or the other would get the entire thing. Chet and his wife will either need to agree to run it together or more likely, the judge will make them sell it and they'll split the proceeds."

"There's no way in hell I'm handing my company over to my wife," Chet said, now coming back to reality. "I'll run it into the ground before I let her have any of it."

"Of course," Sophie said to Angie. "From what I've read, Chet here's already taken out a ton of loans against the company. I don't think either side will get a lot out of it when they sell it."

"Well shit," Angie said. "I was hoping to run the place after the divorce. I have a finance degree and Chet's completely inept when it comes to business."

"What?" Chet stammered as he looked at Angie.

Sophie looked between Chet and Angie. "Sorry, but I'm thinking that's not going to happen now. But if you really want to help run the place, maybe you could contact whoever buys the studio after Chet sells it. They'll probably need help getting the finances back in shape."

"That's a great idea," Angie said. "I already know the business better than anyone."

"Angie?" Chet whined, acting all hurt.

I had a thought. "If you could get a bank to loan you the money, maybe you could buy it yourself."

Angie thought about it for a few seconds, then smiled. "Yeah, you know, I bet I probably could. My credit's pretty good and I have a paid-off house I could use as collateral."

Chet seemed to have pulled himself together and was becoming angry. "What if I grabbed your phone and tossed it out the window?" he asked in a snotty voice. "Then you'd have nothing. It would be my word against yours."

"Oh," Sophie said, "while everyone was standing around talking, I uploaded a copy of the video to the computer at the law office. You can break the phone into a thousand pieces and it won't change anything." Sophie held it out to him. "Here, if it'll make you feel better, go ahead and smash it. The battery's starting to go and I wouldn't mind if my boss bought me a new one."

Hearing this seemed to deflate Chet. He let out a long sigh and slowly fell back against the pillows.

Angie looked at Chet and then over to us.

"Um, I'm on my lunch hour at the studio," she said. "After I get dressed, can I get a ride back with you guys?"

"Sure," Sophie said. "As long as you don't mind being seen in a piece of crap car."

"Hey," I said. "That's my car you're talking about." I looked over at Angie. "I'll be glad to give you a ride, but would you mind taking a shower before we go? Because, you know, eeewww."

~~~~

My name's Laura Black. I'm a Scottsdale native and I can't see myself living anywhere else. I got a bachelor's degree in philosophy from Arizona State University in Tempe and I put it to use as a bartender at Greasewood Flat, one of the more popular bars with tourists in the Valley of the Sun. A few years ago, I happened to meet Sophie at a Paradise Park concert. As we talked, she said there was an opening as an investigator at the law firm she worked at. I got the position, but I was terrible at it. I hated the job and I was always on the verge of quitting or being fired by Lenny. But then, Gina took me under her wing and spent six months training me in the basics of investigation, legal theory, and self-defense. Since then, I've moved from terrible to passable. I usually enjoy the job, but some of the people I have to deal with sometimes get me a little down.

~~~~

The next morning, I was sitting in the reception area of the law office, talking with Sophie. Getting the evidence of Chet's unfaithfulness had been my only assignment. With Sophie's video safely stored on the office computer system, I was free until a new assignment came in. I decided to stop by the office and see if Sophie or Gina would be around for lunch.

"Was it just me?" Sophie asked. "Or, yesterday, did Chet seem a little pudgy for someone who owned a Pilates studio?"

"Yeah," I said. "I was thinking the same thing. I guess I was expecting someone who looked a little more motivating. Maybe that's why the finances of the place were in such bad shape."

I looked around the office. In the week since I'd last been in, the stacks of files on Sophie's desk and on the end tables had started to grow again. I looked into the conference room and file folders were covering the conference table again. "Are you still protesting Lenny not hiring another admin to do the filing?"

"Yup. My work load keeps growing. He knows that. He didn't have a problem hiring Annie to help me over the summer. She was great. She kept the place looking good and I was able to concentrate on the paralegal and the billing. But when she quit, Lenny suddenly didn't want to pay to have anyone else help me. He even started to bitch when Danielle was here for those couple of days last month. If he doesn't want to pay to have the files taken care of the way he likes, I'll use my own system. The important files are here on my desk. The ones I'll need soon are there on the coffee table. And long-term storage is in the conference room."

"How do you keep track of everything?"

"As long as no one moves anything, I can pretty much remember where I put what I need."

"Well, I hope Lenny gets someone in for you soon. It looks like a disaster in here."

Sophie looked at me and I could see her thinking. "Why are you being so grumpy today?" she asked. "You finished your assignment in under a week. That's like a record. I thought you'd be thrilled."

"Sure, I'm done, but the only reason I'm done is because you decided to go rogue and film them having sex directly."

"I know. Although, I think we told Lenny too much about our visit at Chet's. He's already lectured me about our methods. He went on about how we shouldn't have discussed details of the case with Chet, especially with a third party in the room. But hey, it worked. I'm thinking you should make it part of your standard procedure. Hide in the house and pop out with your camera whenever you hear someone having sex. It would save you a lot of time."

"Yes, but it would eventually get me shot, or at the very least get me into fights with sweaty naked men. Eeewww."

Sophie paused, stared into space for a moment, then her lips quirked up in a slight smile. Apparently, fighting with sweaty naked men was something she'd never considered before. After a moment she shook it off. "Okay, but that still doesn't explain why you're so glum. Normally you're happy between assignments. Is it because you changed your hair back? I loved the way it came out when you were trying to make yourself look like Danielle. You two looked like identical twins."

"I know, and that's part of the reason I changed it back. I didn't want someone on the street mistaking me for the head of a vicious drug smuggling gang. Actually, I'm glad my hair's back to the way it was. I didn't mind the color so much, but the extensions felt weird. Besides, Lenny kept looking at me. He never said anything, but he could tell something was up."

"So, why so moody?"

"Honestly, it's because each new assignment is as bad as the last. I'm getting tired of hiding in closets and filming naked people having sex. It's frustrating and a little depressing. Every once in a while, I'd like to work an assignment that's different, maybe with a little adventure."

"What, like James Bond or Lara Croft? Are you looking to go somewhere exotic and dangerous? Meet some hot men, then get into all sorts of life and death situations? Maybe you'd like to have some gun battles and high-speed chases, then kick the bad guy's ass and save the world?"

"I'm not trying to save the world, but I'd like to do something that would allow me to actually make a difference and really help someone. Sneaking around with a camera isn't working so much for me anymore."

"You helped our client yesterday when we filmed her husband having sex with Angie. And we helped Angie realize that she was being taken advantage of by Chet. Those should count as good deeds. Besides, last month we helped Professor Mindy recover an ancient Mexican statue. That was sort of like an adventure and the Mexican government was able to recover an artifact that was stolen almost five hundred years ago. Besides, I'd be careful what you start wishing for. You might get it."

"You're right. I'm probably overthinking things again."

The door to the street opened and a woman walked in. She looked around the office before taking a few tentative steps inside. She was in her mid-twenties, medium height, and was relatively thin. Her hair color was somewhere between dark blonde and light brown and hung down to her shoulders. She wore flat, comfortable shoes, dark slacks, and a long-sleeved cotton top, the typical outfit of a woman who works in a Scottsdale office.

"Hello," Sophie said, in her friendly talking-to-a-client voice. "How can I help you?"

The woman took another two steps towards Sophie's desk. She then paused as she looked at the file folders stacked everywhere. "Um, I need to talk with one of the lawyers. I'm not sure which one. I guess I could start with any of them. Do I make an appointment or how does this work?"

"Well," Sophie said, "we only have one lawyer now, so that part's simple."

The woman looked more confused than ever. "But your sign says there are four of them."

"There used to be four," I said. "One retired and two died. We've never gotten around to changing the name of the business. Leonard Shapiro's the last one."

"Um, well, if he's the only one, I guess I'll need to talk with him."

"I'll be glad to set something up," Sophie said. "Could I get your name?"

"Oh, sorry, it's Susan Monroe."

"Hi, Susan," I said as I walked over and held out my hand. "I'm Laura Black and this is Sophia Rodriguez. I do investigations and Sophie's the paralegal. Gina Rondinelli also does investigations, but she's not here at the moment."

"Are you looking for someone to take naked pictures of your husband while he's having sex with his mistress?" Sophie asked.

"No, I'm not married. Do people want that a lot?"

"You'd be surprised," I said.

"I need to talk with your attorney about a case your law firm handled a long time ago."

"Okay," Sophie said. "Lenny's in the office today, but I don't know if he has any free time. Let me check."

Sophie walked over to Lenny's door, which was open, and went inside. Thirty seconds later she popped her head back out. "He's able to see you now, if you have time."

We walked into Lenny's office and made introductions. He took one look at Susan, who was now visibly trembling, then asked Sophie to pour him a Beam on the rocks. He pointed to the wet bar and asked Susan what she'd like.

"Oh, actually a white wine might help. I didn't realize how stressful coming in here would be."

Sophie poured the drinks and handed them out. As usual, Lenny didn't offer anything to either Sophie or me. Not that I needed a drink before lunch, but it would've been nice if he'd at least asked.

Susan looked at her glass for a moment, then downed about half of it in a long gulp.

"We might as well get started," Lenny said. "Sophie says you have some questions about an old case of ours. Have a seat and tell us a little bit about who you are and what we can do for you."

"There isn't a lot to tell about me. My name's Susan Monroe. I've lived in Scottsdale my entire life, well, except for a year after high school when I shared an apartment in Mesa with a girlfriend. I have an associate's degree in business technology from Maricopa Community College and I work as an admin at an insurance office in South Scottsdale. I've been there for almost three years. I'm taking courses in information technology at Arizona State in Tempe and I hope to graduate with my bachelor's degree next spring. From there, I'm hoping to get a more serious job in I.T."

"Now then," Lenny said. "How can we help you?"

"Did you once represent someone who called himself William Southard? This would have been many years ago."

Lenny sat back and stared into space for several moments.

"That name doesn't ring a bell. Do you have any details of the case? Can you narrow down the year?"

"I don't have a lot of information about it. My mom said it had something to do with a company he owned. Apparently, he sold it and his former partner, Kathleen somebody, thought she'd been treated unfairly and decided to sue him. It was right before I was born so that would have been about twenty-six years ago."

Lenny did a quick calculation in his head to come up with the correct year. "The name doesn't match, but the timing and details sound about right for a case my former partner, Paul Oeding handled."

"Oh, is Paul the lawyer who's still alive? Maybe I could look him up and ask him directly? Do you have a way to get ahold of him?"

"Unfortunately, you can't. Paul died a few years ago in a skiing accident."

"Oh, of course. I understand. Are there still records of the case available or is there anyone else who might know about it?"

"All the records from back then are in long-term digital storage. We'll need to do an electronic search through all the cases from back then to come up with the right one. However, assuming it's the same case, I still remember some of the details of it. May I ask your interest in the matter?"

"I have reason to believe William Southard's my father."

"You no longer communicate with him?"

"To the best of my knowledge, he doesn't know I exist."

"So, why are you trying to find him? At the time we represented him, and you'll have to remember that was many years ago, he was a very wealthy man. Are you perhaps hoping to get ahold of some of his fortune?"

She smiled and slowly shook her head. "No, I'm not interested in that."

"Well, what then?"

"He and my mom were only together for a few months, but he turned out to be the one true love of her life." Susan was talking very fast, as if this was something she'd been thinking about for a long time.

"After he left, mom hasn't ever gotten close to anyone else. She always said she didn't have time for a man, since she had me to take care of. But I remember she used to go out on a lot of dates. The funny thing was, she never went out on more than two or three dates with any one guy. I think she was looking for someone as special as my dad, but she never found anyone. I was hoping if I could meet him and explain things, maybe he'd give her a call. They wouldn't need to get back together or anything, but I know it would mean the world to my mom to hear his voice and know he was okay. I think if she had some sort of closure on it, she could start to move on."

"Again, the names aren't matching up, but you're saying William Southard is your father. Do you have any proof of that? Does your mom also believe he's your father?"

"No, no actual proof. And mom always denies he's my dad. But I don't believe her. I think she's only trying to protect me."

"Do you know where he's living?" Lenny asked. "If you'd like, we could set up an introduction based on our prior association with him. But, honestly, it would be a lot quicker for you to send him an email, explain who you are, and maybe ask to meet face-to-face. I'm sure he's on social media, everybody is these days. He'd likely have where he works listed. You could probably call up the business to set up a meeting. You may have to go through an admin or two, but it probably wouldn't take too long."

"Unfortunately, it's not that simple. About five years ago, my mom tried to track him down. She thought if they could meet again, everything would be like it was. Sort of like in the movie *Mama Mia*."

"I take it she couldn't find him."

"We hired an investigator, but all they could discover was that William Southard wasn't his real name. Back when they were together, he told my mom his entire life's story. Unfortunately, when the investigator checked, it was all made up."

"Well, that would explain why things aren't matching up for me either. What do you have to go on?"

"Not a lot. Mostly pictures. He and mom are in a lot of pictures together. Mom remembers right before he took off, he had some sort of legal issue come up. My mom used to own an art gallery across the street from here and you were the only lawyers she knew of. She recommended you and that's how he ended up here. I was hoping you'd have some records of his case. If he was doing something with the court, I was thinking he would have needed to use his real name. Then I could use that as a starting point."

"Was the art gallery called Desert Vistas?" Lenny asked.

"That's right. My mom, her name's Olivia Monroe, closed it down about fifteen years ago. She said she couldn't afford the rent in Old Town Scottsdale anymore and had plans to open another gallery in downtown Tempe or maybe Chandler. Unfortunately, some financial problems came up and she never did open the new gallery. She still talks about doing it, but after fifteen years, it's pretty obvious it's not happening."

"I remember the woman who ran the gallery," Lenny said. "I never talked to her, but I often saw her going in and out. Tall and thin, with blonde hair down to her waist?"

"Yeah, that was how mom looked back then. She's not quite as thin and her hair's shorter, but you'd probably still recognize her."

"Sure," Lenny said. "We can do a search and recover the original records. That should provide some clues as to who your father really is. It shouldn't take a lot of digging. However, researching something like that will have some costs associated with it."

"I live with my mom, drive an old car, and my expenses are low. I've been able to put some money away. My aunt knows what I'm doing and said she'd help with the expenses. I have two weeks of vacation coming up, so I can be gone if I have to go out looking for him."

"Why now?" Lenny asked. "You said the other investigation was five years ago."

"Ever since the first investigator came up empty, it's been a goal of mine to find my dad. I keep thinking if he could talk to my mom one more time, maybe things would start to go better for her. For the last four or five months, mom's been more moody than usual. She's been spending a lot of time on the couch watching TV. You don't know her, but that's unusual for my mom. She's almost always on the go. I've asked her what's wrong, but she says it's nothing. A few weeks ago, I came home and found her flipping through the old scrap books, the ones with the pictures of her and my dad. It was the first time I'd seen her happy in months. I think this obsession with my dad is starting to get to her."

"Alright," Lenny said. "This first part will be fairly straight-forward. Compile a list of everything you know about him. Where he said he grew up, where he lived, and the places he worked. We'll assume none of the information is correct, but it'll give us a place to start. It would also be helpful if we could get a copy of the report the previous investigator put together. Again, we'll know all his leads were dead ends, but it may keep us from going over the same territory twice. I'll go through the old records from when he worked with us. All of that should give us a starting point."

Susan, Sophie, and I went back into reception. Sophie opened a drawer in her desk and gave Susan the multi-page new-client form. "Let's schedule an appointment for you to come back tomorrow afternoon. I should have the old records first thing in the morning, so by tomorrow afternoon we should have some more information. Then you and Lenny can go over the fees for whatever you want us to do."

"Thanks," Susan said. "I'll fill these out when I get home tonight."

She was about to leave when Gina came up to reception from the back offices. We made introductions, then asked Susan if she'd like to go to lunch with us.

"Unfortunately, I can't," she said. "I came here on my lunch hour and I'm already late. Maybe another time?"

She disappeared out the front door and Gina looked to us for an explanation. Sophie gave her the thirty second download.

"She seems nice," Gina said. "I hope we can help her out. Where should we go for lunch?"

"Anywhere," Sophie said. "I had to watch Lenny and our new client sip drinks for half an hour. That was just mean. I think I need a margarita for lunch."

"Tacos at Old Town Gringos?" I suggested.

"Sounds perfect," Gina said. "We haven't been there in a couple of weeks."

Chapter Two

After we got back from lunch, we gathered around Sophie's desk in reception. Gina hung out with us for a few minutes, then said she was going to take off for the rest of the afternoon to work on her latest assignment. This one involved investigating the alibi of a murder suspect Lenny was representing. Gina thought the guy was probably guilty and she was only chasing her tail.

Sophie's desk phone rang. When she picked it up, we could hear it was Susan. Gina had Sophie put it on speaker and asked Susan if she could start again at the beginning.

"I said I think I wasted your time today. I went back to work and started going over the situation again. I don't know what I've been thinking. My dad doesn't know I exist and I've always suspected mom was just a quick fling for him. He probably has a wife and a family somewhere. I don't think anyone will be happy if I simply show up and announce he's my father. I don't have any proof I'm his daughter. I'm only going on some old pictures and wishful thinking. Realistically, my dad could be any of the guys mom dated back then."

"I understand," Sophie said. "Doing something like that's a pretty big step. Well, if you change your mind, let us know. I've already ordered up the records, but there's no charge for simply ordering them. Everything's digital and we'll have them all by tomorrow morning."

Sophie hung up and there was a moment of silence. I was a little bummed. All through lunch, I'd been looking forward to starting the assignment, one that didn't seem to involve any angry naked people.

"It's a shame," I said. "She seemed nice."

"She'll be back," Gina said.

"I don't know," Sophie said. "Can you imagine? You're sitting around the table having a nice dinner with the family, when a woman knocks on the door and announces she's your long-lost daughter. That's the sorta thing that causes strife in a family. I don't know if I could go through with it."

"Why'd you say she'll be back?" I asked Gina.

"I saw it all the time, back when I worked on the force. She'll hem and haw, but in the end, she'll want to know about her dad. Even if she has no intention of going to see him, she'll still want to know who he is."

We said our goodbyes to Gina and she left through the door that led into the back offices. Sophie watched her leave then turned towards me.

"I didn't get a chance to ask this morning. When are you going out with Max again? You haven't seen him since last week, right? Is he still okay with the fact that Tony hasn't made him the official head of the group yet? The big announcement was supposed to be like three weeks ago, then nothing. You know, if I were Max, I'd be a little pissed."

"I'm hoping to see him in a day or two. He seems to have open evenings early in the week. The last time I talked with him about it, he said Tony was still working out the structure of the group and how he wanted to organize things for the future. Don't forget, you're not supposed to know any of this. Max only told me because, well, I'm me."

"Oh, he already knows you've told me everything. He'd be more surprised if you didn't tell me. It's the way it works. You tell me, I tell

Milo, then he spreads it to his contacts within the group. It's the only way everyone over there can be on the same page."

"I've been avoiding asking him too many questions about it. I'm not sure if it's a sensitive subject and honestly, the less I know about the inner workings of the group, the better off I'll be. The only reason I want to know is because once Max officially takes over, it'll likely affect us, even more than it already does."

"Are you starting to get annoyed that you're dating a guy who's hot and rich and you can't tell anyone about it?"

"Well, maybe a little, but it's not his fault. I knew all about the restrictions involved when we first started seeing each other. But you're right, part of the fun of having a boyfriend is being able to show him off, at least occasionally. Every time Max and I go on a date, we have to do it in private, so no one can see us together."

"I know what you mean. When I'm with Milo, he can only say he works in hotel security. But when I'm with Snake, everyone knows he plays for the Cardinals. There was even a kid the other day who came up and asked for his autograph."

"I haven't been keeping up with the team like I should. Has he gotten to play since the game last month?"

"No, but I was going to tell you. The second-string quarterback broke his hand in the game on Sunday. He'll be out six to eight weeks. Yesterday, they announced Snake's moved up to being the official backup."

"That's great. He might get a chance to play now. Is he happy about it?"

"I'm not sure. He called me last night with the news. Honestly, I think he was starting to enjoy getting a big paycheck for not doing anything. Being the official backup means he actually has to be ready to go in at any time. It's a lot more work than he'd counted on."

~~~~

I was still disappointed that I wouldn't be working on the assignment for Susan, so I hung around the office for another half-hour. I talked with Sophie for a while but she eventually had to start working again, so I decided to go home. I reminded her, for about the third or fourth time, to keep an eye out for any new assignments.

~~~~

I pulled into my apartment parking lot at about three thirty. Grandma Peckham was standing behind her Buick, pulling out bags of groceries, and loading them into her wheeled basket. I parked and walked over to her.

"Well, Laura, thank you," she said, as I pulled out the last two bags and set them in her basket. "It's been pretty quiet around here the past couple of weeks and I haven't talked to you in days. Anything new going on?"

"Not a thing," I said, as we walked through the building and into the elevator. "Work's the same. My friends are the same. Although, I should probably tell you something. I can't give you a lot of details, but I've been seeing someone new lately."

"I thought you were," Grandma said. "I'm glad. I know how frustrated you were while you were dating the policeman. I followed several of the arguments you and he had over the phone and I knew how unhappy you were with him."

I felt my face flush as we walked out of the elevator. "Oh my God, I'm so sorry. I didn't think I was ever that loud."

"Oh, you weren't screaming or anything. But with the thin walls of our building, anything more than an enthusiastic conversation comes through pretty clearly."

"I'm sorry you had to listen to it. I know our discussions sometimes got pretty heated."

"Don't worry about it," Grandma said as she unlocked the door to her apartment and we went in. Marlowe was fast asleep on his chair.

"From what I heard, he didn't seem to value what you did for a living and he thought it was too dangerous. I know how much that frustrated you."

"You're right. That's the main thing we argued over."

We set the groceries on the kitchen counter then started putting everything away. "Well," Grandma said, hopefully the new boyfriend will be more understanding about that."

"So far, so good. Of course, I haven't done anything lately to put myself in danger. At least, nothing over the past three or four weeks. I guess we'll see."

"Speaking of boyfriend problems, I haven't seen your cousin over here since she moved out. Did everything work out okay with her? Did she ever get a job?"

Due to some internal problems within the Black Death, Danielle had been forced to hide out in my apartment for a few days. I'd made up a story about how she was my cousin from Albuquerque and she was sort of in hiding from an angry ex-boyfriend.

"Yes, I should have told you. The boyfriend thing resolved itself and she took a job as the office manager for a truck company here in town. She got an apartment close to where she works. It's not fancy, but she likes it."

"I'm glad everything worked out with her old boyfriend. It was a little strange having those men hanging out in the hallway looking for her."

Don't I know it.

With the groceries put away, Grandma pulled out a Diet Pepsi from the fridge and handed it to me.

"Thanks for helping," she said. "The groceries seem to get heavier every time I go to the store."

"No problem. What about you? Is everything still going alright with the engagement? How are the wedding plans coming along?"

"Honestly, we're still trying to figure out what we're doing. Neither of us wants a big wedding. We're thinking about maybe doing it at one of the smaller chapels. They have a couple here in Scottsdale and there's one he likes in Sedona. But no matter how we do it, it keeps getting bigger. Even if we only invite immediate family, we'd still be talking about twenty people, once you count the spouses and the grandkids. We've even talked about eloping to Las Vegas and getting married in one of the cute little chapels there."

"With Elvis?"

"I don't think so. Even if we get married in Vegas, I think Elvis would be a little too much."

I said my goodbyes to Grandma and told her to keep me posted as she found out more about the wedding. I then walked into my apartment, set the Diet Pepsi on the coffee table and collapsed on the couch.

Picking up the remote, I started flipping channels without much enthusiasm. Thirty seconds later, I heard the cat door in the bedroom swing open and Marlowe strolled into the living room. Apparently, he thought food was more important than sleep.

He jumped up on my lap and started to rub against me and purr. This seemed friendly enough, but I knew from experience he wouldn't stop until I fed him.

I got up, pulled a half-full can of Deluxe Dinner from the fridge, and plopped a spoonful into Marlowe's bowl. As always, he quickly gobbled down the food.

"Do me a favor, don't throw it up this time," I told him as he looked down at his empty bowl, then back up at me.

I went back to the couch and began to sort through my bills. Now that my latest assignment was over, I'd get a paycheck on Friday. But even at that, things were still going to be tight.

A few months ago, I'd helped the owner of the apartment building, a woman named Suzie Lu, with a problem she was having. As a thank you, she said I could live in the apartment, rent-free, for as long as I'd like. Not having a rent payment has helped, and I'm grateful to Suzie for that, but I'm still not able to save more than about two or three hundred dollars each month. I'm working on a down payment for a new car, but at this rate, it'll be two years until I can afford to get something different.

Over the last year or so, I've picked up a few souvenirs from some of the work assignments I've been on. Some of the items are rather valuable. Sophie keeps telling me to sell something and buy myself a new car. I know she's probably right, but to me these things are more than simple souvenirs or pieces of jewelry. I look at each of them as a keepsake of a different adventure I've had in my life. They're symbols that I'm strong enough to have gone through a really crappy situation and yet managed to come through it all okay.

The only one I was on the fence about was the gold nugget Professor Mindy had given me the month before. It was pretty, but the real souvenir of the assignment was the ancient gold statue of a young woman, one of seven sisters, now sitting in the National Museum in Mexico City. Maybe I'd go down there someday and see her again. Maybe Sophie and Professor Mindy would want to come along and make a girls' weekend out of it.

As I was daydreaming about Mexico, I heard a familiar noise from the kitchen. *Aaack! Aaaaack!* This was followed by a retching sound, then by the *splat* sound of something wet landing on the tile floor.

The only thing I didn't like about Marlowe was his need to suck down his food, then throw it back up in the corner of the kitchen. If I ever get another cat, I'll need to ask the previous owner about his eating habits.

~~~~

I ended up having a frozen thing for dinner, half a pint of mint chocolate chip ice cream for dessert, and then I binge-watched three episodes of *Chopped.*

A few minutes before ten, my phone started playing the theme from *The Love Boat.* I couldn't stop myself from smiling as I answered.

"Hey you," I said.

"Laura, how's your day been?" Max asked in his deep and steady voice. "Are you in bed yet or still on the couch?"

As always, hearing him talk gave me X-rated thoughts of us marooned together on a desert island. Well, a desert island with room service and air conditioning.

"Still on the couch. My day was pretty typical. I got an interesting new assignment before lunch but then lost it in the afternoon. I'm hoping something new comes in so I can get out of the apartment. I usually like being off work, but this time, I get the feeling that sitting around for more than two or three days will drive me nuts."

"Does that mean you'll have time for dinner tomorrow? Six o'clock? Maybe I can make up for not being able to see you over the weekend."

"Don't worry about the weekend. I understand your schedule. I should be good for dinner. Did you want to go somewhere or should I meet you at the resort?"

"I'll need to meet you at the Paradise. My last meeting is at five and I have a conference call at nine. That should leave us about three hours for dinner."

"You know," I said. "Three hours is time for more than dinner."

"Yes, but I didn't want to be too obvious about it."

Yum.

"I can't wait. Where should I meet you?"

"I've reserved the Mesquite Suite. Try not to be late. I'll have champagne and dinner waiting for us in the room."

"Dinner in a hotel suite? I didn't think you were trying to be too obvious about it."

"Well, with only three hours, I do need to be a little obvious."

"Um, are you going to bring your toys with you?"

"Maybe."

"Only maybe?" I asked.

"Fine. Definitely."

Oh my.

I had a flashback to the last time Max brought his bag of toys along on one of our dates. It had led to an interesting evening and I tingled with excitement just thinking about it.

"You know," I said, "it's going to be hard for me to concentrate tomorrow."

"That's the idea. I also wanted to talk with you about the weekend after next. The only thing going on over here's a golf tournament at the Blue Palms and the resort's director of golfing will take care of that. Tony told me to take the weekend off. I know it's hard for you to plan a week out, but do you think you'll be available? Maybe we could go someplace far away where nobody knows either of us? We could act like we're actually a couple."

"I'd love that. Of course, no guarantees I'll be free. That's a long way off and with the Snowbirds back in town, I assume I'll get a new assignment between now and then. But I'll do my best to block off the weekend. We haven't gone anyplace since San Diego and that was a couple of months ago."

"Good. I'll see about setting something up. Let me know if you have any preferences."

"Well, if you're asking, I've never been to a place with a lot of snow. I've seen pictures of mountain villages covered in snow and they're so beautiful. But other than Christmas shopping in Flagstaff a couple of times, I've never made snow a destination. It might be fun to go somewhere like that."

Max started laughing. "Most people want a tropical beach when they take a vacation, you want snow."

"Hey, I'm from the desert. I know all about palm trees and the heat. If we're going on a vacation, I'd like to visit the snow."

Max laughed. "Okay, we'll go to the snow. You'll have a week to find everything you need. But remember, snow may be beautiful, but it's also cold."

"How cold could it be?"

"*Really* cold."

"Fine. I'll try to keep that in mind."

~~~~

When I woke up the next morning, it was only seven fifteen. I laid in bed for almost half an hour, but then became fidgety and got up. Normally, I love the first few days between assignments, but today I couldn't see myself flipping channels, waiting for Sophie to call with something new.

I put on a pot of coffee, then got ready to head into the office. I needed to bug Lenny into giving me something to work on. I knew he had a couple of semi-dormant long-term assignments in his files. Maybe I could work on one of those.

On the way out, I poured the rest of the coffee into *The Big Pig*, my oversized travel mug, and fed Marlowe. I made sure to feed him right before I left so I wouldn't have to listen to him tossing up his breakfast. I was still a little grossed out from the night before.

As I was locking my door, Grandma Peckham got out of the elevator and briskly walked down the hall toward her apartment. She had on a bright pink jogging suit and I knew she was just getting back from her morning walk.

"Hi, Grandma," I said. "How is it out there today?"

"It's gorgeous. I love this time of year. You always tell me how much you like the summer, but I like it when I can walk around in the morning without starting to sweat."

"Are you doing anything fun today?"

"I'm meeting Grandpa Bob for lunch at the Old Town Tortilla Factory. We're still trying to decide on the wedding plans."

"I forgot to ask yesterday. Have you set the date yet?"

"Not yet. It'll depend on where we decide to do it. I've forgotten how many details there are, even with a simple wedding."

"I remember mine was pretty simple and it still took months of planning," I said. "Let me know if I can help with anything."

~~~~

When I got to the office, Sophie's yellow Volkswagen convertible was the only car under the carport. The spaces belonging to Lenny's red Porsche and Gina's black Range Rover were empty.

Up in reception, Sophie was sipping a big gas station coffee and flipping pages on her tablet.

"Hey, girlfriend," she said as I sat in one of the wing chairs next to her desk. "How are you feeling? You look happier today."

"Actually, I'm feeling a little better. Max wants to take me on a mini-vacation, the weekend after this. Sort of like when we went to San Diego."

"Nice. Where's he taking you this time? Somewhere romantic and exotic, I hope. The Caribbean? Maybe Mexico? Too bad you only have the weekend. I keep seeing shows on the Travel Channel about Tahiti. That's a place you can't help but have a romantic vacation.

You and Max could go to a tropical beach and snorkel."

"I told him I wanted to go to the snow. Do you have any cold weather clothes that would fit me? I don't have a thing to wear for something like that."

"Snow? You're serious. Of all the beautiful places you could go, you want to visit a blizzard? You know, I keep seeing stories about snow on the news. It's mostly car crashes and people trying to dig themselves out of waist high drifts. Nobody looks happy when it comes to cold weather."

"I don't care, I want to go to the snow. As a kid we'd sometimes go up to the forest along the Rim above Strawberry and make snowmen. But as an adult, I've never done more than drive through the snow, well, if you don't count our daytrips up to Flagstaff. Every year I see pictures of little towns in the mountains covered in snow. They all have lights twinkling in the trees, horse-drawn sleigh rides, and hot drinks by a wood-burning fireplace. I was watching a show about it a couple of weeks ago. They said being outside in a hot tub while it's snowing is a magical experience."

Sophie looked at me like I was nuts. "You want to be outside, like in a bikini, while the temperature's below freezing and it snows on you? That doesn't sound like any fun. Besides, if the hot tub's somewhere outside, how are you going to get to it in the first place? Walk barefoot through the snow?"

"On the TV show, everybody had on slippers and a robe. I guess the hotels there provide them. They showed a group of people in this big hot tub. Everyone was laughing and drinking champagne while it snowed on them. The hot tub had water jets that made bubbles. Steam came up from the water and it seemed to keep everyone warm. It looked fun and romantic and I'd like to try it with Max. I want him to give me the full 'snow' experience."

Sophie shook her head. "No, I'm sorry. Yuck."

"What do you mean, yuck? Weren't you telling me a couple of

months ago how much you wanted to live somewhere cold? Didn't you say the people who live where it freezes probably cheer and dance whenever it starts to snow?"

"Well, yeah. I might have said that. But that was when it was hot as an oven and I only wanted to get out of the heat. Have you been outside lately? It's beautiful here now. We're the place people come to so they can escape their crappy winter weather. Anywhere else you go will either be too hot or too cold."

"I don't care. I've lived here all my life. This will probably be my one chance to vacation in the snow and I want to make the most of it."

"Okay, fine. Go and have fun in the snow with Max. But remember, I'm from So Cal. I have a couple of big sweaters that'll fit you, but I don't have any actual cold weather outfits. Now, if you change your mind and decide to go to a beach, I'll have you covered."

I sighed. "It's my own fault. I didn't think before I told Max I wanted to go to the snow. I could ask Gina, but she's also lived here all her life and I doubt she has anything. Besides, I'd have to tell her why I needed the clothes and then I'd get another lecture about dating a criminal."

"Sounds like we'll need to go shopping."

"I know. I'm good for the hot tub, but I don't have a thing to wear in the cold. This thing with Max is only nine days away." I sighed again. "In the meantime, I've gotta find something to do, well, other than shop. If I sit in my apartment the whole time, I'll go nuts. Plus, I can really use the paycheck. I'm hoping Lenny'll give me some sort of assignment. I'd even work on one of the lost-cause cases in the inactive files."

Sophie looked at me and smiled. I knew what she was thinking.

"As long as it's an assignment without cheating spouses," I said. "And hopefully one I can finish up in a week and a half. I'll be heartbroken if I have to cancel my weekend with Max."

"Well, I might have some good news for you. There's a new client coming in at eleven. His name's Jet."

"Jet? Seriously? What is he, like twelve?"

"I don't think so, he sounded older on the phone. It's something about a fight in a bar. When I talked to him, it didn't seem like it was going to turn into a big deal, but who knows. Maybe you'll get lucky."

The door from the back offices opened and Lenny came in. He looked at the two of us and grunted in a way we both took as 'good morning', then he went into his office and closed the door.

Sophie's desk phone rang. When she answered, I could hear it was Susan Monroe. Sophie looked up at me and shrugged her shoulders. She let Susan know I was also in the office, then put it on speaker.

"I'm glad you're both there," Susan said. "I had a long talk with my mom last night. It turns out she's very sick. She's known about it for months but never told me about it. In fact, it was my aunt who alerted me."

"I'm so sorry," I said. "What happened?"

"Well, I told my aunt about coming to your law office and what I'd wanted Leonard to do. But I also told her I'd backed out. That's when she told me about my mom. Apparently, she's been going to doctors for the last four or five months. Between the disease and the medication, it's draining her strength and starting to make her lose hope."

"That's terrible," Sophie said.

"What can we do?" I asked.

"I'm thinking if I'm ever going to look for my dad, I'll need to do it now. I'm hoping if I could meet him and explain things, he'd come back and see mom one more time before things begin to go downhill."

"We got the old case files in this morning," Sophie said. "I'll tell Lenny you changed your mind and he can review the information. He has an appointment at eleven, but he should be finished by noon or so. I can schedule an appointment for your lunch hour."

"Okay, let's do it before I get nervous and change my mind again."

~~~~

Now that it seemed like I'd have at least one assignment, I decided to stick around until Susan came in. I asked Sophie if there were any files she didn't want laying around anymore. I told her I'd be glad to file them in the cabinets in the storage room.

"Well, you can take the ones sitting on the wet bar in the conference room. I won't need those anytime soon. Make sure not to touch the ones on the conference table. I'll need everything there, plus they look extra messy. I know how much it annoys Lenny when he tries to have a meeting in there. I don't want you to clean anything up too much."

~~~~

Gina came in a little before eleven and was talking with Sophie about someone she wanted her to look up with the secret software. I'd just come out of the conference room with an armful of files when the door to the street opened and a guy walked in.

The first thing I noticed about him was that he was big and cute. He was somewhere in his late thirties, clean shaven, and had short, dark hair. Even though he was big, he moved with the athletic grace of a much smaller man. The black polo shirt he wore showed off the bulging muscles of his arms and chest.

As he walked up to Sophie's desk, I watched his firm tush wiggle in his tight khaki slacks. "I'm Andrew Kramer," he said to Sophie in a deep but friendly voice. "But everyone calls me Jet. I think we talked on the phone yesterday. I have an appointment with Leonard Shapiro at eleven."

Sophie stared at him for a moment, her mouth halfway open. She then gave him elevator-eyes. Her gaze starting at his face, going down to his feet, slowly drifting up to admire how well he filled out the front of his pants, then eventually traveling back to his face.

"Oh, um, sure," she said. She then pulled out a form and handed it to him. "This is the new client paperwork. I've already filled it in with the information you gave me over the phone. I'll check to see if Lenny's ready for you."

We heard a weird noise, almost like a moan. Sophie and I both looked at Gina. She was biting her lower lip and still making the soft noise. Her gaze was intent on the man, not even trying to hide the fact that she was virtually undressing him with her eyes. I'd never seen Gina look at a man like that before and it made me smile.

"Oh," Sophie said, an amused smile on her face. "Before you go in, this is Gina Rondinelli. She's our lead investigator."

He looked over at Gina and paused, his eyes opening wide with obvious interest. He did his own version of elevator-eyes, then they each took a step closer and shook hands. The handshake went on for a long time as they gazed into each other's eyes.

"Jet?" Gina eventually asked. Her voice sounded a little uneven. "That's an unusual name. How'd you get it?"

"I used to be a Navy Seal. I somehow ended up with Jet as my nickname and it sorta stuck."

"Oh, really? A Navy Seal?" Gina asked. Her eyes were unfocused and her breathing was ragged. "We heard you were in a bar fight?"

"Oh, it wasn't a big deal. I saw some guys picking on a woman so I stepped in. There were only five of them and they were mostly drunk."

"And this is Laura Black," Sophie said. "She also does investigations."

The man turned reluctantly away from Gina and shook my hand.

Although, in my case, it was a pretty standard handshake.

"I'll tell Lenny you're here," Sophie said as she got up and walked into his office. Jet and Gina looked at each other and there was a brief, loaded silence. Fortunately, Sophie was only in Lenny's office for about ten seconds before she stuck her head out and waved Jet in.

Jet took a step toward the office, then turned back to look at Gina. "It was very nice meeting you. Maybe we'll see each other again."

"I'd really like that," she said. Her voice had a weird breathiness to it that I'd never heard before.

"Good," he said, as he flashed a gorgeous smile at her. "I look forward to working with you."

He went into Lenny's office. Sophie closed the door and walked back to her desk. When she sat, she started laughing. Once she started, I couldn't help but join in.

"What's so funny?" Gina asked, a little defensively. We couldn't help but notice her face had a rosy pink glow.

"Oh my God," Sophie said. "You were hilarious. You were staring at that guy like you wanted to eat him for lunch. I haven't seen anyone look at a man like that since the first time Laura saw Max."

"Hey," I said, although I couldn't deny it.

"Me?" Gina asked. She was clearly embarrassed and now her face had turned bright red. "What about you? I saw the way you were staring at that big bulge in his pants." She then turned to me. "And I saw the way you were staring at his ass. I wasn't the only one."

"No," I said, "but I could see how he was looking back at you. I think there's some mutual lust going on."

"Um, do you know if Lenny will want us to go in with the client?" Gina asked Sophie.

Sophie smiled and started laughing again. "Lenny didn't say

anything, I think they're just talking fees, but I'll be sure to let you know."

Even though Gina was annoyed at us, she didn't leave the reception area. After a while, she started helping me with the files. I couldn't help but notice she was keeping a close eye on the door to Lenny's office.

~~~~

Susan came in at about a quarter to noon. Unfortunately, she didn't look much better than she had the day before. You could tell that the news about her mother was weighing on her and she was still a little nervous about seeing a lawyer. She handed Sophie the new client paperwork, the previous investigator's report, and a list of everything she and her aunt could remember about the man they knew as William Southard. Susan said she hadn't asked her mom about it because she thought it would only upset her.

A few minutes before noon, the door to Lenny's office opened and Jet came out. He went over to Sophie's desk, where Gina was already standing, watching him as he approached.

"Leonard said to talk with you about making an appointment for tomorrow."

"Sure," Sophie said as she opened the calendar on her computer. "How does ten o'clock sound?"

Gina made a noise of disapproval and shook her head. Sophie looked back at her screen and typed in a few more keystrokes. "Okay, how does one thirty sound?" She then looked at Gina who was smiling and looking at Jet.

"One thirty sounds fine," he said without taking his gaze off Gina. "Looks like we may get to work together on this one after all."

Gina made another sound that we took for happiness.

Jet said his goodbyes, then went out the front door. Gina watched him walk down the street while Sophie showed Susan into Lenny's office.

Gina and I pretended to work on the files while we waited for Lenny to finish going over the costs and fees with the client. Sophie sat at her desk, occasionally glancing at Gina and trying not to laugh.

After twenty minutes, Lenny poked his head out and invited us in. Susan again had a glass of white wine in her hand and he had a glass of Beam on his desk. Once everyone took a seat, Lenny started.

"I've reviewed the case from twenty-six years ago. I can't reveal all the details, but several aspects of it are in the public record. First, the client wasn't named William Southard. He identified himself in the court papers as Michael McKinsey. He came to us to defend himself against a lawsuit brought by his former business partner, a woman named Kathleen Alastor. They'd started a company together and it was apparently doing quite well. The original company charter had given each of them fifty percent ownership of the company, but Michael had somehow gone behind Kathleen's back and transferred control of the company to an outside group. No details on the sale itself are public record. The lawsuit was seeking fifty percent of the net proceeds from the transfer and legal fees. The case was settled out of court and those details also aren't part of the public record."

"He used the Michael McKinsey name on the court documents?" Susan asked.

"That's the name he'd been using when they started the company and all of the documents relating to the company were consistent with that designation. I'm assuming it's his actual name, but at this point nothing's for certain. Unfortunately, Michael McKinsey is a fairly common name. There'll be hundreds if not thousands of them living in the U.S."

"You're saying we're back at square one?"

"Not necessarily," Lenny said. "We'll start to narrow down the list of possible matches based on the McKinsey name. We'll also do some research on the business partner, Kathleen Alastor. If she can be found, it's likely she'll have some additional insights into Michael McKinsey. We'll also start investigating based on what he told your mom about himself."

"But if everything we know about him is a lie, where would you start? The other investigator came up empty. Every lead he had was a dead end."

"Making up an entire life's history is harder than it sounds," Gina said. "You can't help but mix your real life in with the invented one. To be successful, you'd need to have a general idea of what you're talking about. The made-up story has to be at least close to the real one."

"We'll get going on our end starting today," Lenny said. "Sophie will call you to set up our next meeting."

We all stood up and said our goodbyes. Sophie then led Susan back out to reception while Gina and I stayed behind. After the client left, Lenny pulled out a pack of cigarettes and lit one up. I went over to the window and opened it, creating a nice breeze through the office so we wouldn't have to breathe the smoke.

Lenny stared through the window and out into the street as he smoked down the cigarette, occasionally taking a sip of his Jim Beam. Over the years, we've learned that this is his way of going over things in his head. At last, his eyes came back into focus.

"Alright," Lenny said as he stubbed out the cigarette and looked at me. "This'll be your assignment. Tracking down a guy who doesn't want to be found is usually more Gina's line of work, but she's in the middle of an assignment and you're not. So far, I don't see this as anything other than billable hours but keep your eyes open. We've got a nice retainer, but I think it's all she has. Unless you've found a clear path to the father, don't spend a lot of time on this past what the existing funds will cover. Sending her overdue account to collections won't help us if she doesn't have the ability to ever pay off the debt."

He leaned back in his chair and took another sip of his bourbon, looking at both of us. "So, where should we start?"

"I'd start with the other party in the old lawsuit, Kathleen Alastor," Gina said. "Even after twenty-six years, she might still be pissed-off at the guy enough to want some payback. If she knows any dirt on him, I bet she'd spill it."

Lenny looked at me.

"Seems reasonable," I said.

"Very well," Lenny said. "Let me know what you come up with. And don't forget to track your hours. You're on a countdown clock with this one. We'll also need to discuss one more before you go. The guy who was in here before Susan was in a bar fight and we're representing him on five counts of aggravated assault. We could plead it down to a small fine, but the client says it wasn't his fault and wants to keep his clean record. It'll mostly be research in tracking down the witnesses." Lenny looked at me. "This should only be a dozen hours scattered across a week, maybe two, so I want you to have that one as well. It should fit in nicely with the finding-the-father one."

"No!" Gina protested. "That one's mine."

I couldn't help but smile.

Lenny shook his head. "I need you to finish up the alibi. This one's only billable hours. Laura can do it."

"No," Gina said again. "He's mine."

Lenny saw the look on her face and raised his hands in defeat. "Alright, fine. I'm glad you've taken over handing out the assignments. But don't let it slow down your work on the one that actually matters."

Chapter Three

Gina and I went back into reception where Sophie was starting to type up the meeting notes.

"I need the information on Jet," Gina said. I recognized the tone. Gina was using her cop-voice. Sophie heard it too and looked over at me. She then handed Gina a file from the top of a stack on her desk.

"Thanks," Gina said, still with the no-nonsense voice. She grabbed the file and walked briskly through the door leading to the back.

Sophie gave me a questioning look. "What's up with Gina?"

"I think she's hunting."

"Good thing Jet used to be a Seal," Sophie said. "He'll need a strong heart for what Gina's going to do to him."

"Would you mind running a secret search for me?"

"What? On Jet? I already have that one started. I'm sure Gina's going to want to know everything."

"No, on Kathleen Alastor, the other party in the lawsuit. I know it was twenty-six years ago, but hopefully she's still alive and somewhere in the U.S."

"Oh, her. I did that one this morning, as soon as Susan said she wanted to go through with it. It turns out, Kathleen Alastor still lives in Paradise Valley and runs a big company that's headquartered in downtown Phoenix. According to LinkedIn, she started the company a few months after she got the settlement."

"How much did she get?"

"The file didn't have that, but she originally asked for twelve million dollars. If the payment was anywhere close to that, it would've set her up with a nice nest egg."

"I'll also need you to do a search for Michael McKinsey."

"Did that too. I've started filtering based on his approximate age and I've narrowed it down to about a hundred possibilities. I'll next start filtering by job title. If the guy was head of a company when he was thirty-five, he'll probably still be head of a company somewhere."

"True, unless he's retired. What about the company he started with Kathleen Alastor? Do the files have anything on that?"

"Some. It was called McKinsey-Alastor World Incorporated. It was a Delaware company, but the paperwork didn't say what the company did. All I could find out so far was that it mainly operated out of somewhere in Nevada. I've started a more in-depth search on that too, since I knew it'd be something you'd want to know."

"Are you okay with using the secret government software again?"

"Yeah, well, maybe I was being a little paranoid. I'm thinking I'll keep using it until somebody in the deep state realizes we have it. If I try to log on one day and my passwords don't work, then I'll know it's gone."

As part of an investigation Lenny handled for the DEA about a year and a half ago, they'd installed some software that allows Sophie into a secret government database. With only a few keystrokes, she can access whatever the government has in its files for just about anyone or any business. We don't think we're still supposed to have it, but we'll keep using it until they take it away.

"Do you have contact information for Kathleen Alastor?" I asked.

"She only listed her work email and the main company phone

number. But it'll at least give you a starting place. All the information's in a folder on your desk."

"You're efficient today."

"I've been antsy the past few days. Ever since the weather got nice, I've been in the mood to go out and do something. I'm thinking I'll drive out to California for a few days, sit on Huntington Beach, and maybe catch a few waves."

"That sounds like a plan. Let me know if you want any company. I'm up for a road trip. I'd be glad to sit on a beach and watch you surf."

"I'll let you know." Sophie looked at me. "You seem like you're in a good mood all of a sudden."

"Really? I guess I am. Maybe it has something to do with the fact I won't be filming naked people having sex, for at least the next few days."

"Yeah, well, you hope."

I went back to the cubicles where Gina was happily humming to herself as she flipped through the folder on Jet. As promised, the folder on Kathleen Alastor was on my desk. Inside was a three-page printout that had all the basic information of her life. She was currently listed as founder and CEO of *K A Resort Services, Inc.*, a company that provided laundry, housekeeping, and landscaping services to hotels and casinos throughout Arizona and Nevada. Going by her profile picture, she was somewhere in her late fifties or early sixties.

I called the main company number and was transferred to an admin. I told her who I was and that I wanted to set up an appointment for Susan Monroe with Kathleen Alastor. She transferred me to another admin and I repeated my story. This one wanted to know the purpose of the meeting. After I told her a vague story about Susan wanting to see her boss on a personal matter, she asked for my email and my phone number. She said she'd check with

Kathleen the next time she was in the office and then she'd get back with me.

~~~~

Sophie and Gina took off for a late lunch. My stomach wasn't up for food so I told them to go without me.

As I'd been sitting, going over the information on Kathleen Alastor, I started to worry about clothes and what I was going to wear for the trip. After telling Max I wanted to go to the snow, he'd reminded me that it was going to be cold. I knew he was joking, but it made me realize I didn't have more than maybe two outfits that would qualify for cold weather. I didn't have a coat beyond my lightweight jacket and I certainly didn't have any snow gloves, or scarves, or hats. I only have one lightweight sweater and the only time I ever wear that is when my shirt is too low cut and I don't want to show my boobs to everyone.

Since I really hadn't started my assignment for Susan yet, I decided I should get in some shopping. I drove to Scottsdale Fashion Square and went in, determined to get myself ready for snow.

After a frustrating two hours, I started to drive back to my apartment. Along the way, I called Sophie.

"Well, how'd the shopping trip go? Find anything to wear?"

"I'm slowly working on it. I bought two sweaters that seem heavy enough. I also found a pair of black boots that look nice and have a tread on the bottom. According to the tag they're ideal for the snow."

"I'm surprised you found anything winter-related here in Scottsdale."

"They were on clearance. I don't think anyone else wanted boots made for the snow. My main problem's going to be finding a coat. I want something that'll look like I belong in a fancy winter resort, but is still warm enough so I don't freeze. It might be a long walk between the restaurants and the hotel."

"Maybe you should go to one of the sports stores, they'll have winter coats."

"Yes, but I was hoping to find something nice that I could wear around here on the days when it gets down to the thirties. I don't want to look like a ski bum. I'll talk to Max about it again tonight, but I still have a week to gather everything. I think I can put together some decent looking cold weather outfits by the time we leave."

~ ~ ~ ~

I got back to my apartment about three thirty. I had an hour or so until I needed to get ready for my date with Max. I'd just flopped onto the couch when there was a loud knock at my door. I went to the peephole and looked into the hall. Grandma Peckham was leaning against my door frame. I quickly unlocked and opened the door.

"Grandma? Are you okay?"

She looked terrible. In all the time I've known her, I've never seen her truly upset. But looking at her, propped against the wall with her mouth drawn down in a frown, I assumed this was the problem.

"Do you have a minute to come over?" she asked. From the way she was talking, Grandma was not only upset, but she'd already had a Jamaican Jerk or two. Without waiting for my answer, she turned and walked back into her apartment.

I followed Grandma and sat on her couch while she went into the kitchen and made two new drinks. Marlowe was asleep on his afghan on his chair. He didn't think the gathering was important enough to do more than briefly open his eyes before falling back to sleep.

As Grandma sloshed the drink in front of me, I noticed she wasn't wearing her new ring.

"Are you okay?" I asked again. "Did something happen with the wedding?"

Grandma snorted in disgust. "I don't know if there's even going to be a wedding," she said as she gulped down about a third of her drink.

"Oh no. What happened? You aren't wearing your engagement ring."

"You mean his dead wife's ring."

"I don't understand. You told me the engagement ring was his mother's."

"Well, I guess it started out that way. It was his mother's and he inherited it after she died. But then he gave it to his first wife as an engagement ring. She wore it for over forty years. From what Bob said, he took it off her cold dead finger at the funeral home. Now he thinks it will be okay for me to wear it."

"Yuck," I said. "That would make me feel creepy. Didn't Grandpa Bob think about that when he gave it to you?"

"Bob doesn't see anything wrong with it. He still thinks of it as his mother's ring and doesn't see what the fuss is about."

"What are you going to do?"

"I honestly don't know. Bob will feel bad if I don't wear his mother's ring, but I'm not going to wear something his wife had on her finger for forty years. You know I've always been sort of iffy on this whole marriage idea, ever since it came up. If he keeps insisting that I wear the stupid thing, I might not want to do it at all."

Grandma and I talked for another fifteen minutes and that seemed to calm her down a bit. Of course, the fact she was on her third Jamaican Jerk might have had something to do with it. From the way she talked, I suspected Grandma had also taken a couple of her arthritis pills earlier in the day. Whenever she mixes the two, it isn't long before she needs to take a nap.

As I suspected, when Grandma looked down into her empty glass, she carefully slid it onto the coffee table and slowly got up.

"It's been lovely talking with you, dear, but I think I'm going to lay down for a few minutes."

I helped Grandma down the hall, then watched as she kicked off her shoes and lay down on the bed. I think she fell asleep at about the same time her head reached the pillow.

~~~~

I went back to my apartment, took a shower, then went through the ritual of deciding what to wear. I eventually got frustrated and hunted around the far end of the rack in the closet, finally pulling out a mid-length blue print dress. It was one I hadn't worn in several months, and it didn't look all that great on me, but I didn't think Max had seen it before.

I then pulled down my jewelry box and took out the diamond pendant. I'd gotten the diamond as a result of my first adventure with Max. It was my way of reminding him we had a history between us without actually needing to say anything.

~~~~

I got a call at a quarter to five, when I was about halfway through the hair and makeup. It was Kathleen Alastor's admin letting me know Kathleen would see us. She asked if ten o'clock tomorrow morning would be convenient. I gave her a tentative yes and told her I'd confirm with my client.

I called Susan as she was packing up for the day. I let her know the meeting with Kathleen Alastor was set for ten o'clock the next morning and asked if she could get away for it.

"Yes. I've already told my supervisor about my mom and that I'd be needing to take her to doctor appointments on short notice. I also let her know I might need to take a few days of vacation. She's always been great about things like this and I don't think it'll be a problem."

"If you have anything that proves who you are, bring it along. It might help to convince Kathleen you're sincere."

"Um, what about my mom's photo albums? There's a bunch of pictures of my dad and mom together. It doesn't prove he's my dad, but it does show he was more than a friend."

"Perfect," I said. "Come by the office about nine and we'll go in together."

I called Kathleen's admin back and confirmed the appointment. After I hung up, I got a strange feeling about Kathleen Alastor and the entire assignment. I hoped everything would go smoothly, but experience told me that it probably wouldn't.

~ ~ ~ ~

I cruised into the main entrance to the Tropical Paradise, drove past the huge fountain, and parked in guest parking. Max had talked about me using valet, but I thought it'd be more in line with keeping a low profile if I blended in with the other tourists.

I walked up the hill to the resort-sized pool located next to the main lobby building. A sign on the entrance gate had a stern warning that the pool area was for registered guests only, but I ignored it, as I'd done every other time I'd been there.

Looking at the people reclining on poolside lounge chairs and listening to the waterfall splashing into the pool was relaxing. The water was sparkling blue and a light warm breeze ruffled the fronds of the queen palms. There was a man playing a steel drum near the tropical tiki bar. It added a tranquil South Seas feeling to the evening.

The sun had dipped below the horizon, lighting up the few clouds in the sky with a bright iridescent glow. The lights around the pool had already turned on and the entire scene was beautiful. If I didn't know Max was already waiting for me, I would've been tempted to go to the pool bar and order some sort of rum drink, the kind with a slice of pineapple and a paper umbrella.

I strolled behind the noisy pool waterfall and into the back entrance to the main lobby. I was about halfway across the cavernous space when Johnny Scarpazzi came hurrying towards me. Of course,

Johnny is six five and must weigh two hundred and forty pounds. Hurrying for him is relative.

"Miss Black, Tony sent me to get you. I shoulda guessed you weren't going to use valet parking. I saw you walking through the pool area and had to run to catch you over here."

"Hi, Johnny, it's good to see you. Tony wants to talk with me?"

"He let Max know you'd be a few minutes late. But not to worry, I don't think this will take too long."

"Okay, lead on."

As I followed Johnny, we walked through the beautiful main lobby of the resort. True to its name, it was set up to be a miniature tropical paradise, complete with a waterfall and a small river. We were headed towards the broad stairs that led to the mezzanine business offices for Scottsdale Land and Resort Management, Inc., the official name for the business led by Tony and Max.

"How've you been?" I asked. "I haven't talked to Suzie in a while, but I trust things are still going well?"

Suzie Lu was a professor of computer sciences at Arizona State, but she led a secret second life as a professional dominatrix who went by the name of Mistress McNasty. Johnny was one of her main clients.

Johnny slowed and a small smile appeared on his face. "Yes, things are still good between us. After everything that happened a few months ago, we've only grown closer. I still have you to thank for that."

We'd climbed about half of the broad curving stairs that led to the mezzanine level, when Johnny stopped all together and turned to me. He had a faraway look in his eyes and he spoke to me in a low, confidential tone. "To be completely honest with you, if the situation between Mistress and me were different, I'd gladly ask her to marry me. I even hinted that to her a few weeks ago, but she shut me down.

As it is, I believe it's my fate to simply be one of the many men who love her."

"Have you thought about finding someone else? A woman you wouldn't have to share?"

Johnny paused, as if this was something he'd been thinking about as well. "Sure, I could probably find someone else. But honestly, any other woman would be somewhat of a letdown if I compared her to Mistress. I believe her to be unique."

"Well, you're right about that. I've never met anyone like her."

"So, you see my dilemma. I'll need to be satisfied with the time we have together and focus my mind elsewhere when we're apart." He then turned and resumed climbing the stairs.

Johnny led me through the hallways until we reached Tony's office. He knocked twice, then opened the door to let me in.

Tony sat behind his desk, reading through a stack of papers. He carefully stood, tossing his glasses on the desk. I came around to where he was standing and gave him a hug.

"Laura Black," he said. "Forgive me for delaying your dinner date. This will only take a few moments."

"It's no problem, Tony. You're looking good. What can I do for you?"

"As you know, we've been holding negotiations with the Black Death ever since Carlos was killed. Over the past month, there seems to have been a reshuffling of their top people. It now appears the woman who you've been negotiating with has assumed a position of leadership. I don't know if it had anything to do with her role as the negotiator, but I suspect it might. In either case, it only seemed to strengthen our position. The last time you met with her, you gave her what I consider to be my last offer. I believe it to be reasonable for both sides and it should prevent further hostilities between our groups, at least for the foreseeable future. I'd like you to have a final meeting with her and receive her group's answer. If we're in agreement, then your time as our intermediary will be completed."

Thank God.

"That's great news," I said. "I was glad to do it for you as a one-time project, but you know I don't want to be a full-time part of your organization."

"I understand your feelings about this, but I believe this will be the last time you'll need to do us this service. If we ever need you again, Max will be the one to persuade you."

"When's Max taking over the group? I thought it would have happened by now?"

Tony let out a small chuckle, as if he wasn't surprised I'd asked him such a direct question about the group. "That's true," he said. "I'd originally thought the change in leadership would have been wrapped up two or three weeks ago. However, I asked Max to let me complete the talks with our rivals. As soon as that's finalized, the group is his."

"Okay, I'll call Danielle and set up a meeting. I'll get you an answer as soon as I can."

"Thank you," Tony said. "I appreciate the service you've done for me and the company. Now, before you go and meet with Max, I ask you to indulge me for another minute or two. I was talking with Muffy Sternwood a couple of weeks ago. You might recall we're working together on a new resort project on a piece of land she owns. We got to talking about scotch and she mentioned she once bought a bottle of Balvenie Cask-191 for a party that Stig Stevens would be attending. She then told me about how you and her shared a few glasses of it and how much you'd liked it. She said she sent you over a bottle for helping to get her grandson Alex back home in one piece."

"That was the most amazing scotch," I said. "It was easily the best I've ever had. In a weird way, it sort of ruined all of the scotches I've had since then. I always compare whatever I'm drinking to the Cask-

191. And you're right, Muffy did send over a bottle. It came in a beautiful box and it's still in my cubicle drawer at work. We've been waiting for a special occasion to open it."

Tony walked over to the wet bar on the far side of his office. "Well, as you can imagine, once I found out about it, I was intrigued. I had to get a bottle and try it for myself. It turns out to be both hard to find and rather expensive. It came from a barrel that was laid down in 1952 and wasn't bottled until 2002. They only got eighty-three bottles from the cask and most of them are already off the market."

"When she gave me the bottle, I looked up on the internet how much it cost. It was just over twenty thousand dollars."

From the bottom shelf of the bar, Tony picked up a bottle. It looked to be the same scotch that Muffy and I had drunk together, almost a year ago.

"Really?" he asked. "She got a bargain. This bottle was forty-two thousand."

Forty-two thousand dollars, for a bottle of scotch? Are you nuts?

"Wow, that's a lot for some scotch."

"True, but after hearing about it, I had to know for myself. I've waited to open it. Would you take a drink with me? I'd like to thank you for your help with the negotiations."

"Um, sure. I'd love to taste it again. But you don't need to do anything to thank me. I only did it to help keep the peace and prevent people on both sides from getting hurt."

"This I know. But would you still share the drink?"

"Of course, I will. I've been tempted to get into the bottle in my desk half a dozen times. Sophie keeps telling me to sell it and buy a car."

Tony carefully opened the bottle and poured two fingers into a couple of medium snifters. He then opened an ice bucket and delicately dropped a small ice cube into each.

He handed me a glass and I held it for several moments, both to warm it and to help release the flavors. I tried not to think about holding two or three thousand dollars' worth of scotch in my hand.

I swirled it a few times then held it to my nose. As when I'd drank with Muffy, the scotch hit me with half a dozen notes at once.

"That smells so good," I moaned. I then held the glass to my lips and took a sip. The scotch seemed to evaporate in my mouth and a gentle warmth spread throughout my body. This was followed by a soft wave of pleasure flowing through me and relaxing me completely.

Tony lifted his glass and also took a sip. He didn't react for several seconds, then his eyes opened wide and he sucked in a deep breath. "Oh, that's damn remarkable. It's scotch, but it's not exactly like anything I've had before. It's something different, something better."

I closed my eyes, still feeling wonderful, and I took another sip. As with the first time, rather than swallowing it, it seemed to disappear in my mouth. "It's liquid sex," I purred out. "That's what I told Muffy. It's like a sexy hot man is running his hands all over my body."

I then remembered who I was talking to. I opened my eyes and got ahold of myself. "Um, I mean it's wonderful. Thank you so much Tony."

He smiled and let out a small chuckle. "It's okay, Laura Black. This is making me a little emotional as well. I can see what you mean about this ruining all other scotches." He then took another sip and slowly swallowed. "This is going to be what I'll compare everything else to, probably for the rest of my life."

~~~~

After finishing the scotch, I said my goodbyes to Tony, telling him

I'd call as soon as Danielle gave me an answer on his final proposal.

Still feeling wonderful, I told Johnny I could find my way to the room by myself. I then took off, back down to the main lobby.

I made it downstairs without any problems, but once I had to actually find the room, I realized I only had a general idea where the Mesquite Suite was. I walked past the waterfall, past the Headhunter Lounge, then down one of the long side hallways. I eventually found the correct group of guest elevators. Taking the elevator to the top floor, I stepped out into a quiet hallway.

I knew I was in the right place when I saw Gabriella seated on a fancy Victorian styled couch. It was positioned so she could not only see who went in and out of the elevators, but she also had a good view of the doors leading to the stairwells.

She was wearing a black leather jumpsuit with royal blue trim. The front of it was unzipped to expose the cleavage between her oversized boobs. As always, her black Farucci Spy bag was lying open next to her. I knew it contained her Uzi. I often wondered what else she kept in it.

"Hi, Gabriella," I said as I walked up to her. "How've you been?"

"I've been good. Very busy. With Tony still in charge, but Max a little bit in charge too, Johnny and I are both working all the time."

"You must enjoy that. I know you like to keep active."

Gabriella shrugged. "It's okay, but I sometimes miss the old days. Resort security and watching over Tony and Max is very nice, but it's always the same thing. Back when I work for my government, life was never the same from one day to the next."

"But weren't you getting shot at? Like all the time?"

"Yes, but it's okay. I got to shoot back. Now, no more shooting." As she said this, she looked incredibly sad.

"I understand what you mean. I was telling Sophie that my job seems to be nothing but the same thing, over and over. I could go for something different, something like an adventure."

"An adventure would be good. Let me know if you find one. I'll be glad to go too."

"Is Max in there?"

"Yes. We know you were with Tony, so we arrive only a few minutes ago. Milo just left. He brought up dinner and champagne."

Gabriella got up and walked to the door. She knocked twice, then used a keycard to open the door. "You have good dinner. No worries. I'll be here."

I walked into the spacious suite. There was a bottle of champagne in an ice bucket and dinner was on the table, still under silver domes.

The double doors to the outside were open. Max was standing on the balcony, looking out over the resort and talking on his phone. He was discussing something about a convention that wanted to add another block of guest rooms, even though the hotel was already sold out.

Looking at him as he talked made me feel all warm and tingly. I was thrilled we were actually together and dating, even though it came with more than a few restrictions. Thoughts about the evening, and what was about to happen, rushed to the surface. I silently wished he would hurry up and get off the phone. My eyes then drifted down to his firm tush and the tingles became more focused into excitement.

"Sorry about that," he said as he disconnected. "The job never stops."

"Well, put your phone on silent, at least for the next three hours. You'll be busy."

"Yes, I will be."

As he said this, I walked up and flung my arms around him. As always, it felt great to be in his warm embrace. As I reached up to kiss him, everything seemed right with the world.

After I'd kissed him for about five minutes, Max walked over and started peeling the label off the champagne. I got up behind him and put my head against his shoulder. "Have you ever thought about getting an assistant?" I asked. "It seems like you spend a lot of time working on the small stuff."

"As soon as the transition occurs, I'll get someone. I like to think of myself as an organized person, but the details that go into running a group as large as ours can be overwhelming at times."

"I think you already know, but I talked to Tony down in his office before I came up. He said he's waiting for the negotiations to finish up with the Black Death before he makes everything official."

Max pulled the cork out of the bottle and it made a pleasant popping sound. He poured out two glasses and handed one to me.

"That's right," Max said. "He told me the group is mine any time I wanted it, but he said he'd prefer to see things through with the Black Death before he steps down."

"But things are going well with that, right? The last time we had a negotiation meeting, everyone seemed to agree on pretty much everything. Tony said they seemed to be responsive to his latest offer."

"True, everything seems to be going well, at least for the moment. As soon as we finalize our positions, Tony will feel comfortable going into his version of retirement. Although he'll never be completely out of it. I think he'll always want to give me advice."

"If everything's going well, why's he worried about handing over the group?"

"It's not so much that he's worried, I think he just wants the transition to be clean, without me needing to clean up what he feels is his mess. Besides, if I were to make a guess, I think it goes back to when he was shot."

"What about it?"

"Tony's old school about most things. I think he wants to separate his injury from his stepping down. He doesn't want it to seem that he was too weak to hold the position. I can respect him for that."

"Alright, I can see that."

"Plus, in talking with him, I think he wants you and I to have a month or two of relative peace, so we can have some time together and get to know each other better. As I've told you, once the transition occurs, it'll get busy around here."

"This isn't busy?"

"Tony's still doing half the work. Once the change happens, it'll all be on me. Speaking of that, Tony might have already told you, but we need to have another meeting with the negotiator from the Black Death. I'm hoping to get this cleared up quickly. From what our sources tell us, she's assumed a position of leadership in their group. Whatever we negotiate with her has a good chance of being implemented."

"You have sources? In the Black Death?"

Shit, that can't be good.

"Everyone has sources. It wouldn't surprise me if they had someone planted in our organization as well. We're always on the lookout for it, but we hire a lot of people and it's good tactical awareness to assume not all of them are loyal. It's why we always keep the important things on a need-to-know basis."

"I guess that makes sense."

"Are you hungry?"

"Starving. Let's see what they made for us tonight."

The dinner was wonderful, as it always is when Max and I are together. I guess it's considered a perk when you run a five-star Scottsdale resort.

"Have you ever heard of Vail?" Max asked as we were eating. "It's a ski town and resort in Colorado, about an hour and a half west of Denver. At the base of the mountain is a beautiful village. I think you'd like it."

"I've not only heard of it, but I actually went there once. It was in the summer but it was gorgeous."

"How about that for our weekend?"

"You're serious? That'd be perfect. It looked like a European alpine village in the summer, I can't imagine how beautiful it'll look in the winter."

"Okay then. Plan on me picking you up at your place at about eleven o'clock next Friday morning. We'll be in Vail in time to have dinner."

Thoughts of sleigh rides, crackling wood fireplaces, and champagne in an outdoor hot tub filled my head.

"I can't think of anything more wonderful," I said as I leaned over to give him a kiss.

"Do you ski?"

What?

I stopped with my lips halfway to his. "Um, you mean snow ski? No, the only time I ever go into the mountains in the winter is to go shopping."

"Would you like to try? It's a wonderful sport that combines speed with a little danger. You might like it."

Are you nuts?

"I guess, if you want to," I said with a sinking feeling. "Um, do you ski?"

"I've skied most of my life. Living in Arizona has made that somewhat more of a challenge, but I still try to go once or twice a year. Vail's a world class ski resort and they have some beautiful trails. I can't think of a better place to learn to ski."

Great.

~~~~

Twenty minutes later, we'd gotten to coffee and desserts. "You know," Max said, as he stirred the cream into our coffees, "if you ever wanted to change your hair back to the darker color, it would be good with me."

"Really? You liked it?" I asked, momentarily forgetting about skiing as I absentmindedly reached up and started to twirl a strand. Looking at Max was also stirring up some naughty thoughts that had nothing to do with snow. "I tried the darker thing with my hair for a few weeks, but I didn't think it looked good. As soon as it started to grow out, I went back to the salon and had them switch it back to the way it was."

"It was playful. I thought it looked good on you."

"I'm glad you liked the hair. I'll change it back sometime if you want me to." I picked up my coffee and looked at Max as I sipped it. "But honestly, right now, my mind is drifting… elsewhere."

"Oh, really?" Max asked with a knowing smile. "And where exactly is your mind drifting to?"

"Um, did you remember to bring your bag of toys?"

~~~~

Two hours later, it was a quarter to nine and I knew Max had to leave for his conference call. I really didn't want our evening to be over, so I asked if he could do the conference call from the room.

"I suppose I could," he said after thinking about it for a moment. "This is only the daily wrap-up with the resort operations team. We don't talk about big secrets, it's where we bring up problems that have affected the resorts throughout the day." Max looked around the room. "I guess I don't even need to get up. I could do it from here." He then looked over at me. "That is, if you can keep quiet. It wouldn't be very managerial if they think I'm lying in a bed with a woman in one of the rooms."

I gave him a look that said I was shocked at the very idea. "I promise I won't say a word."

Max texted Gabriella to let her know he'd be doing the conference call from the room. He then got on his phone and dialed in.

The meeting was exactly as Max described it would be, dull and rather routine. For the first fifteen minutes, I lay there and didn't do a thing. But then, my bad side got the better of me and I reached over and lightly ran my fingers up his leg. Max sucked in some air but then gave me a look that said he wasn't amused. I held my finger to my lips as a sign we weren't supposed to talk, then I did it again. ~~~~

Chapter Four

I got to the office the next morning at about eight thirty. When I walked up front, Sophie was busily typing away at something on her computer. Stacks of file folders covered her desk. As usual, a big coffee cup sat next to her mousepad. Gina wasn't in yet. Lenny's Porsche was under the carport but his office door was closed.

I sat in a chair close to her desk. She looked at me for a moment and must have seen the panic and desperation in my eyes.

"What's wrong with you? Did something bad happen on your date with Max last night?"

"Max wants to take me to Colorado and go to Vail with him."

"Wow," she said as she picked up her coffee. "Well, you said you wanted snow and he delivered. I bet it'll be beautiful. You know, I'm completely jealous."

"Maybe, but you don't understand. He wants me to go skiing with him."

Sophie was in the middle of sipping her coffee. Her eyes grew big and she tried to hold in her laughter, but after a few seconds it broke through. She laughed so hard that coffee spewed from the sides of her mouth and flew all over her desk. Her face turned red as she tried to hold in the coffee while she laughed. After a few moments, she gradually calmed down and started to fan her face with her hand. She took in a big breath then looked at me.

"I'm sorry. But you? Skiing?" She started laughing again. She laughed so hard she couldn't breathe and tears were in her eyes. She then used one hand to pretend it was me skiing and her other hand was a big tree. She crashed the skier into the tree a couple of times and each time she laughed harder.

I waited it out.

Sophie calmed down again and grabbed a tissue and started to dab at her face. She then sniffed and coughed a couple of times. "Oh my God," she said between sniffles. "You made me shoot coffee out of my nose."

"Hey, if you're done being amused, I need help. I'm not only worried about crashing into a mountain or falling off a ski lift. I've been looking for clothes to survive going to dinner and maybe shopping in the cold. Max didn't say anything about getting a ski outfit. That means a ski jacket, ski pants, ski socks, insulated gloves, plus goggles and probably a helmet. I don't have any of that and I don't even know where I could shop for that stuff around here."

"I don't think the malls will have anything. You might have to go to a ski shop or somewhere like that. But I can't even guess how expensive that'll be." She thought about it for a few seconds. "Well, don't panic. Let's go online. I'm sure we'll find what you need and Amazon can deliver everything in two days."

She got on her computer and started typing. She frowned, went through a couple of pages, typed some more, then slowly flipped through another two or three pages.

"Well?" I asked.

"Well, they have everything, but it's kind of expensive. They have a checklist of everything you'll need for skiing. It says you'll need all the stuff you were talking about, plus you'll need something called a balaclava."

"What's that?"

"It looks like a hood that covers your entire face, except for your eyes. Sort of like what a bank robber or a ninja would wear."

"So, how much for everything?"

Sophie spent a minute typing and punching numbers into her calculator. "Well, getting even a basic ski outfit is like four hundred dollars. Add another hundred if you want everything to be waterproof, which I assume is a good thing, especially since you'll be spending most of the day lying face down in the snow."

"I don't have five hundred dollars for a new outfit. I've already spent what I have just getting enough clothes to get through the weekend. Even getting a normal winter coat was going to be a stretch."

"Hold on," Sophie said, pointing to her screen. "I might have a solution. There's a thrift store up by the airpark called Going North. Their ad says they specialize in winter clothing, including skiing gear. If you'd like, I'll go with you and help you pick out an outfit."

"Okay, that sounds perfect. I'm going to need your help with this. When do you want to go shopping? It's Thursday now and I'd like to get everything done by sometime this weekend. Otherwise, I'll stress about it all next week."

"We can do it on Saturday, if you want to. I don't have anything planned until dinner."

"Thanks," I said, feeling a little better about the trip. I decided to change the subject, mainly so I didn't have to think about crashing into a tree on the side of a mountain.

"Isn't it a little early for Lenny to have his door closed?" I asked. "He usually keeps it open until ten or eleven."

"Oh, that. I think he tried to have a date last night with the receptionist from his dentist's office. You know how that always goes for him."

"Oh no. Did it happen again?"

"Yeah," Sophie said. "I think so."

In court, Lenny presents himself as a smooth well-spoken professional. But that's only because he's had days to prepare his statements and he spends hours in his office practicing his important speeches. When forced to engage in spur-of-the-moment conversation, especially with a woman he's attracted to, he becomes tongue tied and frustrated. The harder he tries to be smooth, the worse he sounds. What usually happens is he blurts out a passionate speech about his true feelings for the woman, the various physical and emotional traits he finds to be attractive about her, and his hopes on where the relationship will go. Unfortunately, since this usually happens mid-way through the first date, things usually go to hell and there's seldom a second date.

"You know what's going to happen now," Sophie said. "Lenny'll be thinking about women again. The last time that happened, he started going commando and walked around the office with a stiffy for three days. It was so gross. Every time I saw him walk by, I wanted to throw up a little bit."

"Yuck, I don't want to see that either. There must be something we can do."

"Short of getting him a hooker, I don't know what we can do."

"Maybe we could set him up with someone?"

Sophie looked at me. "What? Like on a date?"

"Sure, why not. If we can find a woman he's compatible with, maybe he could go out occasionally and have a nice time. If he has an outlet, maybe we won't have to deal with his moods so much."

"Seriously? You want us to find a date? For Lenny?"

"Oh, it can't be that hard to find him someone compatible. What do we know about Lenny?"

"Well," Sophie said as she started counting on her fingers. "He's rude, abrupt, insensitive, uncaring, and he doesn't give a shit about anyone's feelings but his own."

The door to the back offices opened and Gina walked in.

"It sounds like you're talking about our boss," she said as she looked toward his office. "Why's his door closed?"

"Lenny had another first date last night and we're guessing it went like it always does," I said.

"Laura thinks we need to find someone for Lenny to date," Sophie said. "Then we wouldn't have to deal with his shitty moods."

"I don't know," Gina said. "Finding someone for Lenny would be a challenge."

"I know Lenny was once married," Sophie said. "What was she like?"

"I never found out a lot about her," Gina said. "I don't even know her name. Lenny only refers to her as the Soul Grinder."

"Well, opposites sometimes attract," I said. "Maybe that's the way we should go?"

"Are you saying we should find someone who's totally charming and sensitive?" Sophie asked. "Someone who'll appreciate Lenny for the way he completes her?"

Gina and I burst out laughing. "God no," Gina said. "Lenny's tried that before and they never make it through the first date. You know what happens. After his fifth or sixth insensitive comment, she makes up a transparent excuse and leaves. Then we always have to deal with sad-puppy Lenny for a week."

"I could care less if he's sad," Sophie said. "I just don't want another week of dealing with Mr. Stiffy. I seriously can't handle that anymore."

"The only time I can remember Lenny being happy after a date was the time Elle took him home," I said. "That was the night Jackie got the Saguaro Sky."

Elle is one of our Scottsdale cougar friends. The cougars are a group of stunningly beautiful, wealthy, middle-aged women, who like to troll the high-end clubs, looking for athletic younger men for casual hook-up relationships.

Physically, Elle's a tall, graceful woman, somewhere in her late forties, with long dark hair and expressive green eyes. She has the toned body that comes from having a personal trainer and a high-end gym membership. Elle is actually a nickname the bouncers gave her when they couldn't remember Lynaé, her real name. They shortened it to "L" and she's been Elle ever since.

"You're right," Sophie said. "You know, he's asked me about Elle more than once. He's even asked if I have any pictures of her."

"How are we going to find someone like Elle who's willing to date Lenny?" Gina asked. "Women like that can have anyone they want."

"Um," I said. "Instead of finding a woman like Elle, why don't we see if Elle wants to get together with Lenny for a second date?"

"I don't know," Sophie said. "The one time they got together was a fluke. Between the excitement over Jackie getting the resort and the champagne we were drinking, Elle sorta got the inspiration to take Lenny home. Honestly, I think it was only thank-you sex."

"Still," Gina said. "It wouldn't hurt to ask."

"The last couple of times I went out with the cougars," Sophie said, "Elle didn't come with us. I know they're going out again tonight, nine thirty at Nexxus, same as always. I think it's Pammy's birthday today. I was planning on going and you both should too. We could have some fun, and if Elle's there, we could ask her about dating Lenny."

"That's a good idea," Gina said. "But you'll need to go ahead without me. I'm going out with Jet tonight."

"You're going out?" Sophie asked. "Isn't going out with a client sorta against the rules?"

"Sort of," Gina said. "But it's not like he's a suspect in a major crime or anything. The formal meeting is here at one thirty, so I called him up last night. We're going out for coffee after work and we'll talk about the assignment."

"And then you'll take him out to dinner?" I asked. "Maybe share a bottle of wine?"

"That's a distinct possibility," Gina said with a wide smile.

"Well," I said to Sophie. "I should be able to make it to Pam's party with the cougars, as long as nothing comes up. Hopefully Elle comes along as well."

The door to the street opened and Susan walked in. She had a colorful beach bag slung over her shoulder that I assumed held the photo albums. From the look on her face, I could tell she was a little nervous.

"Hey," I said. "Are you ready to start the investigation?"

Susan blew out a deep breath. "I guess. Honestly, I'm totally stressing about this. I didn't sleep a lot last night."

"You'll be fine," Gina said. "Laura's good at this. Besides, you're only at step one. Don't be too surprised if this takes a while to get results."

"I know," Susan said. "I keep telling myself not to get my hopes up. But after all this time, it's hard to wait. Where are we going to meet the woman who sued my dad?"

"She's at One Arizona Center," I said. "Her admin said parking is underneath the building. Are you ready? We can take my car."

"Good luck," Sophie said. "Let me know if you need any help with anything."

I led Susan through the back offices and through the security door. She slowed down a little when she saw my car. I seem to get this reaction a lot, mostly due to the modifications that have been made to it over the past year.

"I know it looks a little rough," I said as I hit the beeper to unlock the doors. "But it still runs great."

~~~~

We drove to downtown Phoenix and made our way to the Arizona Center. We found Building One and took the ramp down to the garage. When I saw the parking rates, I was glad this was for work and Lenny was paying.

We took the garage elevator up to the lobby then waited in line at a crowded security desk. When it was our turn, we each handed over our licenses and let the guard know we had a ten o'clock appointment with Kathleen Alastor at K A Resort Services. She consulted her computer, then scanned our ID's, took our pictures, and printed up two visitor's badges.

Attached to the wall was a huge building directory. We stood in front of it and scanned for Kathleen's company. When we located the business, I was surprised that it took up three entire floors. We took the elevator to the uppermost floor of the business, where I assumed the executive offices would be located.

The elevator opened to a lobby. There was a large door with *K A Resort Services, Inc.* stenciled on it directly across from the elevator. We went in and were directed to a plush reception area. The woman at the desk looked up as we approached.

"May I help you?" she asked.

"We have a ten o'clock with Kathleen Alastor," I said.

She typed our names into a computer and verified we had an appointment. She then picked up the phone and made a call, letting Kathleen know we'd arrived.

"Ms. Alastor's office is at the end of the hall," she said. "It's the one with the big fern next to it."

We walked down the long hallway, passing several nice offices. "I hate doing things like this," Susan said. "I've never been good at meeting new people, especially over something important."

"I'll be there the entire time," I said. "You'll do great."

We found the open door with the fern next to it. We knocked on the door frame and went in.

Kathleen Alastor was a no-nonsense type of woman, somewhere in her early sixties, with short dark hair and a solid body. She eyed us as we came in and coldly offered us the two wooden chairs in front of her desk.

"Which one of you is Susan, the one who wants to see me about the personal matter?" Kathleen asked. From her tone, I knew this wasn't going to be an easy interview.

"I am," Susan replied. "My name's Susan Monroe. I'm sorry to bother you about this, but..."

"So, who are you?" Kathleen interrupted as she thrust a finger towards me.

"Um, I'm Laura Black. I'm an investigator at Halftown, Oeding, Shapiro, and Hopkins in Scottsdale."

"Right," Kathleen said, "I should have guessed. Opposing counsel from back when I had to fight to get my half of the casino profits. The lawyer's name was Paul Oeding as I recall. He was a real prick. How is he? Still making a living off of causing people misery?"

"No," I said. "He's dead. Skiing accident."

Wait, that's right. Paul Oeding actually died while he was skiing.

"Ha," Kathleen barked out. "Well, what's that they say? A dead lawyer's a good start. So, why are you here? Since you were involved in one lawsuit, I assume you're here to try it again. If so, stop right there and call my lawyer, Tom Elliot from Perkins, Elliot, and McMann."

"No," Susan said. "We aren't here for anything like that. I'm trying to locate someone who was either called William Southard or Michael McKinsey. Although, I guess it's possible you knew him under another name."

"What do you want with Michael?" Kathleen asked. "There hasn't been a lot of love lost between us since he betrayed me, but that still doesn't mean I'd send some gold digger after him. What'd he do to you honey, get you pregnant?"

"No," Susan said. "I believe Michael McKinsey's my father."

Kathleen's eyes grew big and she stopped to look at Susan again. Her eyes swept up and down Susan's body, as if she was trying to figure out the truth just by looking at her.

"That's a pretty ridiculous claim," Kathleen said, her voice somewhat quieter. "I assume you have some proof to show me?"

Susan pulled out two photo albums and placed them on the desk. Kathleen took the top one and opened it. She quickly flipped through the first few pages, then stopped, looking at one of the photos of the man we now knew as Michael McKinsey. It was an informal portrait of him with palm trees in the background. He had a playful smile on his face and you could see he was happy. As she looked at the picture, her face softened and her breathing got faster.

"Who's the woman with him in these pictures?" Kathleen quietly asked.

"That's my mom, Olivia Monroe. At the time she owned an art gallery in Old Town Scottsdale. That's where they met. He came in to get some artwork for a company he said he owned."

"How old are these pictures?"

"I'm twenty-five, so most of these are twenty-six years old."

Kathleen slowly flipped through the album. When she got to the end, she asked for the other. As with the first, she flipped pages, stopping to linger over any picture of Michael that showed him looking into the camera. One in particular held her interest. It was of Michael outside somewhere. He was dressed casually and had a broad smile on his face. She lightly touched the picture with the tips of her fingers and looked at it for almost a minute before she turned the page. By the time she got to the last couple of pages, it was obvious that Olivia was showing a large baby bump.

"Do you have any pictures of you together with this woman?" Kathleen asked, her voice barely above a whisper.

"Um, sure," Susan said. She pulled out her phone and pulled up a picture. "This is the two of us back when I was in elementary school. I keep this one on my phone because it's one of my mom's favorites." Kathleen looked between the picture on the phone and the pictures of the woman in the albums. Susan then pulled up another picture of herself with a smiling woman in her mid-fifties.

"This is mom and me from about six months ago."

Kathleen closed the album and slid it back to Susan. "Okay, it seems like you're telling the truth. I remember back when Michael was spending all his weekends in Scottsdale. Your dad told me he'd met someone special. Honestly, I thought it was great that he was finally happy. I was surprised when he ended it. I was especially surprised after I found out that he and the woman had a daughter together. Unfortunately, this was the same time we were getting sued by our financial partners and I didn't spend a lot of thought on Michael's personal life. After that, he stole the casino from me and I had to take him to court. I'm one of the few people who knew Michael had a child. Having a daughter seemed to make him happy, but he asked me never to tell anyone. I've always wondered when I'd meet you. You do have Michael's eyes."

"Tell me about my father," Susan said. "You were business partners for a long time?"

"Your dad and I have a long history together. We started out trying to date, but it was obvious from the start it wasn't going to work out romantically. I thought the relationship had possibilities, but he never did develop feelings towards me. Fortunately, we seemed to get along great when it came to business. We worked on several smaller projects together, but we were always determined to find a big one. Something that would really put us on the map. We ended up buying an old sanitarium on the banks of the Colorado River, one that had previously been converted into a casino. It had already gone through foreclosure twice and had been boarded up for over three years. We were able to get it for next to nothing. Because of the color of the stones used to build it, we called it the Black Castle. The first stage of the project mainly involved paperwork for the gaming license and the permit to build a bridge across the river, so people could get to the casino from the Arizona side more easily. That part took almost two years. Over the next couple of years, we completely refurbished the property and built the actual bridge."

"I've heard of the casino," I said. "It's somewhere in Nevada, right?"

"Yes. It's on a small piece of flat property between a mountain cliff and the banks of the Colorado River, about five miles south of Laughlin."

"I once saw a show about the casino," Susan said. "They said it was mainly a fancy brothel that had high-stakes gambling and catered to every fantasy people could think of."

"Well, maybe that's how it ended up, but when we first started, we mainly focused on the gambling."

"What can you tell us about the lawsuit between you and Michael?" I asked. "All we know is that you both formed a company, then he sold it out from under you. You took him to court to get half the proceeds and settled before trial. The amount wasn't listed."

"Yes, that's the short version. We opened the casino almost thirty years ago and everything was falling into place. Then Michael tells me there's a problem with our loans. Some of the financial things we had to do to make sure the casino opened on time violated the terms of the loans and they were being called in. We eventually learned our financier was a front for a Las Vegas crime organization and they'd done this sort of thing before. We were threatened with violence and told to transfer all of our rights or be killed. Lawyers became involved and control of the casino was moved to the gangsters. The funny thing was, they kept Michael on as the legal owner and general manager of the property. To the outside world, the only thing that changed was that I had left the business. It was only later I found out Michael had facilitated the whole thing and was handsomely paid to do it. That's what I took him to court over. All I wanted was my half."

"Did you get it?"

"Yes. Your dad didn't even fight me on it. Honestly, I got the feeling he ultimately felt bad about what he'd done."

"Do you know where I can find my dad?" Susan asked.

"Sure, that's not a hard one. He still owns the Black Castle Casino and you'll probably find him there. From what I've heard, your dad seldom leaves the place. I guess he's worried it can't run without his personal oversight."

"We're trying to find Susan's dad," I said. "We aren't looking for anything from him other than to introduce him to Susan and maybe exchange phone numbers. If you think he's going to be at the casino, we'll probably go up in a couple of days to look for him. Any help or advice you could give us would be welcome."

Kathleen sat back in her chair and seemed to think. As she did, her smile became mischievous. She then started talking, as if to herself. "So, Michael's long-lost daughter will be going up to the casino to announce herself. That'll really stir the shit up." She paused, looked at Susan, then looked vacantly across the room. It was clear she was thinking intently. After several moments she started talking to herself again. "Well, why not? Maybe it's time to shake things up."

Kathleen seemed to come back to the present and she looked at Susan. "You've told me a very interesting story. But you have to understand that I have a lot of enemies in this world and they're always trying to get at me. You would've needed to give your ID's to the guard to get into the building. Let me run some checks on the both of you. Come back after lunch, say around one thirty. If your backgrounds match with what you've already told me, maybe I can help."

~~~~

We stopped by a Subway that was in the building next door, grabbed some sandwiches, then went outside to eat. It was a beautiful November day. Temperatures were in the mid-seventies, there was a light breeze, and there wasn't a cloud in the sky.

We walked around for two or three minutes before eventually finding an open bench underneath a huge ficus tree. While we were eating, Rihanna's song, *S&M,* started playing from the phone in my back pocket.

"Hey, Sophie," I said when I answered. "What's up?"

"I called Jackie and asked when Elle would be going out with the group again. Jackie's pretty sure she'll be coming tonight for Pammy's birthday. The girls want to set Pam up with an athletic college guy for the night."

"Did you find out why Elle hasn't been going out with the group lately?"

"No, but we'll probably find out tonight. I'm hoping she won't be too annoyed when we ask her about dating Lenny again."

"I hope not." I then spent several minutes downloading Sophie on what we'd been able to find out from Kathleen Alastor.

"Do you think Susan's father really owns a casino? That would be pretty cool."

"I don't know, but it's looking like a possibility. Would you be able to run a secret software check on the casino and see if anything matches up with the story we just got?"

"No problem. It'll give me something that's at least interesting to do today."

~~~~

We arrived back at Kathleen Alastor's office right at one thirty. Kathleen was again seated behind her desk and motioned for us to take the two visitor's chairs. She seemed to have warmed up to us, at least a little.

"I've looked into your backgrounds," she said. "I didn't find anything about either of you that raises any red flags for me. Plus, you're both Scottsdale natives, which is a rare enough thing when everyone I meet anymore seems to be from a state that borders Canada."

"Are you still going to help us?" Susan asked.

"Yes, I'll help you. I'm thinking Michael could probably use some change in his life by now. But I'll be honest, it'll be a challenge even getting you into the casino to see him. It's members only and they won't give you a membership."

"Do you know where he lives?" I asked. "We could wait until he comes home and knock on his front door."

"That won't help. From what I hear, he seldom leaves the property. He had a rather nice apartment on the top floor and I imagine that's where he still lives. I'll tell you what, come to my house tomorrow afternoon at two o'clock. I have something that might help."

She took a pad and wrote down a street address in Paradise Valley. She tore off the paper and handed it to Susan.

"That's it, until tomorrow," Kathleen said as she sat back in her chair. "Anything else you'd like to know?"

"Um," I said, "would you mind validating our parking?"

~~~~

I drove us back to the office and parked out back. We went through the rear door and walked up front to reception. Lenny and Gina were out, but Sophie was still at her desk, working on a stack of documents for Lenny to use at a hearing the next day. She moved a pile of file folders out of the way so she could see us better.

"Well?" Sophie asked. "How'd the second meeting with Kathleen Alastor go?"

"Better than I expected," Susan said. "I think she believes me and she's trying to help."

"That's great," Sophie said. "What's your next step?"

"We're mostly done with the background work on this," I said. "I'm thinking the next step is to go up to the Black Castle Casino in Nevada and see if we can talk with Michael McKinsey directly."

"Okay…" Susan said, looking a little anxious. "When do you want to do that?"

"If Kathleen really does have something that will help us get in, I'm thinking about Monday. Everyone who works in casino administration will probably be there. Plus, the crowds shouldn't be as bad as on the weekend. Would going up three days from now work for you?"

"I thought you were going to say that. Okay, let's go up there and do it. Maybe I can meet with him and we can get this over with."

"With the Monday morning traffic, it'll take us three and a half or four hours to drive up to the casino. If we leave by eight, we can be there by noon. That'll give us the entire afternoon to find your dad. With any luck, we'll be back in Scottsdale by eight or nine o'clock Monday night. Bring along a nice cocktail dress and some shoes. We'll need to look like we belong there if we want to get past casino security."

"Um," Sophie said. "Before you go, I have some information on the casino. Like you asked, I used the secret software and I got back a ton. I put the folder back on your desk. It turns out Michael McKinsey and Kathleen Alastor are still listed as the two official owners, but it's actually run by an organized crime family based out of Las Vegas. They seem to be the criminal remnants from back when all of Vegas was run by gangsters. I've got a dozen police reports from over the last ten years of people who were reported to have gone missing after they were supposed to have visited the casino. The police were never able to prove anything, but there's a pretty definite pattern. If you're able to get in there, you'll need to watch yourselves. It doesn't seem like a nice place."

~~~~

I made plans with Susan to come by the office the next afternoon so we could go over to Kathleen's together. Sophie was going to be working for a while, so I told her I'd see her at Nexxus at nine thirty, then I took off.

I stopped by a Filiberto's and picked up a carne asada burrito and a bag of warm chips. I loaded up on both red and green salsa, along with a container of the chunky pico de gallo for the chips. I then took everything back to the apartment.

As soon as I walked in and set everything on the coffee table in front of the couch, I heard the squeaking of Marlowe's cat door in the bedroom. He came running into the living room, looked up at me, and gave me one of his squeaky meows. I knew this was his way of asking if I'd happened to bring him home a tuna and salmon dinner.

Getting no response to his urgent pleas for food, he jumped up on the coffee table and delicately took a couple of experimental sniffs of the bag. Since spicy Mexican is not on his list of favorite foods, he jumped onto the couch, then just sat there and stared at me with what I could only assume was cat annoyance.

I popped on the TV to *Say Yes to the Dress*, grabbed a Diet Pepsi from the fridge, then spread everything out on the table. Marlowe watched as I ate the chips and the burrito, even getting up a couple of times to make sure there wasn't something on my plate he'd consider eating.

After I was done, I remembered my promise to Tony to talk with Danielle. I called her and she answered right away.

"Hey," I said. "How are you feeling?"

"I'm doing better. Still sore, but I guess that's to be expected."

Danielle's father was Escobar Salazar, head of a violent Mexican drug cartel called the Black Death. He decided that she would take over as leader of the cartel's Arizona operations. Unfortunately, before the handover of power, there'd been an assassination attempt on Danielle. I never did find out exactly what had happened, but her injuries kept her in a hospital bed for over two weeks. While she was laid up from her injuries, and since we looked enough alike to pass for one another, I was asked to take her place at the formal ceremony installing her as the head of the Arizona branch of the group.

In order to fool the rest of the organization into thinking I was Danielle, I had my hair lengthened and colored to match hers. I then did my makeup and clothes to duplicate her style. It seemed to fool everyone, except for my long-term enemy in the group, a vicious man named Raul. He tried to attack me during the ceremony, but was shot by Danielle's protector, a man named Señor Largo.

"I talked with Tony yesterday," I said. "He'd like us to get together for another negotiation meeting."

"Good, I think we're ready to finalize things."

"When do you want to do it?" I asked.

Danielle laughed. "If I know you, your schedule will be the busier one. When do you think you'll have time?"

"Um, maybe Saturday. Either lunch or dinner, whatever works out better for you. No guarantees I won't need to cancel, but as of now I'm good."

"Let's do dinner on Saturday. Back to La Playa Bonita? I love that place."

"Perfect," I said. "Six o'clock?"

"I'll see you there."

Chapter Five

I was in the middle of binge watching my third episode of *Say Yes to the Dress*, this one featuring mothers from hell, when the theme to *The Love Boat* sang out from my phone. Breaking into a wide smile, I hit the accept button.

"Hey you," I said.

"Hello, gorgeous," Max said in his deep and steady voice. "I know I'm earlier than usual. I hope I'm not disturbing you."

"Not at all. If I'm in the middle of something, I usually won't answer the phone. Marlowe and I are on the couch, watching women shop for wedding dresses."

"Really? A show about shopping? For wedding dresses?" I could hear him suppress a laugh. "How is that even a thing? Should I be concerned about you?"

"Hey, it's nothing to make fun of. These women spend thousands of dollars on a dress. Their entire family, along with most of their friends, come along to help pick it out. Everyone has their own ideas on what would look good. There's actually a lot of drama involved in making sure the bride gets the perfect dress."

"Okay, I get that the dresses cost a lot. But they'll only wear it once, for maybe seven or eight hours in total, right? Does it really matter if it's not perfect? Besides, they all sort of look the same. As long as it's the right color and it fits, any of them should work. Or am

I missing something?"

"You should come over here sometime and cuddle with me while we watch the show. You could learn all about it. It'd be fun."

"If I was with you on the couch, we wouldn't be watching TV. I could think of better ways to keep you amused."

Yum. I bet you could.

I smiled at the happy thought.

"Anyway," I said, "I'm glad you called early. I'm going out with Sophie and the cougars later tonight. We're trying to set up Lenny with one of the girls."

"That should be interesting. He could probably afford one, but isn't his personality a little, um, uneven for dating?"

"His personality sucks. But we're hoping if he's dating someone on a regular basis it'll help with that."

"Well, good luck. I sometimes don't see how you can stand working for him."

"He pays me, that's why. I have a question about the skiing. Where do you get the skis and the boots and the poles? Does the hotel have some you can borrow or how does that work?"

"I'm going to bring my own, but since this is your first time, we'll rent everything you'll need. I'll take you to my favorite ski shop. It's close to the lifts and they'll set you up in no time. If you find you like to ski, we can get you some equipment of your own for the next time."

"Okay. I wasn't sure how it was done, but that sounds reasonable. What are you doing tonight?"

"My regular end-of-the-day meetings. I had a few minutes so I thought I'd call. It sounds like you're getting into the winter vacation spirit. I'm glad. It should be fun."

"I've already started shopping. I seriously don't have anything for a skiing weekend."

"You don't have anything? What, no big sweaters? No turtlenecks? Warm pants? Nothing?"

"Did you forget? I've lived in Scottsdale my entire life. For me, cold weather clothing means long sleeves. Sophie and I are going out this weekend to find everything."

"That should be interesting. You and Sophie, shopping with a purpose."

"You know it."

~~~~

For the next two hours, I sat on the couch, watching TV and juggling the finances enough to pay off the monthly bills. By this point, I'd had four or five Diet Pepsis and was buzzing off the caffeine.

I was also thinking about spending the weekend with Max. The more I thought about it, the more uneasy I became. I hadn't really thought it through when I'd said I wanted to go to the snow. It was an impulse decision, something that always gets me into trouble.

In this case, going somewhere to visit the snow had somehow turned into me learning to ski. My thoughts about the trip had changed from finding a coat that was warm enough for shopping in the snow to hoping I survived the weekend without suffering any serious injuries.

~~~~

At about eight thirty, I went to the closet and started looking for an outfit. I'd bought a sexy new green cocktail dress several weeks before, specifically for going out with the girls, but now I was going to need it on Monday for going up to the casino with Susan.

Rather than trying to come up with something different, I grabbed my stand-by evening outfit of my short black skirt with the silver rainbow sparkles and my favorite low-cut red silky blouse. I also pulled out my jewelry box and removed the diamond and ruby tennis bracelet. I held it up to the light and slowly moved it back and forth, simply to watch the sparkles in the gems.

Jackie Wade had given it to me, as a thank-you present, from an assignment I'd worked almost a year ago. As I put it on, it reminded me of the kidnapping and the horrible time we'd both had at the hands of Carlos the Butcher. I was surprised at the relief I still felt just knowing he was dead.

When I'd told Jackie the news, she broke down and confided that he'd been the cause of her continuing nightmares. Two or three nights a week, in her dreams, she would re-live the events of that day, even months after the kidnapping. After she learned of his death, she said the nightmares had vanished.

~~~~~~

Sophie said the cougars were going to start out at Nexxus at around nine thirty. This is where they usually gathered before deciding where to go for the night. I drove over to Shoeman Lane and cruised up and down the nearby streets until I found a parking space. I then walked over to Nexxus. Fortunately, it was still too early for the crowds to have gathered in full force and I didn't have to wait in line for more than a couple of minutes. I paid the outrageous cover then went inside.

The cougars usually met on the lounge side of Nexxus to get their nights started. I think this was because it was walking distance to most of the nightclubs they liked to go to. I liked it because the music was always up-tempo, but not so loud that you had to shout to talk.

As always, the girls weren't hard to spot. So far, only Jackie, Pammy, and Cindy had arrived. Annie and Sophie were also there as the two pumas, or cougars-in-training. I was also considered a puma of sorts, but I didn't go out with the girls often enough to have picked up the official title with the bouncers.

The girls had their usual corner of the lounge to themselves and there were already several good-looking guys hovering around the group. As I walked closer, the delicate aroma of several mingled high-end perfumes filled the air. Everybody said hello and Jackie waved me over to the spot she'd saved for me next to her.

"Hi, Jackie," I said as I sat down. "I haven't seen you in a while. How are you and how's everything going over at the resort?"

Through a strange set of circumstances during an assignment I'd had earlier in the year, Jackie found herself as the sole owner of the upscale Saguaro Sky golf resort in North Scottsdale. While having this much responsibility thrust upon someone would intimidate most people, Jackie took it all in stride. Rather than delegating the day-to-day operations to a manager, she seemed to enjoy handling everything herself. From what I've been able to tell, she's good at it.

"Oh, it's one thing after another," she laughed. "They raised my water rates again. The margins on the golf operations are already thin and this only squeezes them more. Plus, the past couple of months I've been critically short on staff. Everyone I try to hire is either illegal or incompetent. I used to be able to hire college students for part-time work, but now they won't even call me back unless I start them off as a manager or offer to pay them twenty dollars an hour." She shook her head. "But you don't want to hear about my problems."

She looked down at my wrist, at the diamond and ruby tennis bracelet she'd given me months ago. "I'm glad to see you're wearing it," she said. "I hope you still like it."

"Are you kidding? I only have three pieces of real jewelry and this is the most beautiful."

"How've you been," she asked. "Sophie says you stopped dating the cop. Jackson Reno, wasn't it?"

"Yeah, that ended a couple of months ago."

"I'm sorry to hear that. I only met him the one time, when you rescued me from that awful man, Carlos, but he seemed nice. Are you with anyone new yet?"

"Well, nothing official."

"Let me know when you start looking again. I'm always running into single guys your age who have good jobs or at least a large trust fund."

"I'll do that," I said. "I hear it's Pammy's birthday today."

"Yes, and you know how much she likes hooking up with college athletes. As it turns out, ASU is hosting a basketball tournament all week. It's tradition that when a team loses, they let their players have a night on the town before they fly them back home. We've asked a few of our bouncer friends to give us a call if they see a group of them coming in to any of the clubs. We'll then head over to wherever they are and let Pam take her pick."

"Won't it be a challenge if the guys are together in a group?"

Jackie looked at me like I'd said something ridiculous. "Oh, we know how to separate a stray from the rest of the herd. Horny college guys, especially horny college guys away from home, are easy pickings."

Within about fifteen minutes, Elle, Sonia, and Shannon also arrived. Three or four minutes later, two of the guys near the table had started up a conversation with Shannon and Cindy. One by one, the rest of the cougars began to strike up conversations with the men.

I was about to move over next to Elle when Jackie's phone buzzed with an incoming text. She looked at it and smiled. "Ladies," she said to everyone. "A group of basketball players from Florida State just showed up at Shade. Pammy, what do you think?"

Pam's smile was huge. "Florida State? That sounds delightful. I'd love to have a tall southern gentleman keep me company tonight."

~~~~

Shade is a classy upscale lounge at W Scottsdale, a high-end hotel down the street from Nexxus. The club surrounds a swimming pool and there's usually a band or a DJ. There's also a lower level lounge called the Living Room. It's beautiful, somewhat quieter, and is always a great place to talk.

We walked over to the hotel and made our way to the lower lounge. As usual, once the bouncers had discovered we were coming over, they'd reserved a corner couch for the group. Jackie slipped a tip to the lead bouncer and we made ourselves comfortable on one of the big sofas. The music was at a perfect volume and fortunately I was able to position myself next to Elle.

As always, she was dressed to impress in an outfit I assumed was this season's Donna Karan, her favorite designer. Her makeup looked like it'd been professionally applied and her hair was flawless. As with every other time I'd seen her, she was wearing forty or fifty thousand dollars' worth of jewelry. Tonight, it was sapphires and diamonds in what looked to be platinum settings. As I sat down next to her, I could smell her Coco Chanel.

A group of handsome men silently approached, then began to hover around our group. Within three minutes, as if by magic, everyone's favorite drink was placed in front of them. I noticed Sophie had started up a conversation with a good-looking guy who appeared to be a few years older than her. The man seemed to come from money and was dressed as if he were some sort of business professional.

"Hi, Elle," I said when we'd settled back with our drinks in hand. "I'm glad you're here tonight. Sophie says you don't go out with the girls as often as you used to."

"Oh, she's right. This is probably the first time in a month. But it's Pammy's birthday and I didn't want to miss it."

"Why haven't you been going out as much? Is it interfering with work?"

Elle gave me a puzzled look, then shook her head and laughed. "Sorry, I thought you were talking about my charity groups. No, I haven't worked an actual job in years. After my divorce, I had more money than I'd ever need. I put everything into some safe investments and I can't find a way to spend even the interest income it generates."

"Wow, that must be nice. But then, why aren't you going out with the girls?"

"Honestly? I'm starting to lose interest in hooking up with these younger guys. Yes, they're full of energy and they're always eager to please, but lately I haven't been as interested in quick flings. Most of these boys can't hold a conversation and even the ones who know how to talk have nothing in common with me. I don't speak Millennial very well and they don't speak my language at all. The thing that finally got to me was the last guy I hooked up with. He'd never heard of either Duran Duran or Wham!, two of my favorite bands from high school. It made me a little sad. The last couple of times I've gone out has been with guys my own age. Oh, don't get me wrong, I love being with everyone and I'll still go out with the group whenever there's something special going on. But I probably won't hook up with anyone tonight."

"You know," I said as I sipped my scotch, "Lenny told us he had a nice time when he went out with you. I know that was a few months ago, but have you ever thought about seeing him again?"

Elle stared off into space for a moment, as if trying to recall who Lenny was and when she'd gone out with him. "Oh, sure," she finally said. "Leonard the attorney. I remember him. That was the night of the party over at your office, wasn't it? The night Jackie became the owner of the Saguaro Sky. Everyone was so thrilled for her. We were drinking champagne and with all the excitement, I started feeling turned on. I remember grabbing him and dragging him back to my house. Yeah, he was alright. It was actually sort of cute how he kept asking my permission before he did anything." She motioned me closer and spoke in a quiet voice: "Honestly, I think it'd been a while since he'd been with a woman."

"Well, I don't know a lot about his love life, but I know he's not dating anyone in particular at the moment."

"Okay, let me think about it. I seem to be into dating guys my age at the moment."

As we were talking, I remembered that Elle came from up north somewhere. I thought maybe she'd have some advice on clothes for a ski trip to somewhere like Vail.

"You know most of the nice stores in Scottsdale," I said. "Where do they carry actual winter clothing? I'm going to need a couple of outfits."

"Are you going somewhere?"

"I'm going to Vail next weekend for a ski trip. The only problem is I've never skied and I don't have anything that is close to warm enough for the mountains of Colorado. The outfits don't need to be designer, just nice enough to go to a fancy resort."

"I'm originally from Vermont and I grew up skiing. When I moved down here, I got rid of most of my stuff, but I still have a box or two of winter clothing in one of my closets. Why don't you stop by my house sometime this weekend and you can go through them? It might save you some shopping."

"Really? That would be a lifesaver. Thanks, I'll give you a call and we can work out a time for me to come over."

A waitress brought a fresh drink, set it in front of Elle, then pointed out the guy who'd sent it. He was a college-age boy in his early twenties, with a nice body and a sweet smile. Elle spent a few moments looking him up and down, then made a little noise of appreciation.

"Oh my, doesn't he look yummy," she said, then flashed him a smile and waved him over. As he approached our table, Elle had a look on her face I'd seen before. She'd become a hungry lioness, looking at the boy as if he was a wounded gazelle.

"I didn't think you were going to hook up with anyone tonight," I said.

"Well…" she said with a big grin. "You know me. Never say never."

The guy sat down on the other side of Elle. She looked him up and down, then turned back to me. "Sure," she said. "About Leonard. Give him my number. Tell him if he wants to go out again to give me a call. I'd be up for it."

She then turned her full attention on the guy. From the way she was looking at him, I knew he didn't have a chance of getting home until after breakfast the next morning.

~~~~

I stayed with the girls until about eleven forty-five. The party was still in full swing, but I wanted to get some things done in the morning and I needed to get some sleep. I said my goodbyes to the girls and started making my way to the exit. I'd switched to ginger ale after the second scotch, so I was still able to drive.

On my way out, I passed by Sophie, who was still deep in discussion with the same guy. From the scattered shot glasses and the plate of lime wedges, it looked like she'd switched from piña coladas to doing shots of tequila. I interrupted their discussion long enough to tell her I'd see her in the morning.

She looked at me and I could see her face had taken on a light rosy glow. "Okay, Laura," she said in a happy voice. "I'll see you in the morning. Drive safe." She then turned back to her conversation with the man.

~~~~

I woke up relatively early and took a long, hot shower to clear out the cobwebs from the night before. I'd only had a couple of drinks, but it'd been a few days since I'd stayed up past midnight and I was still feeling a little groggy.

When I reached the office, it was sometime around eight and Gina's car was the only one parked in the assigned spaces underneath the carport. I went through the back door and found her in her cubicle typing up a report.

"Hey, Laura," she said. "How's the assignment going so far?"

"We're making progress. We were able to confirm that Michael McKinsey is the actual name of Susan's father and that he's listed as the owner of the Black Castle Casino in Nevada. I took your advice and we went to see his former business partner, Kathleen Alastor."

"That's what Sophie said. How'd that go?"

"She's an odd one. Apparently, they tried to date back when she first formed the business partnership with Michael. She was into the romantic side of the relationship but he never returned her affection. From the way she acted, she still has some lingering feelings for him. At the same time, she's never gotten over how badly he screwed her with the business. I think she's looking at Susan reuniting with her father as some sort of way to get back at him. Considering all of this happened twenty-five years ago, it was a little strange how she kept flipping back and forth between affection and disdain for the guy."

"Love and hate are the same emotion seen from different viewpoints," Gina said. "I saw it all the time during my homicide investigations."

"In addition to confirming the identity of Susan's father, she's also going out of her way to help us. We're going to her house today to talk more about it. Like I said, I'm not so sure of her motivations, but she says she has a way of getting around a membership requirement and for getting us inside the casino. After that, we'll have to trust to luck."

"Sophie was filling me in about Kathleen Alastor and her background. She seems like a good resource."

"She's a great resource, at least to this point. But I'm not sure how far I trust her. It's pretty obvious she isn't doing any of this for Susan's benefit."

We heard the scraping of keys and the sound of the security door opening. Sophie came walking into the cubicles, looking a little out of sorts. Her eyes were bloodshot, her hair wasn't brushed out, and her outfit was crumpled. She appeared to still be wearing last night's makeup and was holding a McDonald's bag and a big coffee.

"Oh my God," Gina said. "What happened to you?"

"Oh, hey, Gina," she said with a big yawn. "Sorry, I didn't get a lot of sleep last night. How was your date?"

"Um, my date was fine," Gina said as she blushed red.

"Oh my God," I said. "You and Jet?"

"No, not what you're both thinking in your dirty little minds. But I don't want to talk about it. At least, not while he's an active client."

I could see Gina wanted to change the subject. She turned to me with a questioning look. "You both went out with the girls last night, right? What happened?"

"I think Sophie stayed out a bit longer than I did," I said.

Sophie dropped into a chair and took a noisy sip of the big coffee. Her eyes had a distant and unfocused look.

"How much sleep did you get?" I asked.

"Um, about an hour," she mumbled. "I went home to change before work and I sort of fell asleep between getting out of last night's outfit and putting this on. My alarm went off and I kept hitting the snooze until it was time to come in."

"What happened with the guy you were with?" I asked. "What was his name?"

"Um, well, we sort of spent all night together. I don't remember his name. Lorenzo, or something like that. He runs some kind of business back east somewhere and he's only in town for a couple of days. We hung out in his room until the sky in the east started to brighten up, then I took off."

"You aren't going to be very focused today," Gina said. "Maybe you should go home and sleep for a couple of hours."

"Naah, Lenny'll be in court most of the day. I can fall asleep at my desk if I need to."

Gina shook her head but didn't say anything. "Were either of you able to talk with Elle?"

Sophie's eyes grew big and she looked really guilty. She'd obviously forgotten the reason we'd gone out with the cougars in the first place.

"I talked with her," I said. "She doesn't go out with the group as much anymore because she's starting to lose interest in the cougar lifestyle. Except for the guy she hooked up with last night at the bar, she's mostly been going out with men her own age."

"Did you ask her about dating Lenny?" Gina asked.

"I did," I said with a laugh. "I was surprised, but she said she had a nice time when they went out and she'd be willing to do it again."

"Really?" Sophie asked. "Huh, I would've thought she'd have higher standards."

"I'd be thrilled if we can change Lenny's perspective on dating to something more positive," Gina said. "Did Elle say anything about where or when would be good?"

"She said to give Lenny her number and for him to give her a call."

"Okay," Gina said. "We can work with that."

"You know," Sophie said with a yawn. "For this even to have a chance, we'll need to start working on Lenny right away. It'll take him a couple of days of practice and rehearsal before he'll be ready to talk with Elle, even on the phone."

"Oh, I think we'll be able to get Lenny ready to ask Elle out," Gina said. "That'll be the easy part. The tough part will be getting him ready for the actual date."

"The first time they went out, it was only for drinks and a hook up," Sophie said. "Are we going for that again or will this be a real date?"

"I'm thinking more actual date than hook up," Gina said. "If we only get Lenny ready for cocktails and sex, I can see it ending badly. If we approach this as a real date, with no expectations of intimacy, it'll open up more possibilities."

"I guess you're right," Sophie said. "We'll leave that side of the evening to Elle. If she wants to take Lenny home, I don't think she'll have a problem making it happen."

"I'm not sure how we're going to get him ready to go out with Elle," I said. "I know this was my idea in the first place, but we're going to need to completely retrain him on how to act on a date. He's been having thoughts about Elle for months. If he gets frustrated and ends up pouring out his soul to her halfway through dinner, it'll ruin everything. He'd be devastated and then it'll be worse than ever around here."

"Lenny on a date with Elle?" Sophie mused. "Oh, it'll be a disaster."

"We have one thing going for us," I said. "When I talked with Elle, she recognized it'd been a while since Lenny had been with a woman. I think she cut him some slack because of it. If they go out again, her expectations will be pretty low."

"I think we can make this work," Gina said. "We'll just need to prepare him properly. It'll be like getting him ready for court. If we give him the facts on what makes a woman uncomfortable on a date, he can come up with a winning strategy. If we can teach him to read a woman, like he already knows how to read a jury, he might be able to pull it off."

~~~~

Lenny came through the back door and saw us sitting together in Gina's cubicle. He didn't look like he was in a good mood.

He was about to say something when he looked at Sophie. "What happened to you?" he asked.

"Late night," she said as she loudly sipped her coffee.

"Huh," he said with a shake of his head. "Do you have everything ready for today?"

"It's all laid out on your desk, in the usual order," she said. "Plus, the secret software found out opposing counsel filed for personal bankruptcy last week and he has almost three hundred thousand dollars in credit card debts. His mistress left him and his wife filed for divorce three weeks ago. That may make him distracted today. The file for all of that is on the top of the stack."

Lenny grunted approval. "Nice. Alright, maybe this hearing won't take all day, but I won't be counting on anything. If anyone calls, don't schedule any new appointments until at least Tuesday. Better make that Tuesday afternoon."

He looked over at Gina. "I know you'd rather be working on Jet's assignment, but I'm expecting a report from you today. Is that still in the works? Were you able to establish an alibi for our client or do I have to turn everything over to the DA again?" He looked closer at her. "Is something wrong with you? You look different; happier maybe."

"Nothing I know of," Gina said with a wide smile. "The finished report will be on your desk when you get back today. I was able to establish an alibi, although it's not quite as tight as I'd like it to be. The witnesses are shaky and the timing is slightly off. But, yes, you should be able to work with it."

Lenny perked up. "Well, that's the best news I've had all day. Stop by my office when I get back and we'll go over your next assignment, assuming you can fit it into your schedule. I'll give Sophie what I have on it before I leave and she can start to organize things."

Gina and Lenny looked over at Sophie, who was again noisily sipping her coffee. Sophie gave them a sleepy thumbs-up.

Lenny then looked at me. "How are you doing with yours? Where are you with finding the father? Was the Alastor woman helpful?"

"She was," I said. "She still seems to hold a grudge against Michael McKinsey. It turns out he's the owner of the Black Castle Casino in Nevada. We're meeting with her again today and she says she'll be able to help us get in to see him. If everything goes well, I imagine we'll be driving up to the casino on Monday to talk with him."

"Alright, that's great. But don't forget, you're on a clock. I'm guessing you spent three or four hours on this yesterday. If you spend two or three more hours today, then spend the entire day with the client, hunting around for her dad in Nevada, it'll chew up whatever's left on the retainer. Make sure she knows this is her one shot."

"Will do," I said.

"Sophie," he said. "I'll be taking off in about half an hour. Don't let any calls through unless they're important."

Sophie still had the coffee to her lips and her eyes were halfway closed, but she gave him a salute to acknowledge his order.

"Before you go," Gina said. "Laura picked up some interesting news last night." Then she looked over at me.

I hate it when she does that.

"Okay," Lenny said, now looking at me. "What is it?"

"Um," I said. "Sophie and I ended up going out with the cougars last night. You remember them? Well, it was Pam's birthday and we all ended up at Shade lounge at the W Scottsdale. The girls were trying to find a basketball player for Pam to hook up with."

Lenny twirled his fingers and gave me a look that said he didn't have time for this.

"Anyway, I was talking with Elle and she mentioned that she had a nice time when she went out with you the night of the party over here for Jackie Wade. She said she'd like to go out again. She wanted me to give you her number and asked for you to give her a call."

Lenny turned pale and his eyes went out of focus. His mouth dropped open, his arms fell to his sides, and every muscle in his body went slack. It was like someone had shot him with a Taser. I was surprised he was still able to stand upright. He looked back and forth between the three of us, as if not knowing what to say or do next. Finally, his eyes focused on Sophie.

"I guess you made a good impression on her," Sophie said. "It sounds like maybe she's missing you."

"Really?" he squeaked. "Elle? She misses me?"

"Yes," Gina said. "Now, I know you've gone out with her before, but we might have some additional insights into her personality that could be helpful to know before you call her. You wouldn't want to veer into any areas we know she's sensitive to."

"From the way she talked," I said, "she's interested in getting to know you better, not just for sex, but as a person. So, since the first date with her might only be talking over dinner, we were thinking we could maybe give you some tips on women in general. That way, you'd have less of a chance at having a, um, misunderstanding during the date."

"Yeah," Lenny said in a dreamlike voice. "Good thinking. You're right. That sometimes happens with me and I don't want to mess this up." He turned and slowly walked up to the front offices.

"Okay, that went well," Sophie said. "Although I don't think it'll help him focus at the hearing today. Maybe we shouldn't have told him until after it was over."

"Well," Gina said. "The good news is he's receptive to learning how to date Elle. We'll need to start prepping him right away."

"How are we going to stop him from calling Elle until he's ready?" Sophie asked.

"Simple," I said. "We won't give him Elle's number until he's ready. We'll say we don't have it and we need to get it from Jackie. That'll keep him in a positive mood, but he won't be able to blow everything by talking to her too soon."

~~~~

By eight forty-five, Sophie and I had moved up to reception. Lenny was still in his office, no doubt thinking about Elle. Gina was back at her cubicle, finishing up her report. Sophie had stopped by the bathroom to brush out her hair and touch up her makeup. Between that, and the coffee, she was starting to look a little better.

"I've gotta stop these late nights," she said. "I always feel like crap the next day. I'm thinking maybe I should only go out with the girls on the weekends. That way I can sleep until noon."

"Since I have the morning free, I thought I'd try the malls again. Susan's going to get here around one thirty. Then we're going to Kathleen Alastor's house. I looked up the address, it's in Paradise Valley, not too far from Johnny Scarpazzi's. Do you want to do lunch before I have to head over there?"

"Sounds lovely," she said with a yawn. "Lenny will be out of here in a few minutes and I know Gina has stuff to do all day. I'm thinking I'm going to pull down the shades, lock the door, and take a desk nap for a couple of hours. Swing by around noon. I should be good to go by then."

~~~~

I made it back to the office a little after noon. Sophie's Volkswagen was still under the carport, but Lenny and Gina were out. I went in through the back door and then up to reception. The sun shades on the windows had all been pulled down and the door to the street was locked. Sophie was asleep at her desk. She must have heard the squeak of the door opening though because she gave a jerk and sat up.

"Oh, hey Laura," she said as she yawned. Her eyes were unfocused and her hair was bunched over to one side. It looked like she'd been sleeping for quite a while.

"Sorry to wake you," I said. "Did you still want to do lunch?"

"Yeah, no problem. Lunch sounds good. Give me a few minutes to wake up. How was shopping? Did you find anything?"

"No, I don't think I'm going to be able to find anything in the malls. I think I'm going to need to go to an actual sports store or start shopping on Amazon. If you're still up for it tomorrow, let's go to that thrift store you found. If they don't have anything, I'll need to bite the bullet and dump everything on a credit card. I hate spending that much on an outfit I'll only wear a few times, but I might have to do it anyway."

"Would you mind if we went down the street for tacos?" she asked. The walk will wake me up and I could use a Corona to clear my head."

Chapter Six

We were back in the office by one fifteen. Susan walked into the office five minutes later. She looked somewhat better than the day before, but you could tell she was still fighting nerves.

"Are you ready?" I asked.

"No, but now that we're starting, I'm hoping it gets easier."

~ ~ ~ ~

We drove to the north side of Camelback Mountain, then twisted around the curvy roads as they climbed up the side of the hill. Kathleen's house was beautiful but not as large as some of the houses further down the mountain. I could only guess at what the land to build a house here would have cost.

When we pulled into the driveway, there was a dark blue Buick with a guy in a dark suit leaning against it, reading a paper. He glanced up at us, then folded his paper and flicked it through the driver's window of his car.

"Ladies," he said to us through our open windows. "Go on up. Miss Alastor's expecting you."

We walked up the path to the house and rang the doorbell. A moment later, another beefy guy in a suit opened the door.

"Before I let you in," he said in a rough smoker's voice, "I'll need to search your bags."

Susan looked at me and I could see this request was freaking her out a little bit.

"Why do you need to do that?" I asked calmly.

"Orders," the man said. "I can't let any weapons into the house."

Kathleen walked into view from what looked like the living room. "Please forgive the security precautions," she said from behind the man. "What I have to show you today is rather valuable. Even though I believe your story, there're some people out there who wouldn't think twice at using your situation as a way to try to take what I have, through force if necessary."

I looked at Susan, shrugged my shoulders, and handed my bag over to the goon. He efficiently went through our things and pocketed my Baby Glock. "I'll return it when you leave," he said.

Feeling a little naked with the loss of my gun, we followed Kathleen into a beautiful living room. It had high ceilings and bright original oil paintings on the walls.

"Drinks?" Kathleen asked.

"Um, I'll have a glass of wine," Susan said, "If it's not too much trouble."

Kathleen looked at me. "Wine sounds great," I echoed.

We followed her into an immaculate kitchen and she pulled a bottle from the refrigerator. There was a professional looking bottle opener bolted to the counter and she pulled the cork with one smooth motion.

Kathleen poured out three glasses, then led us out to a wide balcony overlooking Paradise Valley. It was a beautiful day and the view of the city was great. I could only imagine what the sunsets were like from up here.

We made small talk for another five minutes while we slowly sipped our drinks. Kathleen then tilted her glass and drained the rest of her wine.

"Well," she said. "I know you didn't come here to admire the view. You know where the wine is, feel free to get some more. Then have a seat in the living room while I get what you came for."

Following her instructions, we refilled our glasses and took a seat on a couch.

Two minutes later, Kathleen walked back into the living room carrying a battered leather case. It was the size of a small suitcase and from the way she was carrying it, it looked heavy.

"I've had to go back into my history for this," she said. "I've been keeping it locked away in a safe."

She set the case onto the coffee table, unzipped the thick metal zipper, and lifted the lid. Inside were several hundred casino chips, all in stacks of different colors. There were also several stacks of strange looking rectangular chips, each about the size of a playing card.

"From the start, Michael and I decided to make the casino a private club. We thought it would give it some added mystique. Plus, it let us skirt around some of the rules of being a public business. Players had to apply for a membership. We charged a hefty fee and only let in people with a certain level of wealth. I'm sure that part hasn't changed. I've heard they've lowered the standards somewhat over the years, but anyone who has to work for a living will have a tough time becoming a member."

She pulled out a stack of about twenty purple casino chips and a similar stack of orange ones. "Take a look."

We each took a few and examined them. The purple ones were valued at five hundred dollars and the orange ones were a thousand dollars each. The backside of the chips had an engraving of the Black Castle and the bridge leading to it. They looked and felt like plastic but seemed heavier than I would have expected. They made a pleasant clinking sound when they fell against each other.

"What are those? I asked, pointing to the stacks of the large rectangular chips.

"Those are called plaques. The round chips, like the ones you're holding, are valued up to five thousand dollars. After that, we used these." She reached into the case and pulled one out. It was valued at one hundred thousand dollars. It was beautifully made and again had a picture of the castle and the bridge.

"These go from ten thousand to five hundred thousand. We even had some million-dollar plaques made up, but those were mainly as a publicity stunt. I don't think we ever were able to put them into circulation. Before they closed, I heard the London Club at the Aladdin casino in Vegas had a ten-million-dollar plaque."

"I've never understood the chip thing," Susan said. "Why can't people use money to bet?"

"Casinos never like players to hold actual money," Kathleen said. "Betting cash makes the loss of it seem too real and it actually cheapens the experience. That's why casinos insist you exchange your money for chips when you first walk in the door. That way, instead of betting your mortgage or your kid's college fund on a hand of blackjack, you're simply betting some brown chips with green stripes."

"Huh," Susan said. "I never thought of it that way."

"One other thing you may never have thought of, you'd be surprised at how many people keep their chips as souvenirs."

"Doesn't the casino try to stop them. You'd think it'd cause some sort of problem."

"Not at all. If a player takes home a hundred-dollar chip to keep on his desk, the casino just made about ninety-eight dollars. They need to keep those chips on their books as an outstanding liability, but the reality is we made over a hundred thousand dollars the first year from people simply taking home their chips."

Kathleen again seemed to be thinking as she stared into space. She then looked down at the table and smiled. "Here, take these with you," she said as she motioned to the stacks of purple and orange chips we'd been looking at. "There's thirty thousand dollars there. It's not a lot by the standards of the Black Castle, but it might get you in the front door without a membership. Just bring back what you don't use."

"Oh my," Susan said. "We can't take thirty thousand dollars from you."

"Look, if you're serious about getting into the casino, you'll need something to show you're legitimate. It's a member's only club and it'll be damn tricky finding a way into the place. There's only one way for you to get in and that's over the bridge. Besides, I was an owner and each of those round chips cost less than two dollars to make. They're only valuable because the casino says they are. I happened to have these at my house when I learned I'd been forced out, so I kept them. I don't think I'll ever go back into the casino, so they're only pieces of clay and plastic to me. But they've all been registered in the system as live chips. They're completely valid. It always makes me smile when I think about having twenty-two million dollars of the casino's assets sitting in my safe."

"Do they know that you have them?" I asked.

"Oh yes. They weren't happy about it, but I told them I considered it part of my payoff for losing the casino."

"Aren't you worried they might try to come and take them back?" Susan asked.

"Of course, they've wanted to get them back for years. It's why I always keep everything in a safety deposit box. When I pulled the case out today, I realized I hadn't touched it since the lawsuit. I've gone so far as to let the casino know I have a letter at one of my attorney's offices that will be released to the authorities if I'm ever attacked or if I die and it seems suspicious. It's a shame I have to take so many precautions, but you don't know the types of people these are."

Kathleen paused for a minute, as if having an internal debate. She then reached into the case, took out a black leather pouch, and untied the lacings. She pulled out two large gold coins and set them in front of us on the table. Each was about the size of an old silver dollar. Susan and I each took one. On the front was an eagle with its wings outstretched. The backside had the same view of the castle and bridge that was on the chips. From the weight, I had to conclude they were made of real gold. Holding the gold made me think of Professor Mindy and our recent adventure in the Superstition Mountains. At a gesture from Kathleen, we returned them.

"They're beautiful," Susan said. "But what are they?"

"These are markers, a token that shows one person owes another person a favor. The favor could be collected by returning the marker to the person who gave it to you."

"I know about personal favors," I said.

I shuddered a little at the mention of a marker. Through some adventures over the past year, Tough Tony DiCenzo owed me two favors. I knew better than to ever use them, but they were still floating around. It made me wonder if his group had ever used these types of markers.

"Back when Michael and I first started the casino, we knew we'd need something special for our markers," Kathleen said. "Michael had some connections and we ended up going through a mint in Switzerland. We had them make up ten of these out of solid twenty-four karat gold. We each took five and I've ended up giving out two over the years." Kathleen stopped, and with a small crooked smile, stared into space again, as if reliving past events. "Ah, I used to live an interesting life."

"But then both your markers and my dad's would be exactly alike," Susan said. "Wasn't that confusing? How would you be able to tell them apart?"

"We stamped marks on the backside, a little above the picture of the casino. His is an 'X' and mine's an 'O'. See?"

Kathleen held up one of the gold markers and we could see the small "O" stamped above the picture of the casino.

"Were you and my dad the only people there to use markers?" Susan asked.

"No," Kathleen said. She then dug around in the leather pouch and came up with a new coin, roughly the same size, but this one was made of a brilliant silvery metal. The picture on the front was a skull and there was a lightning bolt on the back. "This is the marker of a man I knew a long time ago named Marcus. This one's made from platinum. Even after all these years, I could present it to him and he'd be obliged to do anything I asked." As she said this, she had a slightly faraway and unfocused look to her eyes.

"I imagine people didn't haphazardly hand them out," I said.

"Oh no, you really needed to owe someone to give them a marker. It's usually because they helped you in a life and death situation. When a marker's returned to collect on the favor, it's usually because of something just as serious. Markers were big back in the day, but I'm sure they don't use them anymore. They'd be looked at as too old fashioned, now that everything's digital. Still, there's something about holding a hunk of actual gold or platinum that makes them special."

Kathleen picked up one of her markers and held it up for us to look at. She turned it slowly back and forth so the edges caught the light. "Knowing it can be exchanged for a guaranteed favor, gives a marker an almost magical quality."

Kathleen looked at the marker in her hand, then she put it on the table and slid it over to Susan. "Take one of my markers," she said. "I don't know if it will be useful or not, but I suspect you could show it and get a response. It's traditional not to block someone when they're in the process of presenting a marker to ask for the favor to be returned, maybe you can use that. The new people there won't know what they are, but the old timers, the people you'll need to convince, will recognize the marker for what it is. They'll assume it's Michael's marker and they might even help you get to him."

"But if we're holding your marker, does that mean you owe us a favor?" Susan asked.

"Well, technically yes, but not in a practical sense. When you hand out or receive a marker, it's traditional to let everyone involved know the circumstances. When the marker's returned for a favor, you again let everyone know what you're doing. That way, if the person refuses the favor, everyone will know and that person would be shunned or even killed. The marker's only a reminder of the favor, not the favor itself. It's a system that keeps people from stealing each other's markers to get what they want."

As Kathleen looked at the marker in Susan's hand, a look of concern appeared on her face. "Even though I'm not officially giving you the marker for a favor, don't give it away to anyone unless there's the greatest need; I'm talking life and death. I expect to get this back when you return."

"I'll get it back to you," Susan said. "Honestly, I don't ever plan on even taking it out of my purse."

"One last thing," Kathleen said, all humor now gone from her voice. "If you do manage to get into the casino to find your father, you'll need to be careful. Some of the people who go in, don't come back out. I suppose I should also tell you, for the past year or so, I've suspected the casino has been monitoring me. Maybe it has something to do with the chips I have, I don't know for sure. But several months ago, I found a tracker on my car, and a couple of weeks ago I found a spy camera actually inside my office. I can't explain why I think it's Michael, maybe it's only my competition doing some industrial spying, but someone's going through great pains to find out what I'm up to. If it's the casino, you'll both need to be cautious. One more thing to keep in mind. Michael may still be listed as the owner, but it's the old-school gangsters that actually run the place."

"Thanks," Susan said. "But I'm hoping not to have anything to do with the actual casino or anyone else. I'm only trying to find my dad."

~ ~ ~ ~

We got back to the office a little after four. I dropped Susan off at her car in the front, letting her know I'd give her a call on Sunday to finalize the details of our trip to Nevada, but she should plan on leaving first thing Monday morning. I then drove around and parked in the back.

When I walked into the office, I found Gina in the back breakroom, breathing deeply and pacing back and forth. She looked terrible, like she'd been in an argument or something.

"What's wrong?" I asked.

"I think we've created a monster with this whole getting Lenny to date thing. He got back from his hearing an hour ago and he's been giving Sophie and me the third degree on how to date a woman. He wants to call up Elle and ask her out. He wanted to do it right away, but I kept to the plan and told him I didn't have her phone number."

"Is he ready for that yet?" I asked.

"I think we can get him ready for the call by tomorrow, but we'll need another couple of days before the actual date. Honestly, I'm not sure if it's worth it. Answering Lenny's questions on how to date a woman is making me a little queasy."

"Really? What's he asking about?"

"Mainly questions on the mechanics of intimacy and how he should bring up the subject of sex with a woman. He has some messed up ideas about what turns a woman on. I finally had enough and came back here to grab a soda and clear my head. I hated to do it since Sophie's all alone up there with Lenny, but I'll go back up as soon as I calm down a little. In the meantime, you should probably go and rescue her."

Great.

I walked up to the front and, as Gina had said, Lenny was leaning over the reception desk talking with Sophie. She had the dazed look that comes from lack of sleep and maybe still being a little hung over. She looked at me with a sense of desperation.

"There's something else I don't get," Lenny said. "Who's supposed to pay for the first dinner? I know women nowadays want to be treated equally. Fine, I can respect that. I don't want to insult the woman by trying to pay for everything. But honestly, all it does is confuse me. You see, back when I was dating, the guy always paid for the checks at the restaurants, then after a few dates, the woman would invite him to her house and cook him dinner. But what should I do now? When I ask the waiter for separate checks, it seems to disappoint them, like I wasn't having a good enough time to even buy her dinner. Should I keep everything on one check and wait for her to pick it up half the time? I mean, the last thing I want to discuss on the first date is who's going to pay the fricken dinner bill."

Sophie looked at me and I could see she was tired of answering Lenny's questions.

"Well," I said, "for a first date, the safe thing is for you to get the check. If the woman's classy, she might offer to split it with you, but if you want to impress her, you'll pay it like it's no big deal. If she keeps offering to take care of it, tell her she can get it the next time, if she really wants to."

"Okay," Lenny said, barely pausing to take a breath. "Yeah, that's good information. There's one more thing I always wanted to know. On the first date, how long should I kiss the woman before I stick my tongue in her mouth? Should I do it right away or wait a couple of minutes? How far should it go in to turn her on?"

Eeeewww.

My stomach gave a twist and I felt it twinge a couple of times. Sophie turned a little green and her lip curled up at the thought of

Lenny shoving in his tongue during a kiss. She then started coughing, like she'd thrown-up in her mouth a little bit.

"Um, I'd suggest waiting for her to start something like that," I said. "Some women aren't into a lot of tongue, especially on a first date."

Sophie picked up her trashcan and spit into it a couple of times.

"Really?" Lenny asked thoughtfully, not even noticing Sophie. "Okay, that explains some things. Thanks. I'll need to keep that in mind."

Oh my God.

"Honestly," I said. "Most women like a strong, take charge personality in a man, but when it comes to touching situations, it's better if he takes his cues from the way she acts. It's almost always a good idea to take it slow in the beginning. Be polite, listen to what she has to say, share your feelings, show tenderness, and remember not to be overly aggressive on the first date."

Lenny's eyes started to glaze over as I talked about sharing feelings and showing tenderness, but he came out of it when he thought of something else to ask.

"I also have a question about underwear," he said. "Do women like it when the guy doesn't wear anything under his slacks? My thinking is, if she sees I've gone commando, she might want to do something to get me going. You know, so she could get a sneak preview of the merchandise. Should I wear tight pants to make it easier for her to get a peek or is that too much for a first date?"

The thought of Lenny showing off Mr. Wrinkles completely grossed me out. I felt my stomach muscles spasm a couple of times. Sophie started coughing again.

"Wearing underwear's always a good thing," I said. "You really don't want to show off everything during dinner. It helps add some mystery to the date."

"Okay, that's good advice, but I still have a lot of questions about the bedroom," Lenny said to me. "Maybe I should tell you what I like to do with a woman and you tell me if it's okay or not. Then tell me everything I should do to make a woman go wild."

"I gotta go," Sophie said as she got up. She hurried across the reception area and went through the door leading to the back.

"Um, maybe we should skip on the bedroom part," I said, my stomach still twitching. "Every woman's different and I might not give you good advice on that."

"Okay," he said. "I suppose that actually makes sense. Besides, I'm already pretty good in the bedroom, so I'm not all that worried. I think I'm about ready to call Elle. I don't want to wait too long, or else she might think I'm not interested. Gina said you had her phone number."

"Actually, I heard she changed it a couple of weeks ago. I'll need to call Jackie and get the new one. Besides, I think they're all going out again tonight, so she wouldn't be able to talk in either case. If you can wait until tomorrow, I'll get you the number and you can call her tomorrow night."

Lenny's face fell, but then he perked up. "That's probably a good thing. There's still a lot of questions I have about dating. I know tomorrow's Saturday, but keep your phone on. I'll want to prep for my phone call, then I'll need to cram for the actual date. We still have a lot of work to do on this."

Great.

~~~~

I stopped by Char's Thai for take-out and got back to my apartment about six thirty. For my dinner entertainment, I watched an episode of *Fixer Upper*. I marveled how Chip and Joanne could take a crappy house in the middle of Waco, Texas and make it beautiful again. It made me wonder what would happen when there weren't any more crappy houses left in Waco for them to fix up.

As I finished dinner, I felt vaguely disappointed. This was something that had been happening a lot over the past couple of weekends. Fortunately, I didn't need to analyze myself too closely to know what the problem was. Even though I kept telling Sophie I understood the restrictions I'd imposed on myself by dating Max, the reality of the situation was that I ended up spending most of my Friday and Saturday nights alone.

That's okay, I told myself. *It's worth it.*

Thinking about Max also made me think about the ski trip, now only a week away. I still didn't have any of the clothing or equipment I'd need. Sophie and I were going to the thrift store tomorrow afternoon, but I was looking at that as a last resort. I wasn't opposed to buying clothes in a thrift store, about a third of my closet had come from one thrift store or another. But whatever I wore had to look nice. It was putting a lot of pressure on me to get it right. I knew if I couldn't find anything in town, I'd need to order everything off of Amazon. I'd then need to spend the next three or four months paying off the credit card.

Before going to the internet, I decided to go for broke. I pulled out my phone and looked up ski shops. I honestly didn't think there would be one in the entire Phoenix metropolitan area. I was more than a little surprised when I discovered there was one about fifteen minutes away called Ski Pro. I went to their website and found out they were open until nine o'clock.

~~~~

I drove over to Mesa Riverview Mall and cruised around the parking lot until I found the shop. I went in and immediately knew this was the right place. There were racks of colorful ski parkas, ski pants, gloves, helmets, goggles, and even balaclavas.

I went to the rack of ski parkas and picked out a colorful one that was my size. When I tried it on, it turned out to be too small. Feeling a little sad, I pulled a coat the next size up and it seemed to fit me better.

I spent the next hour trying on the coats and the ski pants. I'd hoped the first jacket had simply run a little small, but unfortunately, I eventually had to admit I seemed to have grown a size, both in the jacket and in the pants.

When I'd picked out everything I'd need for the trip, I mentally added up the cost. The results were depressing. Even though the total cost was less than I would find on the internet, this was still going to keep me in hock until spring.

That's okay, I told myself. *It's worth it.*

Standing in the shop, I formulated a game plan. I'd first go shopping at the thrift store with Sophie. I'd keep an open mind and get things if they seemed okay. Then, whatever I couldn't find there, I'd get here. It might be more expensive, but I knew whatever I got would last for several years. Well, assuming I stayed at my new larger size.

~~~~

I woke up sort of late and laid in bed for half an hour. Saturday's are one of the few times I can actually sleep in without guilt and I wanted to take advantage of it.

I knew I'd need to give Lenny Elle's phone number and then he'd want to ask me a lot of personal questions. It wasn't that I didn't want the date to be successful, but I really hadn't counted on learning that much personal information about my boss.

My plan was to text him the number sometime after lunch. That way, if he had any questions, he could text the three of us. Unfortunately, Lenny had other plans. He called at five minutes to nine. I ignored it and rolled over in bed. Thirty seconds later, my phone pinged me to let me know he'd left a voicemail.

I listened to the message: "Call me when you get up."

I went to the kitchen and put on a pot of coffee. Once I had a cup in my hand, I dialed Lenny.

"I've still got a ton of questions about Elle," he said. "I need you, Gina, and Sophie to meet me at the office. We'll need to have a strategy session on this."

On a Saturday?

"Yeah," I said. "I guess I can come in. What time?"

"It's nine fifteen now. See if everyone can make it at noon. I'll bring a pizza."

~~~~

I waited until almost ten, then called Sophie. It took her a while to answer and when she did, she sounded sleepy. "Hey," I said. "Sorry to wake you. Lenny's still stressing about Elle. He wants us to come in and work with him some more."

"Yeah," she said as she let out a loud yawn. "I figured he'd want something like that. He rang my phone about an hour ago and I ignored it. You know, sending Lenny out on a date was supposed to make things better for us, but so far all it's doing is messing up my weekend."

"Do you know what Gina's up to today?" I asked. "Lenny said he wanted all three of us."

"You can try her phone, but I think she's on a hike with Jet. They're up in the Superstition Mountains somewhere. She asked if I wanted to go too, but after hiking around up there with Professor Mindy last month, I've had about all the hiking fun I can stand for a while."

"Gina's with Jet? That makes date number two. What do you think? Is she serious about this one?"

"That's right, you've been out most of the week. Gina broke down and has been telling me all about her dinner with Jet the other night. At first, I think she was only looking at his body, but after hearing about his work with the Seals, she's all hot for him on an emotional level, at least that's what she's telling me."

"Good," I said. "It's about time she did more than date random guys from her gym. Are you coming into the office? Lenny said he's bringing pizza."

"Fine, I'll come in. But do you know where he's getting the pizza? I hope he learned from the last time he tried to feed us. A pizza's supposed to have pepperoni, sausage, and green peppers. Stuff like that. If I have to come in on a Saturday and all he's brought is another brie, artichoke, and arugula piece of trash, I'll make him go out and get us another one."

~~~~

When we got to the office, Lenny had two pizzas waiting for us. Fortunately, he'd gone to a normal pizza place. One was pepperoni and one had everything.

Lenny spent the next half-hour asking us how to act around Elle. For the most part, his questions were reasonable, and we were able to give him some practical advice.

"You'll also need to brush up on your eighties pop bands," I said. "Especially Wham! and Duran Duran. Those were two of Elle's favorites when she was in high school."

"Maybe you should watch some VH1 Classic before Tuesday and spend an hour or two watching some of the old videos," Sophie added.

"Hey," Lenny said, sounding a little offended. "I was in high school in the eighties too. I played Duran Duran and Wham! all the time. I had cassettes of both groups that I always kept in my car. I probably still have them in a box somewhere. Same for Talking Heads, Culture Club, a-ha, Devo, Blondie, and The Police. The eighties were about the only time in my life I enjoyed pop music. Not like the crap they play now. There aren't even any bands in pop music anymore, just generic sounding vocalists singing over computerized rhythm tracks."

"Okay," I said. "It sounds like you're good to go with that. If you can't figure out what else to talk about, you can always fall back to music. She seems pretty passionate about it."

"I also need to ask you about hair," Lenny said.

"Um, what about hair?" I asked.

"The last woman I was with told me it looked like I had a Pekinese sitting in my lap. From the way she said it, I'm guessing it wasn't a complement."

Gross.

Sophie had a piece of pizza halfway to her mouth. She turned a little pale and her face scrunched up in disgust. She slowly put the pizza back on her plate. I was worried she'd throw up in her mouth a little bit again, but fortunately she managed to get through it.

"Yeah," I said, thankful my stomach was still doing okay. "It's called manscaping and it's a thing."

"I looked up waxing this morning," Lenny said. "They have all sorts of styles. There's the American, the French, the Brazilian, and the Hollywood. Which one do women think is sexy? They had one called the landing strip that sounded interesting."

"Um, I think those styles are mainly for women," I said.

"Well, the pictures were all of women, but does it make a difference? Wouldn't the ones for guys be pretty much the same?"

"Oh no," Sophie said, color slowly returning to her face. "Guys have completely different styles. You gotta go somewhere where they specialize in boykini waxes. They'll be able to do all the men's styles. From what I can tell, most of the cougars prefer either the hairless mister, billiard balls, or the boyzilian."

Lenny looked at Sophie like she was speaking another language.

"It would probably be best if you go to a parlor where they specialize in men," I said. "They'll help you figure out what to do. Although, waxing can be a little uncomfortable, especially if it's your first time. Rather than going somewhere, I think most guys just touch up at home with an electric trimmer. You might want to consider it."

"Naah," Lenny said. "I'm all thumbs when it comes to things like that. I'd rather go to a professional, so it looks like I know what I'm doing."

After yet another half-hour of questions, Lenny felt he was ready. He told us we were free to go, then went into his office to make the call. We heard the sound of ice cubes dropping into a glass then the sound of the Jim Beam bottle clinking on the rim. As Lenny was pouring himself some liquid courage, Sophie looked at me.

"Are you doing anything now? I'm free until dinner. Do you want to go shopping for your ski trip?"

"After being cross-examined by Lenny for the past hour, I could stand to do something fun. Do you still want to try the winter clothing store you found on the internet? Although, I went to a ski shop in Mesa last night. I went up a size, in both jackets and pants."

"Like what? Like you went from a size four to a six?"

"I don't want to talk about it."

Chapter Seven

Going North was a store in a strip mall near the Scottsdale Airpark. When we walked in, I knew the place had possibilities. It was larger than I expected and looked clean and well organized. A lady was stocking one of the racks near the front and she looked up as we came in.

"Welcome, ladies," she said. "Are you both headed up to the snow?"

"Just me," I said. "I'm going to Colorado next weekend to go skiing. But I've lived in Arizona my whole life and I don't own a thing for being in the mountains in winter."

"Not to worry," she said. "Most people in Arizona have the opposite problem. They've moved here after living in the snow and find their winter outfits do nothing but take up space in their closets. After a while, everything trickles down to us. We're affiliated with one of the big thrift store chains and they sort out their nicer winter items to send to us. They don't want everything taking up space on their racks either."

"Okay," I said. "How does it work?"

"Skis, boots, and poles are in the back, the clothing's up front. Everything's sorted by size and type. The racks in front of you have matching sets of ladies' ski parkas and snow pants. I'd start with those. The gloves and hats are in the bins over there," she said as she pointed.

"Do you have balaclavas?" Sophie asked.

"Well, yes," the woman said, her voice dropping to a confidential tone. "But honestly, I'd buy that item new, same for the ski socks. We wash and sanitize everything that comes into the store, but I'd still feel a little creepy wearing something that somebody had on their face and was breathing into."

I heard a small retching noise, like a cat trying to cough up a hairball. I looked over at Sophie. Her upper lip was scrunched up and I could tell she agreed with the sales person.

"That's okay," I said. "I know where I can get both of those."

Sophie and I went down the list and in less than an hour we had everything. The total bill was a more manageable eighty-seven dollars. I found the bargain of the day when I'd come across, then fallen in love with, a matching ski jacket and pants outfit. It was blood red and had a black-widow spider embroidered on the back of the jacket. The salesperson said it was a high-end ski outfit and was completely waterproof. It didn't have any tags on it but it looked like it'd never been worn. I held my breath as I tried it on, but it fit perfectly. Looking at myself in the mirror made me feel bold and adventurous.

"Damn," Sophie said. "You look good. You know, this opens up all sorts of winter shopping opportunities. Maybe I should take up skiing too."

~~~~

By the time we were done at the thrift store, it was time for me to meet with Danielle and time for Sophie to get ready for her date with Milo. I told her to have fun and I'd see her on Monday, well, assuming Lenny didn't try to call us together before then.

~~~~

I pulled into the parking lot for La Playa Bonita a few minutes after six. Although the food is typically a little blander than I like, it's one of the nicer chain Mexican restaurants in town. I hadn't been here since the meeting I'd had with Danielle, almost two months ago, and the only thing that had changed was the size of the crowds.

The last time I'd met face-to-face with her was two weeks ago at the group's safe house in North Scottsdale. She was still recovering in her bed when I'd given her Tony's final proposal.

I walked into the restaurant and asked for Danielle Ortega at the busy hostess stand. As with most places that cater to tourists in November, the front of the restaurant was packed with Snowbirds. I got the stink-eye from more than one of them as the hostess immediately handed me off to a woman in a fluffy red dress, who led me through the restaurant to one of the banquet rooms in the back.

As with the last time I'd been here, I noticed that the music and decorations were nice, but not too over the top. The theme of the restaurant was that of a Mexican beach bar and it gave the place a festive feeling. As always happens at these places, a waiter walked by with a plate of sizzling fajitas and I was immediately hungry.

The music from the front faded and the mood quickly changed as we went down a short hallway towards the back. Standing at a red door leading into the banquet room were two grim looking men, one of whom sent a chill down my spine.

His name was Señor Largo and I'd met him about a month ago. He was the head enforcer for the Black Death. As with the last time I'd met him, he reminded me of the actor Sam Elliot when he was in The Big Lebowski or when he played Virgil Earp in the movie Tombstone. He was in his late fifties or early sixties, had a big gray mustache, and piercing blue eyes. A brown leather satchel was again hanging over his shoulder, the bag resting against his hip. I noticed the wound he'd suffered a few weeks ago had started to fade to a pink scar. It wasn't the only one he had on his face.

As I walked closer to the two men, the woman in the red dress turned and returned to the front. Señor Largo held up a hand to stop me. As I came to a halt, he looked at me for several moments with his cold blue eyes, then introduced me to the other man standing at the door.

"Laura Black," he said quietly. "I'll be returning to Mexico soon. This is Diego. He'll be assuming some of my duties in protecting Señorita Ortega." He then turned to the man. "This is Laura Black. She is a *friend* of our organization."

His voice had a strange inflection when he said the word 'friend'. As if it carried some special meaning. Diego looked me up and down then nodded his head.

"I'll need you to leave your purse out here," Largo said. "I'll see that no one touches it."

I took my bag off my shoulder and set it on a table. I was about to reach for the door when Largo again stopped me.

"One moment," he said.

Diego pulled out a small electronic device that seemed to have some sort of antenna sticking out of the top. He passed it up and down my body, both in the front and in the back. Satisfied I wasn't wearing a wire, Señor Largo let me in.

As with the last time I'd been here, the large room was filled with tables, chairs, and decorations, but was otherwise empty. Roberto was standing next to the entrance, watching over the entire space. Danielle had started dating him the month before and it seemed like he'd moved up to full-time bodyguard.

Danielle sat alone at a table on the far side of the room with her back against the wall. She slowly stood up, and as I walked closer, she held open her arms for a hug. Concerned for the injuries she'd received less than a month ago, I was careful about how enthusiastically I held her.

I've always had a mixed relationship with Danielle. At first, I thought she was a friend, but then I found out she was the daughter of the head of a vicious drug cartel. That soured the relationship for a time. But last month, she'd come to me with a problem that only I could help her with. I did what I had to do, mostly to keep her from getting hurt, and it seemed to bring us closer together again.

"I hope you don't mind we came back here," Danielle said as we sat down. "I really like this place. I still think it's wonderful how Americans interpret Mexican food." There was a bowl of chunky salsa with a basket of chips in front of us and we both started munching.

"I like it here too," I said as I stuffed a chip into my mouth. "You're right, it's different from what I'd call a real Mexican place. It's a chain that's mostly for the tourists. But the decorations are fun and I do love the smell of the fajitas. How are you feeling? You look good."

"I'm so much better. I don't think I told you last time, but I had several broken ribs and those weren't any fun. One of the bullets tore a big gash in my side. It was sewn and stapled back together, but they told me it would rip open if I tried to get up. That was the main reason I had to stay in bed when we last met. Once the wound healed, I was able to move around. I should show you the scar someday. It's a doosy."

"It's a doosy?"

"I'm studying how to talk like an American. Do you like it?"

"You sound great."

There was a brief awkward silence, then Danielle became serious. She reached across the table and took my hand. "Thank you again for everything you did for me. I know it was difficult and the risks were high, but everything worked out. I'm officially head of the group and no one has voiced any concern about how it was handled. Señor Largo is leaving next week, but he's leaving some of his top men here, to make sure no one gets any ideas about trying to challenge me."

"What happened to Raul? The creep who tried to shoot me."

"Well, he's going to live, although it was touch and go for a while."

Shit.

"He saw through the disguise and tried to kill me," I said.

"I know, but it doesn't matter. Once he recovers to the point he can travel, we're sending him back to headquarters in Mexico. That way, he can't cause any more trouble up here."

A feeling of relief swept through me, as if a weight had been taken off my shoulders. I hadn't even been aware of how much anxiety I'd been feeling at the prospect of Raul coming after me for revenge. If I was being honest with myself, I'd been hoping he was dead.

"You changed your hair back," Danielle said. "That was a good idea. It's probably best if people don't realize how much we look like each other."

"There's one thing I wanted to talk with you about," I said. "My fingerprint is in the Black Death book of leadership. It's in my own blood. I've been stressing that the police will raid your office sometime and find the book. Then they'll do a DNA trace and come knocking down my door."

"I think you're okay on that one. My uncle took the book back down with him to Mexico. And honestly, of all the things the authorities would want to know about our group, whose DNA is in the book would be pretty low on their list."

As she said it out loud, I knew she was probably right. But knowing the book was down in Mexico still made me feel relieved.

"I know Tony wants to finalize things with you," I said. "They don't want a war, but they also want to protect their positions. Last time we met, I told you about his offer. He wants to know if you'll accept it or not."

"I've had talks with Escobar about this. From our perspective, the solutions Tony came up with will benefit both of our groups. Tell Max and Tony we agree to the division of activities he proposed. The only concession we request is that he uses us for the transportation of merchandise into Mexico when we have excess capacity. Otherwise, our trucks would return with only legitimate cargo and it would be a shame to waste such a valuable resource. Both Tony and Max are good businessmen, I think they'll see the wisdom of sharing resources."

"Good. I'll pass along both your acceptance and the request."

A pitcher of margaritas had been sitting on the table. Danielle picked it up and poured each of us a drink.

"Okay then," Danielle said as she raised her glass. "To the end of our negotiations."

"I'm glad it's over," I said as I clinked my glass against hers.

"That should finish this. Hopefully this is the last time we'll have to discuss anything having to do with business. I know you didn't want to be involved with this and I appreciate all of your help.

Danielle shouted our something in Spanish to Roberto, I only caught the word waitress. "Are you hungry?" she asked. "After talking about them, I'm going to get the fajitas."

"That sounds perfect."

~~~~

After I left the restaurant, I called Tony and asked to meet. He said he'd be in his office for the next hour or so and I could come up anytime. I said I'd be there in about twenty minutes.

When I got to his office, I was a little disappointed that Max wasn't there. Tony must have read my mind.

"I'm sure you're wondering why Max isn't here. Unfortunately, he's in the middle of another meeting at the moment. I'll relay what you tell me. Of course, feel free to discuss everything with him as you would with me. When it comes to the group, Max and I have no secrets."

I then downloaded what Danielle had told me while Tony listened intently. When I was finished, he leaned back in his chair, a small grin on his face.

"Good," he said. "Let her know we'll accept her accommodations. Also let her know we'll need to set up a line of communication, in case conflicts happen to occur. Whatever she suggests is fine. Pass on the information to Max, he'll be the one who'll need to implement everything. Well now, it seems like the negotiations are complete."

I breathed out a sigh of relief. I hadn't been eager to be this involved with Tony's group and I was happy it was finally over.

"I'd like to thank you for your service to our organization. It seems as though I am again in your debt.

Conscience of the way Tony always waved away my concerns, I gave my hand a small wave of dismissal.

"You don't owe me anything Tony, it's simply something that one friend would do for another."

At that, Tony actually laughed. "Very well, Laura Black. Very well."

~~~~

I was lying in bed, awake but not yet ready to get up on a Sunday morning. Marlowe was curled up at my feet, sleeping peacefully. I was having vague thoughts about getting up and maybe heading over to church when my phone rang with Lenny's ringtone. I looked at the clock and saw it was only seven twenty.

What the hell?

I ignored it, but thirty seconds later, the phone beeped, telling me he'd left another message.

I rolled over, picked up the phone, and played the message. "Hey," he said. "You sleep a lot. Do you know that? Call me when you get up."

The phone had woken Marlowe and he was now pacing back and

forth over my legs, waiting for me to get up and feed him. Now fully awake myself, I got up and stretched for a minute. I then punched in Lenny's number.

"Hey, what's up? It's kinda early."

"I called Elle yesterday," he said, ignoring my comment about the time.

"How'd it go?"

"It's weird, but I think it went okay. I took your advice and kept it short and to the point. I told her you'd given me her number and I'd like to see her again."

"So far so good. What'd she say?"

"She said she was glad I called and she wouldn't mind seeing me again. We talked for a while then decided to go out for drinks and dinner on Tuesday."

"That's great. Where are you going?"

"I suggested Mastro's Steakhouse over on Pinnacle Peak. She said it wasn't too far from her place and she really liked it there."

"It sounds like everything's going well, at least so far."

"Yeah," he said, but then his voice trailed off in a weird way.

"What's wrong?"

"Look, I've been up half the night stressing about this. I'm not so sure about dating Elle. She's out of my league and I know how my dates always go. This is going to get screwed up, then I'm going to feel like crap for the rest of the week."

"It'll be okay," I said with a yawn. "Wait until Monday. We'll help you get through it."

~~~~

I tried to go back to sleep, but it was soon obvious I was up for the day. I made myself a real breakfast and watched the local news as I ate. Marlowe sat at my feet and reminded me it was time for his breakfast as well, but I was in a good mood and didn't want my breakfast ruined by listening to him throwing up.

~~~~

I didn't know if Elle would be at church or not, so I waited until eleven thirty to give her a call. The other night she'd offered to let me come over and go through her boxes of winter clothes. I was hoping she'd have at least one or two things that would work. I'd pretty much blown the budget already and I was still an outfit or two short for a weekend in Vail.

When she answered, she said she'd just come back from taking a fitness class and I could come over anytime. We then agreed on one thirty.

She gave me her address at the Desert Highlands Golf Club in North Scottsdale. I looked it up and it was three or four miles north of where Jackie lived.

~~~~

I left my place a little after one and went down to the parking lot. When I got to my car and hit the beeper, it already seemed to be unlocked. I thought this was odd, but I wasn't overly concerned about anyone breaking in. The only things of value in the car were my CD's. I gave everything the quick once over, but nothing seemed to be missing or amiss. Even though everything seemed okay, it did bug me a little as I drove up to Elle's. I was pretty sure I'd locked it the night before.

~~~~

Twenty-five minutes later, I'd made it to the main entrance at Desert Highlands. Fortunately, Elle had already given my name to the guards and I was allowed to enter.

I followed the navigator until I made it to Elle's street. As the road began to wind up the base of Pinnacle Peak, I noticed the houses here were slightly larger and had better views than the houses lower down.

I found Elle's house and it was stunning. It maybe wasn't quite as big as some of the mansions I'd driven by, but I guessed it probably had four bedrooms and five thousand square feet of space.

Elle answered the door and I realized this was the first time I'd seen her when she wasn't dressed for a night at the clubs. Instead of the designer outfits I was used to seeing her in, she was wearing navy blue shorts and a white cotton blouse. I'm not sure why, but I immediately felt less intimidated than I'd been a few minutes before.

She led me to a huge gourmet kitchen and showed me some of the features. She then opened her Sub-Zero refrigerator and pulled out a bottle of rosé wine.

"Is it too early?" she asked.

"Not at all."

Glass of wine in my hand, she led me out to the living room. It had a curved floor-to-ceiling window that looked out over the pool and the valley below. Going through a sliding glass door, we moved out onto the patio.

Although some people in Scottsdale close up their pools around the end of September, a lot of people keep them going all year round. Elle's patio had a six person hot tub that overflowed into the main pool and was no doubt used to heat it.

We walked to the edge of the railing surrounding the patio and looked down upon the valley and across to the McDowell Mountains to the south. Behind us was a great view of the bulk of Pinnacle Peak. I noticed that from this angle, the pointed top of the mountain looked a little like the Matterhorn in Switzerland.

"Wow," I said. "It's so beautiful here. Your house is really great."

"Thanks," she said. "I don't know if you've heard the story, but my ex-husband was one of the nerds in Silicon Valley who happened to be working for a start-up that went public. As luck would have it, he had a falling out with his boss and was fired a few months before the dot-com crash. He cashed out his stock, we moved out here, and bought this place for cash. After our divorce, he moved back to Los Gatos and is now working for another start-up. From his pictures on Facebook, he seems to be happy and is doing well."

We both stood at the railing, sipping the wine and enjoying the view.

"I should tell you," Elle said. "Leonard called me yesterday. We agreed to go out on Tuesday."

"That's great, I hope everything goes okay. Keep in mind, I don't think Lenny goes out a lot. He might be a little rusty at the whole dating thing."

"Oh, I don't mind. We've already been together and I know about that. Um, I'm sure everything will be fine." Her voice sounded a little unsure, as if she'd already changed her mind about the date.

"Is everything alright?" I asked.

"Remember I told you I'm starting to get tired of these quick hook ups with the young guys and how I'm starting to date guys my own age?"

"Yeah, you mentioned that."

"Well, between you and me, I'm finding I've gotten somewhat of a reputation in my social circles as someone who's only after sex. The guys I've gone out with over the past couple of months only seem to want to buy me dinner, then get laid. With the last one, I told him during dinner that I was only looking for an actual relationship, but then he tried to undress me in his car in the parking lot. Honestly, if this keeps up, I might have to move to a city where they've never heard of me."

"I can see how that'd be a problem."

"Oh, don't get me wrong. You know me, I'm not shy when it comes to no-strings sex. But I've also reached the point where I'm craving a longer-term relationship. If I can find that, I'll be thrilled. But if all I can find in Scottsdale is men who look at me as their latest sex toy, I might need to give up on the dating idea and just stick to hooking up with boys from the college."

We spent several more minutes drinking wine and making crude remarks about college guys, what we liked them to do to us, and what we liked to do to them. Although, since it had been several years since I'd been in college, I had to reach back in time for most of my memories.

We went back to the kitchen where Elle refilled our glasses. She led me up a wide spiral staircase to an upper floor, then down a hallway to the master bedroom.

The room featured the same wrap-around picture windows as the living room, along with a spacious balcony that looked out over the pool and the valley. The far end of the room had two massive walk-in closets, each the size of my living room. Both were completely filled with clothes and shoes. I noticed the bedroom had the faint scent of Chanel.

We walked into one of the closets and Elle pointed to a rack with ten or fifteen outfits, all arranged by color.

"Here you go, take a look and see if you like anything."

"Wow, I thought you only had two boxes of clothes."

"I thought I only had the two boxes, but it turned out I had a few. We used to go skiing a lot and I guess I kept more than I remembered. I thought it'd be easier for you to go through everything if I hung them up. These are the outfits I got before I had my boobs done, so most of them should fit you okay."

Ouch.

We spent the next twenty minutes taking clothes off of hangers and comparing outfits. It reminded me of being a kid and going through my mom's closet.

In the end, we decided on five outfits, three Donna Karan, a Ralph Lauren, and a Calvin Klein.

"Take them home and make sure everything fits," Elle said. "If they look okay, go ahead and keep the outfits. If something doesn't work for you, bring it back sometime. It'd be a good excuse for us to get together again."

"Are you sure?" I asked. "These are so beautiful, and they don't even look like they've been worn."

"I'm pretty sure I wore everything, well, once or twice anyway. But yes, I'm sure. I know the outfits are going to someone who appreciates clothes like I do. Honestly, I'm not sure why I kept them, since the tops are too small for me now. I guess I'm just a collector when it comes to clothes."

~~~~

On the drive back home, I gave Susan a call. I thought she might be a little nervous about heading up to Nevada in the morning and I wanted to check on her.

"Hey," I said when she answered. "How are you doing? Are you ready for our road trip tomorrow?"

"I guess," she said. "I'm mostly terrified. I've been second-guessing myself on this ever since we came back from Kathleen's house. But I'm also a little excited. I'm hoping we can find my dad and talk with him. If we can accomplish that, I'll be good with it. I'll try to talk him into calling mom, but if he only acknowledges I exist, I think it'll bring some closure."

"Did you find anything to wear to the casino? Something that makes you look like you do this sort of thing every day?"

"Well, I went through my closet and picked out a nice cocktail dress, like you said. It's one I sometimes wear on a second or third date, you know, when I'm thinking we might end up over at his place and I want to look my best."

"Sounds good," I said. "Wear something comfortable for the drive up. I'm sure we can find somewhere to change before we try to bluff our way in."

"The only thing I'm stuck on is the shoes. When I wear the dress, I usually wear heels. But I'm thinking if we're going to a big casino somewhere, heels might not be the best thing."

"I'd go with something comfortable you can walk in, that's what I'm going with. We don't know how much hiking we're going to do and I don't want either of us to end up with blisters."

~~~~

I turned on an episode of *The Big Bang Theory*, grabbed a Corona from the fridge, and pulled out my tablet. I thought it would be a good idea to learn as much as I could about the layout of both the casino and the area surrounding it.

I eventually found a satellite map of Laughlin, Nevada and the Colorado River next to it. I slowly scrolled the map down, following the river until I'd gone five or six miles. The Black Castle eventually came into view. It was a large structure and it dominated the western side of the river. Several smaller buildings were attached to the main bulk of the castle. These were spread out and they mostly filled the hundred yards of flat space between the castle and the steep side of a mountain that sharply rose to the west.

As Kathleen had said, the only way in from the Arizona side was over a pedestrian bridge that spanned the Colorado River. Next to the bridge was a large parking lot with several shops, fast food restaurants, and a bar.

From the Nevada side, there only seemed to be one road in, a long winding journey down from Laughlin. From the road, the only way in or out of the grounds of the casino was through a very secure looking guard station.

It appeared there was a high fence surrounding the property. Near the river, the fence was replaced with a stone wall. From the images, it was at least fifteen feet high. If Susan and I couldn't find a way over the bridge, we were pretty much screwed.

I then looked up the Black Castle web site and eventually found a floor plan. It showed where the gaming floors, the restaurants, the shops, and the guest rooms were located. It didn't give any clue where the business offices were. I hadn't thought they'd be hard to find, but I realized I should have asked Kathleen when I'd had the chance.

As usually happens when I'm drinking and not doing anything, I started texting Max. At first, he only answered sporadically and I knew he was busy with work. But a little after eight o'clock, we had a quick flurry of texts, most of them involving various things I wanted him to do to my body while we were in our hotel in Vail. I'd just texted him with a rather naughty request when he called my phone.

"Hey," I said. "I'm glad you could call. I've been wanting to hear your voice."

"I had a few minutes and thought it would be more productive to talk, rather than sending texts back and forth."

"So, are you going to answer me? Would you be willing to do that one little thing for me? Or is that outside your comfort zone?"

"In other words, you want me to bring the bag of toys to Vail."

"Well, I'm sure we could put everything to good use."

"I don't doubt that. But you know, I'll need to pack everything away in my suitcase. It wouldn't be a good idea to let anyone else see what I'm bringing with me on what's supposed to be a skiing weekend."

"True, but think of the fun we could have. After a long day of skiing and a relaxing soak in an outdoor hot tub, wouldn't you love to spend the night playing with me and the toys?"

"I think you already know the answer to that. Although, I'm not sure I can wait that long. Are you doing anything tomorrow night? My schedule opened up and I'd love to spend some time with you."

Oh, why didn't you ask me sooner?

"I don't think I can tomorrow, or at least I won't know until late tomorrow afternoon. I'm heading up to the Black Castle Casino in Nevada tomorrow morning with a client. It turns out her father is the owner of the place and she wants to meet him. He doesn't know she exists so it will be a surprise family reunion, of sorts."

"That sounds like an interesting time. It'll be like living out an episode of Jerry Springer. Although, I've heard of that casino; *Every fantasy satisfied.* That's the place, right?"

"Yes, but we aren't looking to fulfill any fantasies, we're only looking to find the owner. The goal for tomorrow is for our client to introduce herself to her father, then have a nice conversation with him. It should be relatively straight forward, at least I hope so. Besides, I've been itching to go out and do something different, you know, have a real adventure. Maybe this will work for that."

"As I recall, the Black Castle's a private casino run out of Las Vegas. Have fun on your adventure but be careful how many rules you break. They might not like it and it's outside of my area of influence."

"You sound like Sophie, but we'll be careful. I'll call you when we leave the casino to come back to Scottsdale. Maybe we can still set something up for later tomorrow night?"

"Alright, I'll leave it open."

~~~~

I'd set the alarm for five thirty and quickly woke up when it went off. I realized I was actually looking forward to the road trip with Susan.

I put on a practical outfit and did my hair for the day. I then packed my sexy new dress, some extra makeup, and a pair of nice, but practical, shoes into a small overnight bag.

As I'd discussed with Susan, the dress and makeup were for when we were going to attempt to bluff our way into the Black Castle. I honestly didn't know how the casino members dressed when they were there, but I thought we'd have more luck making it past security if we slutted ourselves up a bit when we showed them the bag of casino chips.

As I was organizing everything, I went over the day in my head. Once inside the castle, the plan was to blend in with the other gamblers, find Susan's father, and have a conversation with him. Hopefully we could find him before they found out we didn't belong there and threw us out.

The more I thought about it, the less confident I became. Everything rested on us being able to sneak inside. I was assuming we could get in over the bridge, but what if we couldn't? What if we got in, but couldn't find Susan's father? What if we could find him, but he refused to talk with us?

Damn, get a grip.

Now that I'd worked myself into a rather depressed mood, I finished packing. I then fed Marlowe, filled *The Big Pig* with the remaining half-pot of coffee, and headed out the door.

~~~~

When I got to the office, Gina's Range Rover and Sophie's Volkswagen were the only vehicles under the carport. I parked and went in through the back-security door. As I suspected, Gina was sitting in her cubicle, working on a report.

"Hey," I said. "You're here early."

"I know. The assignment for Jet is turning out to be a lot more work than Lenny originally let on. I've tracked down most of the witnesses but some of them are giving contradictory stories. It's going to be a busy couple of days for me."

"I heard you and Jet went hiking yesterday. How'd that go?"

Gina's broad smile lit up her face, but I could see she was trying hard to keep everything neutral. "Um, it was good. We seem to be pretty compatible."

"He was a Navy Seal, right? I suppose that gave you and him some things to talk about as you compared your old jobs. I bet you both have stories about chasing down the bad guys."

"Yes, we seem to have lots to talk about."

She was trying so hard to be casual, I started laughing. After a moment, Gina broke down and started laughing too.

"Alright, fine," she said. "He's adorable, sweet, sexy, and I'm already so crazy for him."

"So, have you and him, um, you know?"

"No, not yet. He says he wants to get to know me before things get clouded with sex. He implied that once we started, we'd be doing nothing else for a couple of weeks. But damn, I just want to eat him up, starting now."

Gina sighed, seemed to pull herself together, then looked back at me. "Isn't this the day you and Susan are going to the casino in Nevada?"

"Yeah, she should be here by eight. With any luck, we'll be at the casino around noon."

"It sounds like things are coming along nicely. So, why do you sound hesitant?"

How does she always know?

"Okay, you're right. I'm feeling a little uneasy about having to sneak into a casino, then more or less bully our way through the place to find Susan's father. Plus, I'm used to working in Scottsdale where I know the area and I feel relatively safe. Usually when I go to Nevada, I stay in cheap hotels, eat too much at the buffets, and lose money in the slot machines. I've never tried to work an assignment there before."

"You'll do great. The only real downside is you'll be working alone. You won't have your usual backup available if things go wrong. I'll keep my phone on until you return to Scottsdale, so call me if I can help. I know you also have, um, other resources available to you, if you need them."

"Thanks for watching out for me. But I'm hoping not to need anyone's help with this. It should be a simple in-and-out. It'll be in the middle of the afternoon and it's a public place with lots of people."

"Yes, but keep in mind casinos are very security conscious. If you don't find a way in the front door, if might not be so easy to find a way in through the back."

I went up front to say hello to Sophie and to wait for Susan. Sophie was at her desk, sipping a gas station coffee and flipping through her tablet.

"Hey, Laura," she said. "You and Susan still heading up to Nevada today?"

"That's the plan. She should be here in about twenty minutes."

"It's a shame there's so much going on over here, otherwise I'd go with you. I could use a road trip to a casino."

"I don't think this will be as much fun as our journey down to Rocky Point. This is going to be a long drive for what I hope will be a short meeting."

The door to the back swung open and Lenny came in. He was hunched over and walking a little funny, with short shuffling steps. He went into his office without talking to either of us.

Gina came up to reception a minute later. "What's wrong with

Lenny?" she asked.

"Don't know," Sophie said. "When he came in, he was walking like he'd been kicked in the nuts or something."

"We'd better find out," Gina said. "There might be a problem."

The three of us walked into Lenny's office. He was sitting at his desk absentmindedly shuffling papers.

"Are you okay?" Gina asked.

"Not hardly," he said. "I took your advice and went to a freaking waxing parlor."

"What happened?" I asked, even though I already knew.

"You told me it'd be uncomfortable. But if I knew it was going to hurt that much, I would've done a couple of shots of Beam first."

I resisted the urge to remind him that we'd talked about using an electric trimmer at home.

"I found a place that specialized in guys and it seemed classy enough. I talked to this hot looking woman at the front desk and she suggested I go with the boyzilian. She said it was the most popular style for men and the ladies really loved it. So, I said 'sure, let's do that one'. She then led me to a room in the back and had me get undressed."

"That seems pretty standard," Gina said. "What happened?"

"This young guy comes in. He's all smiles and happy, like we're best friends about to have a fun time together. He had me get on a table with harnesses for my legs to go over, like I'm a woman about to have a baby. He then smears wax on places I assumed he wouldn't touch, and then starts yanking on everything. It seriously felt like he was punching me in the junk. Then, after he was done with the wax, he started going after the ones he'd missed with a pair of tweezers. Every time he found a stray, he'd laugh and say, 'found another one', then he'd rip it out. I'm rolling back and forth in pain and he's looking at it like a freaking treasure hunt. The swelling's mostly gone down today, but I could hardly walk last night. I'm only hoping everything will be back to normal for the date with Elle tomorrow."

Sophie snorted a laugh through her nose, which she quickly tried to disguise as a cough. Lenny glanced at her with an annoyed look.

"I hope Elle appreciates what I'm going through for this date. But from what you said, she might not even want any action this time, just talking and stuff."

"Getting ready for a date where you only talk is probably the safe bet," I said. "She'll appreciate that you have more on your mind than just sex. But don't worry, you know Elle. If she's in the mood for something more, she'll let you know."

"Speaking of getting her in the mood," Lenny said. "From what I could tell, all of those gals like to drink. I know a little champagne seemed to get her going last time, but how much is too much?"

"Don't worry about Elle," Sophie said. "I've seen her drink college boys under the table and still be ready to go. I'd be more worried about you. I know how guys are. They start drinking and they get all loud and boastful about how great the night will be, but when it counts, they're too wasted to do more than make a half-assed effort then fall asleep. You definitely don't want that to happen on your date."

Lenny's face turned red and he hung his head down, like Sophie had hit on a sensitive subject. "Yeah," he said with a weak laugh. "I wouldn't ever want that to happen. Um, that'd be really embarrassing."

Chapter Eight

We walked out of Lenny's office as Susan came in through the front door. She was dressed in a comfortable office outfit and seemed to be a little anxious. As we'd discussed, she was carrying a bag with a dress and a pair of shoes.

"Hey Susan," Sophie said, as everyone gathered around her desk. "It sounds like you might get to meet your father today."

Susan gave a weak smile. "I hope so. I'm trying not to get my hopes up too much. After all, we don't even know if he'll be there today. He might be out of town or something."

"Keep in mind," Gina said, now with her big-sister tone. "These investigations can take some time. You might get lucky today or this might only be a step on the journey. But, from what I hear, you have a pretty good shot at it."

"Well, from what the Alastor woman said, I think we're on the right track."

~~~~

We left Scottsdale a little after eight and by nine fifteen we'd made it to the village of Wickenburg. I always think of the town as a sort of dividing line between the Phoenix metro area and the vast deserts beyond.

"Would you mind if we grabbed something to eat?" Susan asked as we were driving through the town. "We've got that long stretch of nothing coming up. My stomach is still doing flip-flops, but I'm starting to get lightheaded. I'll need to eat something before we cross the desert."

"Sure, what are you in the mood for?"

"The only thing I'll be able to eat is probably something that's bad for me, pie or something like that."

We parked and considered Bedoian's Bakery & Bistro and the Horseshoe Café, two cute places next to each other on the old-fashioned main street in the center of town. At first, Susan was leaning toward biscuits and gravy at the Horseshoe, but finally decided on the bakery to get a piece of Dutch apple pie.

We walked in and had a look around. It was a cute place with maybe a dozen tables. We grabbed a couple of seats at a table against the wall.

A waitress came over and Susan ordered the pie and what the menu described as the World's Best coffee. I ordered a cinnamon roll and a cup of the famous coffee as well.

"Where you ladies headed?" the waitress asked. "Vegas or Phoenix?"

"We're going up to the Black Castle Casino," Susan said.

"Yeah, a lot of people head north from here," the waitress said as she poured our coffees. "Not me though. Haven't been that way in a couple of years. I've seen too many crazy things happen out there, especially in the summer. It's a hundred and thirty miles of mean unforgiving desert between here and the next town. Well, unless you want to call Wikieup a town. Keep in mind your phones won't work most places out there. You're just in the middle of a big fricking lot of dusty nothing. The first part of the crossing's the worst. There ain't shit between here and Wikieup."

"You said crazy things happen out there," Susan said. "What kinds of things?"

"Well, there's lots of side roads between here and there and for some reason, people seem to get an urge to drive down them. None of them lead anywhere, I don't know why they do it. Maybe people think they're shortcuts or something. I'm not only talking about the illegals, it's people from Phoenix too. It's always the same. Sheriff finds an abandoned car somewhere out on the desert. Then they'll do a big search, helicopters and everything. They find some of them alive, some of them they don't find for a year or two, and some of them they never find at all."

Susan looked up at her with concern on her face.

"Oh, don't mind me," the waitress said. "It's a nice day today. I'm sure you'll do fine. What are you doing up at the casino? Taking a few days off?"

"No," Susan said. "Actually, we're going up to find my father. He works up there and I've never met him before."

"I once had a family reunion with my father, that was after I hadn't seen him for like fifteen years," the waitress said. "I thought it was going to turn out great, but he was nothing but a disillusioned old man who didn't give a shit about anybody or anything. You want my advice? Stick to your memories and fantasies. Don't worry about reality. It can be a real bitch."

~~~~

After the pie, the cinnamon roll, and the coffee, we drove north onto US-93 and the road again narrowed down as we entered the long stretch of deep desert. Within the first ten miles, the terrain had broadened out to wide vistas of creosote bushes and Joshua trees. Other than the occasional string of electrical towers and power lines, no sign of civilization could be seen from horizon to horizon.

The weather was beautiful, with temperatures in the seventies, and a light gentle breeze. The sky was clear, and traffic was light to non-existent. We made good time as we started our drive across the desert.

"I think I agree with the waitress," Susan said, as civilization disappeared into the rearview mirror. "I always hate this part of the drive. I've been to both Laughlin and Las Vegas several times. This stretch of desert between Wickenburg and Kingman always gives me the creeps. There's the little village of Wikieup about halfway there. I always called it Wakey-Up when I was a kid. I always made my mom stop at the Trading Post. Looking at the Indian jewelry was fun and it gave us something interesting to do before we had to drive across the desert again. Even as an adult, I still stop at the trading post, just to top off my tank and be off the creepy road for a few minutes.

I handed over my CD case and asked Susan to pick out something to listen to as we drove across the desert. After flipping through the dozen or so disks, she pulled one out and shoved it into the slot in the dash. Within a few seconds, the sound of the Beastie Boys blasted out of the speakers.

"Good choice," I said.

"Woo hoo!" she laughed. "With music like this, the desert's going to be a piece of cake."

~~~~

After about forty-five minutes, we'd made it roughly fifty miles into the desert. Other than the occasional teenager zooming past us in a pickup truck, or a few big-rigs that were headed south, we hadn't seen anyone on the road for the last ten or fifteen minutes.

The music had gone from the Beastie Boys to Tori Amos. Susan was in the middle of telling me about a guy she'd been dating a few months back, when there was a loud bang, almost like a backfire. It happened in the front part of the car, somewhere near the engine. The explosion was big enough to cause the hood to jump.

Shit.

"What was that?" Susan called out, panic in her voice.

"I don't know, but it can't be good."

Even as I spoke, white smoke started to billow out from under the hood.

"Okay, this definitely isn't good," I said. "We've got to get off the road before the rest of my engine blows up."

"There's a group of buildings coming up," Susan said, pointing to a spot further down the road. "It looks like the main building even has some sort of parking lot in front of it."

About half a mile ahead was what looked to be a gas station and a few outbuildings, but even from this distance I could tell it'd been abandoned for some time. I put the car in neutral and switched off the engine, hoping we had enough speed to coast all the way to the buildings.

~~~~

It turned out the buildings were farther away than they looked. Fortunately, the highway was on a slight decline and we were able to make it thirty yards into the huge dirt parking lot before we stopped completely.

I twisted the key the rest of the way off and the music abruptly died.

Susan had started to recover her composure after the banging noise. "Of all places to be stranded," she moaned. "See, I told you how creepy this desert is."

Ignoring the client for a moment, I popped the hood and climbed out of the car. We were in a dirt parking lot, maybe two hundred yards long and almost a hundred yards deep. There were several decrepit buildings at the back of the lot. They looked abandoned, but it was possible someone could have been living in one of the bigger ones. There were six or seven cars scattered near the buildings. Some were missing their glass and tires, but some of them looked like they could possibly be drivable.

After listening to the music for almost an hour, it seemed eerily quiet, the only sound being the wind, which seemed to have kicked up a notch since we'd left Wickenburg.

Whatever had happened to my engine had put a big crease in the hood. It also had knocked it out of alignment with the latch release. It took me three or four hard yanks to free it.

Raising the hood resulted in a cloud of sweet-smelling white smoke. I looked in to see what'd blown. I hoped it was only a coolant hose that had become detached from the engine. I knew I had a pair of pliers and a screwdriver in the trunk so maybe I had a prayer of fixing something like that. I was hoping none of the hoses had burst. I had a roll of duct tape somewhere in the trunk, but it wouldn't be waterproof and at best would provide only a temporary patch. Any repairs more than that would be way above my high school automotive shop class skill level.

Instead of a detached hose, the entire area between the radiator and the engine was a tangle of leaking cooling hoses and broken fan belts. The hoses had a blackened and burnt look, but there didn't seem to be any other signs of a fire. The engine itself appeared to be undamaged and I was grateful. The repair bill to fix everything would likely be several hundred dollars, but I didn't think I'd need to scrap the entire car.

"Well?" Susan asked as she climbed out and joined me under the hood.

"It's beyond anything I can do. We're going to need to call someone."

Susan looked devastated, but I could see it was the answer she'd expected. "I have auto club, but I don't know if they'd come all the way out here."

"I'm hoping we can get a signal," I said. "We're a long way from anywhere."

Susan reached into the car and pulled her phone from her bag. "I'm not getting anything, but I use the cheap phone service."

I started thinking of options. We were roughly halfway between Wickenburg and Wikieup and it was too far to walk in either direction. I'd brought enough snacks and sodas to last the day and probably the night if we absolutely had to. We could wait for a sheriff to drive by or try to flag somebody down. Neither option sounded very appealing.

Susan started walking around the parking lot with her phone held over her head. "Nope, my phone's dead. No signal at all. What about yours?"

As if in response, my phone in the car started ringing with *S&M,* by Rihanna. I retrieved the phone and answered.

"I'm so tired," Sophie said. "I should've gone with you. All I've done so far today is paperwork for Lenny. I've typed so much the last two hours my eyes are starting to cross. Plus, I'm probably on my fifth or sixth coffee. I have so much caffeine in my system it's making my hands shake."

"Sophie," I said. "Trust me, you aren't missing anything. Actually, I'm sort of having a shitty day."

"Really?" she asked, now perked up. "What happened this time? Did some big car force you off the road again? Did you get shot at again? Is our client alright?"

"The client's fine, but my car's having issues. Something under the hood blew and it's pretty much dead."

"Well, that sucks. Where are you?"

"We're in the parking lot of an abandoned gas station about halfway between Wickenburg and Wikieup."

"Hold on," she said as she started typing. "Okay, I pulled up a map. I think you're at a place called Nothing. Does it look like a mostly abandoned store or maybe it's a gas station, along with a couple of little buildings behind it? Is the main building a nasty piss-yellow color with graffiti all over it?"

"Yeah, how'd you know?"

"I'm looking at street view on Google maps. Think you could have picked a crappier place to get stranded?"

"At least it's not August. It's actually a pretty day out here. Would you look up mechanics in Wickenburg and see if any of them have time to work on a car today?"

"No problem, let me check. I'll call you back in a few."

As I hung up with Sophie, a dark blue Toyota Four Runner slowed down as it drove past our parking lot. The SUV came to a stop on the side of the highway, a hundred yards past where we were parked, then began to back up.

I reached into the car, pulled out my bag, and slung it over my shoulder. I wasn't expecting trouble, but I always feel better knowing my Baby Glock is within easy reach.

As the SUV pulled to a stop next to us, the driver's window lowered to reveal a gorgeous man. He was in his mid to late thirties, had long dark hair, a three-day beard, and a great tan. As we walked closer, he took off his sunglasses and flashed us a beautiful smile that made his deep blue eyes sparkle.

"I'm Jonathan," the man said as he hung his arm out of the window. There was a tattoo of a red rose on his forearm. "It looks like you're having some car trouble. Can I give you ladies a hand?"

"I'm Laura and this is Susan," I said. "You're right about the trouble."

"Unfortunately, I don't have my tools with me, so I won't be able to do anything with your car. But I can drop you off at the next town and you can send someone out to get it taken care of."

"Thanks," Susan said. "We were headed up to the Black Castle Casino, but it looks like that'll be delayed a day or two."

"Really? You're serious? I work at the Black Castle. That's where

I'm going now."

"We really need to get to the casino sometime today," I said. "If I could arrange to have my car towed to a garage, would you mind giving us a ride? I know it's an imposition, but we'd really appreciate it."

"No hassle at all. The drive through the desert is God-awful boring and I'd love the company of two beautiful ladies."

At that, Susan blushed and I also felt my face get a little warm. I knew it was only his way of talking, but it still felt great to hear a sexy guy call us beautiful.

I held up a finger to let him know I'd be a minute, then pulled my phone out and called Sophie. As it was ringing, I took a few steps toward the yellow building so I could talk without being overheard.

"Sophie, it looks like we've got a ride to the casino, and oh my God, you should see the guy who's going to give us a lift. I'm glad I'm dating Max or else I'd have a serious case of the hots right now. This guy is delicious."

"Well, don't get your hopes up, remember the last guy you thought looked hot?"

"I don't care if he's gay or straight, I don't want to have sex with him. I'm just going to look at him and maybe smell his cologne."

"Did you only call to tell me about Mr. Yummy Pants or did you want to know about the mechanic?"

"Both, actually."

"Well, so far the mechanic thing's a bust. They'll be glad to come out and get your car, but everyone wants a couple of days to get it looked at."

"I was afraid of that. Well, since it's not going to get fixed out here, would you call a tow truck and have it hauled back to Scottsdale? You know the garage I use. I'll put the car key in an old Maxwell

House coffee can that's on the left-hand side of the yellow building here."

"I can do that, but are you sure you want me to? I already looked it up and it will be a hundred and twenty-six miles one-way for a tow back to Scottsdale. Sending a truck all the way out there will cost at least three hundred dollars. That's more than your car's worth. Are you sure you don't want to pull the plate and then, you know, sort of leave it there?"

"Hey, my car's worth more than that and it usually runs great. I'm not going to abandon it because of one little hiccup."

"Fine, I'll call your shop and have them go up and get it. Hey, you know what? Since this is for an assignment, I can put it on the office credit card. We'll let Lenny pay for the tow."

"Won't he mind?"

"Nah, you know our accounting system. I'm the one who pays the credit card bill. Lenny never does more than glance at the statement. Besides, it's actually a legitimate charge. I keep telling Lenny that you and Gina need company cars for what you do."

"Well, then sure, that'd be great. Hold on a second and I'll tell Susan."

I walked over to where Susan was talking to Jonathan through the window of his SUV. "While we're driving up to the casino, Sophie's going to arrange for a truck to come up and get my car."

"Wow, that's a really long tow," she said, a little doubtfully. "But I guess it's probably best not to leave it here. Does Sophie have your license plate number to give to the driver? There're half a dozen cars here and honestly, some of them look better than yours. It'd be a shame if they towed the wrong one all the way back to Scottsdale."

I was about to get annoyed when I looked around and saw she was right. The old gas station and the buildings behind it seemed to be a popular place for people to abandon cars.

"Um, Sophie, let me give you my license plate number. Make sure the tow truck driver gets the right car."

~ ~ ~ ~

We transferred the overnight bags containing our casino clothes into the Toyota. I offered Susan the front seat so she could talk with Jonathan, but she only blushed, shyly shook her head, and said she'd rather stretch out in the back.

We drove in silence for the first ten minutes or so. I was thinking about my car and how I was going to afford another repair bill. If it was too high, I was going to have to break down and sell the nugget of gold I'd gotten the month before from Professor Mindy. I mentally crossed my fingers that it would only be a simple repair.

"What do you do at the casino?" I asked Jonathan, mostly to break the silence.

"I work as an escort," he said in a matter-of-fact voice.

"Is that what it sounds like?" Susan asked as she leaned between the front seats. "I've heard prostitution is legal in Nevada."

"Oh no," he said. "There're plenty of people who'll do that, both men and women, but I'm an actual escort. A lot of wealthy women come to the casino to relax and it helps if they have someone to go to dinner with and escort them to the shows. I'll do whatever they want to do, but it's mostly hanging out with them while they gamble and when they're at the pool. It's not unusual for me to spend three or four days with someone."

"That's it?" I asked. "You just hang out with them? Do you mind if I ask how much you make doing that?"

"It's not a secret. Escorts make a hundred dollars an hour. The client pays the casino one-fifty, the house keeps fifty and I get the rest."

Damn, I'm in the wrong business.

"Wait a minute," Susan said. "You hang out with these women, for days at a time. Drinking, eating, and talking, but you don't have sex with them? How does that work?"

"Well, I'm not saying I never have sex with a client. In fact, I often do, but it's totally my choice. I'm not required to be intimate with them or anything, they know that up front. I'll turn down a client's request for sex if I'm not into them."

"Doesn't that piss them off?"

"Sometimes, and it always shoots my tip all to hell, but I'm never rude about turning them down. I usually say I'm flattered but I'm saving myself for marriage."

"They're okay with that?"

"Mostly, but I've also gotten two serious marriage proposals over the years. That's always a little awkward."

"I can imagine."

"Um, this is our first time at the casino," I said. "I've seen pictures of it, but how do you get in?"

"That part's easy. There's only one way. You take the bridge from the Arizona side over the Colorado River. There's a big parking lot next to the bridge and it's obvious which way to go."

"I know it's member's only. Do you know if they ever break that rule?"

"Not as far as I know. But you're both already members, aren't you?"

"Um, of course we are. But suppose somebody showed up with a big bag of casino chips. Do you think they'd let them over the bridge to gamble, even without a membership?"

"I really don't know," he said. "Maybe. I'd think all they'd really want would be for the person to gamble all the chips back to the house."

~~~~

Twenty minutes later, we drove into the village of Wikieup. From the back seat, Susan perked up. "I'd like to stop at the trading post. Do you mind?"

"Not at all," Jonathan said. "I was thinking about stopping there anyway. I could use a break."

~~~~

The Wikieup Trading Post is the only nice-looking building along the entire hundred-and-thirty-mile stretch of desert between Wickenburg and Kingman. It has a good restaurant and for countless years has been used as a bathroom break by people travelling between Scottsdale and Las Vegas.

We pulled into the parking lot and found a place near the entrance. I grabbed my overnight bag before I went in and Susan did the same. Jonathan seemed like a nice guy, but I didn't want to take the chance he'd decide to take off with our bags while we were in the bathroom.

After we'd used the facilities, we went out to look in the display cases, which were full of Native American jewelry. As always, my eyes drifted to the turquoise and silver pieces, especially the intricate squash blossom necklaces.

Susan was eyeing a silver ankle bracelet and the lady behind the counter pulled it out so she could take a better look at it. It had a woven silver pattern with a carved turquoise charm hanging down from it.

"That's beautiful," Jonathan said as he came up behind us.

"I've been coming here since I was a kid," Susan said. "I always love looking at the turquoise jewelry."

"Why don't I get it for you?" he said. "I'd like to get you both something. That way, instead of remembering this as the day your car died, you can remember this as the day you got your turquoise jewelry."

"Oh, I couldn't let you do that," Susan said.

"Sure, you could. Trust me, I make a ton and I have virtually no living expenses. It would be my pleasure."

Susan looked at me. "Well," I said, "if he's willing."

"Perfect," he said as he flashed us another of his great smiles.

Susan got the anklet and I found a matching bracelet. We showed Jonathan the price of the pieces, but he only laughed and took them to the register.

~~~~

After passing through Kingman, a small city along Interstate 40, we drove northwest, in the direction of Las Vegas. After a few miles along this road, we turned due west towards Bullhead City and the Black Castle Casino.

After about fifteen minutes, the road climbed up through a small pass, between two barren rock mountains, then dipped sharply as it twisted the twelve miles down to the Colorado River. As we descended, the landscape rapidly changed. Unlike the Grand Canyon, sixty miles to the north, which is a vast rainbow of colors, the scenery here was merely bleak and depressing. All traces of vegetation disappeared. What was left were heaps of jagged black boulders, rugged hills, and dusty canyons of ash-gray rock.

"I bet this is what Mordor looks like," I said, half to myself.

"Mordor at least had Mount Doom, belching fire and stuff to give the place some color," Susan said. "Have you ever used that self-cleaning function on your oven? After four or five hours, you open the door and everything's clean except for some gray and black crunchy chunks on the bottom. That's what it looks like here, the crusty burnt-on stuff in an oven."

~~~~

Twenty minutes later, we'd arrived at Bullhead City, the little town directly across the river from the gambling oasis of Laughlin, Nevada. Unlike its flashier sister city of Las Vegas, sixty miles to the north, Laughlin is all about penny slots, convenient parking, and cheap all-you-can-eat buffets. We turned south and drove the five or six miles to our destination.

As we got closer, we could see the casino parking area in the distance. But what really drew our eyes was the black castle, now visible on the far side. It sat on a flat piece of land between the Colorado River and a sheer cliff on a barren hill in the Dead Mountain range.

I shivered as I got my first good look at the casino. Maybe the black color was their way of going for elegance in the design, but to me it only looked ominous, like an evil version of Cinderella's castle.

~~~~

Jonathan followed the brightly colored signs for the casino, drove past two overflow lots, an employee lot, and eventually pulled into the main parking area. There were spaces for three or four hundred cars, reminding me of long-term parking at an airport, only with nicer landscaping.

The parking area sat on a flattened hill and was about a hundred feet above the river. Stretching between the bluff on our side and the Black Castle on the other side was an ornate white concrete bridge.

I'd read about the bridge and knew it only carried foot traffic and electric carts. All service vehicles had to come in from the Nevada side, after travelling along a winding seven-mile road that connected the casino with Laughlin to the north. The bridge had a single massive span that arched over the green-colored river, which, at this point, was two or three hundred yards across.

Jonathan dropped us off next to a long white building that contained several restaurants and shops.

"There're bathrooms in there, if you'd like to freshen up," he said, pointing toward the building. He then waived toward the bridge on the far side of the parking lot. "The entrance to the bridge is through that building over there. Good luck at the casino. Maybe I'll see you both again."

We thanked him again for the ride, for the beautiful jewelry, and for pulling us out of a jam. We then got out of the car to stretch and look around. Jonathan took off and headed back toward the employee parking lot.

"He was nice," Susan said. "I wouldn't mind running into him again, once we're in the casino."

"If you had a hundred and fifty dollars an hour, you could do more than just run into him."

From the smile on Susan's face, I knew she was considering it.

"We've got a bag full of casino chips," I said. "Are you ready to put on some clothes and try our luck at getting across?"

"Before we try, I could use a bathroom break and maybe some lunch."

As soon as she mentioned food, I realized how hungry I was. The cinnamon roll I'd had in Wickenburg was good, but it wasn't a lot in terms of breakfast. Being so close to the casino had taken my mind off eating for a while, but now it sounded like a good idea.

We went into the white building that included several businesses strung together, like an indoor mini-mall. We first stopped at a central bathroom facility and changed into the clothes we'd brought. Susan put on a low-cut blue cocktail dress, while I changed into the short green dress.

The next step was to get rid of our bags. We wouldn't be staying at a room at the casino and it would be obvious we didn't belong there if we were carrying bags full of clothes. I also needed to stash my Baby Glock somewhere. Nevada would require a concealed carry permit, something I didn't need in Arizona, plus I didn't think the casino would be very happy if I tried to bring a gun in.

Fortunately, there was a coat and bag check room next to the main bathroom. We walked up to the woman working there. She was reading a romance novel and seemed happy to have someone to talk with.

"How long can I keep something in here?" I asked.

"Well," the woman said, "officially, coats and bags can only be checked for thirty days at a time. But honestly, we have stuff that's been sitting here for years. There's a room in the back they use for long-term storage. Every couple of months, someone'll show up with an old claim ticket and we'll have to dig through the pile to pull out some lost bag. The only time we ever get rid of anything is if it starts to stink. You'd be surprised at how many of the bags are filled with food."

We checked our bags then headed down the mall to the High Roller Cantina, a classy looking bar and grill. As we walked in, we couldn't help but notice the band on a small stage against the far wall. They were playing some type of modern fusion music that sounded more like something from a science fiction movie than anything I'd want to listen to.

We took a table as far away from the stage as possible, next to a picture window overlooking the river, the bridge, and the castle beyond. From our perch against the window, it was a good fifty or seventy-five feet down to the river below.

"Wow," Susan said. "It's all so beautiful from here. I hope we don't have a problem crossing over the bridge. If they don't let us in that way, I think we're pretty much screwed."

A waitress came by and we both ordered a cheeseburger and fries, along with a local beer. She quickly brought the drinks and said it would only be a few minutes for the food.

For a Monday afternoon, the bar was surprisingly lively. Many of the tables were filled with couples, most of whom were laughing and talking.

I looked closer and spotted two Elvis impersonators at one of the tables. They were both smiling and having a lively conversation. One of them was pounding his arms up and down, like he was playing the drums, and the other one was doing an energetic air guitar.

There were several singles at the bar and they all seemed to be talking, either with the bartenders, the waitresses, or each other.

A nearby table of five women in their fifties each had a drink and were working on a huge plate of nachos. In addition to their drinks, they seemed to be doing shots of tequila while they waited for the rest of their group to arrive. They were all laughing loudly and seemed to be having a great time.

There were also a few tables of people who seemed to be in a quiet reflective mood. The person who seemed to be the most unhappy was a man at the table next to us. He was nursing a beer and wasn't paying attention to either the beautiful view or the people around him. As I was watching him, he looked up and caught my eye.

"Don't bother going to the casino," he said. "You'll have better luck in Las Vegas or even Laughlin."

"You didn't do so well?" I asked.

The man snorted a laugh. "They cleaned me out. The worst part is, I think they cheated me. I'm not sure how, but I've been to a lot of casinos and this is the first time I've lost that much, that fast. I sort of feel lucky to have made it out of there at all. Save yourself some trouble and stay on this side of the river. Trust me, it's not worth it over there. You'll end up thanking me in the long run."

When the food came out, I asked the waitress why the bar was so crowded.

"Oh, it's always this way in the afternoon. The hotel won't let anyone check in until four o'clock and the food here's about half the price as it is across the river. People tend to gather here and have lunch before heading over."

I started in on my food and found everything to be delicious. The burger tasted like it had been grilled over real charcoal and the fries were homemade, not frozen. When I looked at Susan, she was picking at her fries and only sipping on the beer but wasn't touching her burger.

"Are you okay?" I asked.

"I'm hungry, but I think I'm too nervous to eat. I had the pie earlier and that should hold me for a while."

I wasn't having that problem and had already wolfed down my burger and was most of the way through the fries.

"That's okay," I said. "Ask them to wrap it up so you can have it whenever you get hungry again."

Chapter Nine

We walked out of the building, then along a landscaped path towards the bridge. The trail led past a high-tech-looking helicopter pad, a valet parking stand, and an ornate limousine drop-off area.

We walked past several tropical plants and up a thick red carpet to the lavish building that served as the bridge entrance. A red velvet rope was stretched across the entryway. The opening in the rope was flanked by two good-looking security guards.

"Good afternoon, ladies," one of the guards said as we walked up to his security podium. He wore a short-sleeved button-down shirt with Black Castle Casino Security embroidered in crimson red above the right breast pocket. "I'll need to verify your ID's and check your purses."

We handed him our licenses and he ran them through a scanner on his security podium. His friendly demeanor stepped down slightly as he handed us back our licenses.

"I'm sorry, ladies, but entry to the casino is restricted to members or by pre-arranged invitation. You'll need to go to the website and fill out the membership application. That'll put you in the system and you can obtain entry."

"But we've already got our Black Castle chips," Susan said, pulling a clear plastic sandwich-bag out of her purse that contained the purple and orange casino chips. "Isn't that the only reason to fill out the forms?"

"Let me get a supervisor over here," he said. "He'll get you both sorted out."

The guard wore an earpiece and had a microphone clipped to the collar of his shirt. He pushed the button to activate the microphone and quietly spoke into it. Within two minutes, a good-looking athletic guy in an inexpensive suit came from the far side of the bridge. He walked over to where we were standing, and the guard told him what we were trying to do.

"I'm sorry, ladies," the supervisor said. "But unless you're a registered member, you can't pass over the bridge." He then gave us a friendly and understanding smile. "It doesn't take too long to fill out the membership forms and there are courtesy computer terminals over in the hospitality lounge. That's in the white building across the parking lot, between the shops and the restaurants. The hostesses there will be glad to assist you."

The supervisor took a step back and it was clear he was done talking with us. The guard shrugged his shoulders as a way of saying he was sorry we couldn't get in.

We slowly walked back to the main parking area. Once there, we walked to an overlook that had a spectacular view of the river below, the bridge next to us, and the Black Castle rising on the far side. From where we stood, it somehow looked more formidable than it had before.

"What are we going to do now?" Susan asked. "We can try again later tonight when a new shift comes on, but I don't think they're ever going to let us across the bridge. The guard said all we had to do was fill out the forms. Do you think it could be as easy as that?"

"From what Kathleen said, we wouldn't qualify. Besides, I was reading on the internet last night and it said the membership fee is twenty thousand dollars."

"Crap, there's no way I could afford that. But there must be a way to get into the castle."

"What about a boat?" I asked, pointing down to the river. "There're boats on the river all the time."

"Yeah," Susan said. "But look at the part of the castle next to the river. That's a really high wall and it looks like coils of barbed wire are on top of it. Besides, isn't that a casino security boat?"

We watched as a large black boat slowly idled down the river past the casino. The boat was painted with the Black Castle Casino logo and had three uniformed security guards on it. We watched for two or three minutes until it disappeared around a slight bend in the river.

"Is that a dock?" I asked, shading my eyes with my hand, squinting to get a better look. "It looks like a boat dock at the very end of the wall. There must be some sort of gate there to let people into the castle. It would be pretty hard for someone to get there. You'd need to have a boat and avoid the river patrol. Maybe they don't keep it locked?"

Susan made a noise, clearly skeptical about the gate being unlocked. I was skeptical as well but didn't say anything since we were running out of options.

"If there's a dock on that side of the river," I said. "Maybe there's a similar dock on this side. It would make sense if they needed to ferry things across. If it exists, it would be a couple of hundred yards up-river from here. If we can find a dock, maybe we'll also find a boat."

"Alright," Susan said, sweeping her arm out to let me go first. "Let's go find a boat."

~~~~

We walked through the parking area, then past the shops and restaurants. We crossed over a dirt-covered field, then found a road that seemed to lead down to the river. Unlike the parking lot and the area around the bridge, which had been landscaped to perfection, the road and the grounds around it were nothing but dirt and broken rocks. I also noticed that the wind had started to pick up again.

We followed the road as it curved down to a wide dirt clearing. Unlike the pristine upper parking lot, this was clearly a service area. There were smaller trash bins, larger trash containers, fork lifts, and stacks of wooden pallets. Half a dozen garbage trucks and a couple of flat-beds were parked along the side of the lot. Some of the more beat-up looking trucks had deflated tires and piles of tumbleweeds lodged under them. They seemed to have been there for a very long time.

We walked down to the river and found a dock. Tied up next to it was a rusted metal boat that had seen better days. It was fifty or sixty feet long and had a flat open cargo area. From the tracks in the dirt and scattered bits of trash, it seemed the boat was used to bring dumpster bins full of garbage from across the river.

The only person visible was a big man with long grey hair and a scraggly beard. It was hard to judge his exact age, but he was likely somewhere in his sixties or seventies. He wore leather work boots, dusty grey overalls, and a filthy grey jacket with a long hood. He was sitting on a wooden stool on the dock and was in the process of fixing some sort of electrical part with a screwdriver.

As we walked closer, a dog on the boat stood up and eyed us warily. He was big and looked mean. The thick black leather collar studded with metal spikes which wrapped around his neck added to his threat level. His tail was only seven or eight inches long and stood straight up. I guessed he'd been in a lot of fights, since he had several thick scars along his face and body.

"I don't haul passengers," the man growled as we walked closer. "I only haul freight. If you want to cross the river, you'll need to use the bridge, same as everyone else."

"We're having some problems getting across the bridge," I said. "Would you be able to give us a ride to the other side? We'll be glad to pay you."

"I'm the only one who has a key to the gate on the far dock, everybody here knows that. Once a week, somebody'll come along, just like you, and ask me to take 'em over. One guy last year offered me ten thousand dollars, but I turned him down, same as you. It wouldn't be enough, since I'd lose my job, or worse, if they found out I was sneaking people over. Besides, Chopper didn't like the fella. Him and me are partners. No one gets on the boat unless Chopper allows it."

"We've got to get across today," I said. "Is there anything you can do?"

"Well, if I was you," he said in a confidential tone as he leaned towards us, "I'd try to sneak in from the Nevada, side. Although you'll need to bring some mountain climbing equipment. Other than the main gate, the only way to the castle is up the mountain then down the cliff. Every few months somebody tries to sneak in that way. Sometimes they make it, sometimes they find 'em smashed on the rocks at the bottom of the cliff." He must have thought that was hilarious because he started chuckling to himself.

I had a sudden thought. "Susan, show him the coin."

Susan seemed puzzled for a moment, then realized what I was talking about. She reached into her bag and pulled out Kathleen's marker. In the bright sunlight, it sparkled like fire was dancing along the edges.

The man looked at the coin and stopped laughing. His mouth opened as though he was going to say something, but nothing came out. He reached up and scratched the side of his face and looked at Susan. Finally, he spoke in a puzzled voice. "A marker?" The man bent down and looked closer at it. "That's an owner's marker. I haven't seen one of those in twenty years." He held out his hand. "May I?"

Susan handed him the shining gold coin and he took it reverently. He felt the weight of it and turned it over in his hand a couple of times. He then solemnly returned it.

"I've held a few markers over the years and I once saw an owner's marker up close. I'd say yours feels real enough. But what would you be doing with an owner's marker? You don't look old enough to have done the owner of the casino a favor. At least, not one of *those* favors."

"How I got it's none of your business," Susan said, a little angrily. "I'm trying to get to the owner so I can present him with his marker. I was told people wouldn't purposefully try to hinder me."

"You're right," the man said, a little defensively. "Ain't none of my business how you got it. Although, it's funny you came to me with this. You could've shown the marker to any of these young security guards but they wouldn't have any idea what it even was, never mind what it meant. I still respect the old ways, even if no one else here remembers how it was, back when the castle first opened. I'll honor the marker and take you over."

He stood up and climbed onto the boat. We followed and took two steps onto the deck. When we did, the dog started to growl. It was a low rumbling sound. He took a step towards us; his teeth were now visible and the hair on his back was starting to rise.

"I don't think Chopper likes you," the man said. "I told you, him and me are partners. Owner's marker or not, you don't get on the boat unless he approves."

The dog took a step closer, then stopped growling. He stretched his neck out, looked up at Susan, and sniffed a couple of times. A glop of drool splatted onto the deck, then the dog licked his slobbery lips. He reminded me a of a dog I'd met on an assignment several months before named Buddy.

"I think he can smell your cheeseburger," I said.

"I don't care what he can smell," Susan said. "I'm looking forward to eating it, all by myself."

"A cheeseburger?" the man asked with a small chuckle. "Chopper does like cheeseburgers. You might change his opinion of you with one of those."

"Susan," I said through gritted teeth, "give the dog your cheeseburger so we can get to the other side."

Susan sighed with defeat. Shaking her head at the loss of her lunch, she pulled the cheeseburger out of the bag and handed it to me.

"Fine," she said. "But you feed it to him. I don't want my hands anywhere near that mouth. There're too many teeth and that slobbering is gross."

I unwrapped the cheeseburger and held it out to the dog. Again, reminding me of Buddy, he carefully reached out and delicately took the burger. He dropped it to the deck and devoured it in three bites. He then looked up at me and licked his slobbery dog lips again.

"That's all I have," I told the dog. Apparently not understanding, he whined, then gave a couple of good-natured yips. When I didn't respond, he looked up at me and whined again, expecting more. Without thinking about the wisdom of what I was doing, I reached down and petted the dog's scarred head. This seemed to be what he'd been looking for, because the dog closed his eyes and let me scratch him behind the ears.

After a few moments of pampering, he came out of his doggie trance. He opened his eyes and his tongue rolled out as he started to pant. Now satisfied, he trotted to the front of the boat and sat down.

"Huh," the man said. "Looks like we're good to go. Those bastards in the patrol boat went by ten minutes ago, but you'll need to keep out of sight in case they make a sudden appearance. We've had some bad blood between us over the years and I know they'd like to nail me to a cross for breaking some of their precious rules. Plus," he quietly said as he pointed down river, "you never know who might be watching from the bridge."

We both scrambled to find somewhere to hide as he untied the boat from the dock and walked to the controls. There was a low grumble from the engines and we slowly began to glide across the river. We watched as the Black Castle began to tower above our heads, until we were looking directly up at it.

"It looks a lot bigger from down here," Susan said. "Are you sure about this?"

"I kind of think we're committed now," I said.

It was only about four or five minutes before the boat gently settled against the far dock. The man cut the engines and tied up the boat.

He led us down the dock to where a huge, black wrought-iron gate was set in the stone wall. It looked very solid.

He pulled a tarnished brass key out of his pocket. "I always keep the gate locked," he said. "Once or twice a month, kids up in Laughlin get drunk, then think they can take a boat downriver and get into the casino through the dock. Whenever I see a tourist boat tied up and a bunch of college kids trying to open the gate, I radio security to clean 'em off the dock. It'd be my ass if people started sneaking in this way."

He walked up to the gate and inserted the key. It smoothly turned in the lock and he pulled open the massive gate. It made a loud, screeching, metal-on-metal sound and I knew everyone on this side of the castle could hear we'd arrived.

"From here," he said, "take the path until you get up to the castle. There's only one way in from down here, that's through the garbage dock. Once you get in, follow the main corridor, and don't make any detours. You'll eventually find yourself in the main part of the casino with the other players. If you're looking for the owner, he'll likely be in the executive offices. Never been there myself, but they're supposedly up in the Tower of the Guard. All the towers have different names. Best get yourself a map once you make it in. But you've got to watch yourself, it's obvious you don't belong in this part of the castle. Most of the people back here will ignore you, but a few might turn you in, just for the fun of it. You especially don't want to be caught by casino security. They may look like choir boys, but they aren't nice people. That goes double for the head of security. He's a real shit."

We nodded and tried to step through the gate. But before we could go through, the man held out a hand to stop us. "Now then," he said, "even though you carry an owner's marker, best not be telling anyone how you got into the casino if you're caught. They might not look too favorably on what I did."

"We won't say a word," Susan said. "Thank you. You're a very kind man." She reached up and kissed him on the cheek. The man smiled and blushed red.

Realizing what he was doing, his scowl returned. He then growled at us to get off his dock before someone spotted what he was doing.

We thanked him again and stepped through the wide opening in the stone wall. With the same loud screeching sound, the man shut the gate. When it closed, there was an ominous sound of the lock snapping back into place.

We watched as he untied the boat and jumped back on. Chopper stood at the back of the ferry, watching us, the stump of his tail slowly moving back and forth. As the man turned back to his controls, I watched as he touched his cheek where Susan had kissed him.

~~~~

As the man had said, there was a long concrete ramp that went from the river up to a loading dock. This was in one of several large steel and cinderblock buildings at the base of the castle. These buildings seemed to be recent add-ons to the original construction. From the outside, I guessed they were mainly storage and warehousing.

The loading dock had a large garbage container attached to it, along with a machine that looked like it would crush and compact whatever trash was thrown into it. Off to the side of the compactor, a set of six or seven metal stairs led to a dented door that seemed to be the only way inside the building.

We made our way up the ramp and climbed the stairs without incident. As with most of the back entrances I've seen over the past few years, there were two metal folding chairs sitting on either side of a wooden crate in front of this entry door. A bucket, containing about a hundred cigarette butts, sat on top of the crate. I assumed the door was supposed to be locked, but there was a rock holding it ajar.

"Are you ready?" I asked.

Susan looked like she was rethinking the entire thing. "No," she said. "But we've gone too far to stop now."

I pulled open the door and we stepped into the castle.

~~~~

The space inside seemed to be a staging area for the casino garbage. On the stained concrete floor were seven or eight trash bins, lined up to be compacted into the larger container on the dock. Fortunately, there didn't seem to be anyone working back here, at least not at the moment.

Susan looked around and wrinkled her nose. "Oh, jeeze, this place stinks."

The stench coming from the garbage bins was intense and only got worse as we walked further into the room. It seemed like the bins had been sitting on the garbage dock for quite a while. "I'm assuming the rest of the casino isn't as bad," I said. "But let's get away from here as quickly as we can. It's not just the smell, the man on the boat was right, we don't look like we belong here."

"We were supposed to blend in with the other players, not look like people who work on a garbage dock. We can't change the way we look now."

I looked around for some overalls or something that would make us look more like workers. Instead, I found a small metal desk against a wall. There was a clipboard, a couple of dirty notebooks, and several pieces of paper scattered across the top. I picked up the clipboard and shoved a blank piece of paper under the clasp. I then rooted around the drawers until I found a pen. Satisfied, I handed everything to Susan.

"This isn't much of a disguise, but if you're holding a clipboard it looks like you have a purpose for being here. A leather folder would have been even better, but I didn't see one in the desk."

Although there were large rooms on either side, there seemed to be a main walkway through the area. I remembered what the man had said about not veering off the path and it seemed like good advice.

We walked until we came to a garage-type roll-up door that was large enough to accommodate forklifts and garbage bins. A sign on it said "No Pedestrians." Next to it was a regular-sized entrance. From the marks on the floor, this smaller door was often used by people going from one room to the other.

"Okay," I said. "We seem to be going in the right direction."

"How long do you think it'll take to get up to the gaming area? Even with the clipboard, it's obvious we don't belong down here."

"I don't know. I suppose it depends on our luck. I don't even think we're in the castle part of the casino yet. These buildings look relatively new."

I pulled opened the pedestrian door and we stepped into a large room filled with high steel racks. It appeared to be a warehouse for the dry goods of the casino. The racks were five shelves high and each space had a wooden pallet with some sort of shrink-wrapped cardboard boxes on it.

"Well, it's not the gaming floor," Susan said, "but at least this room doesn't smell as bad."

"We're making progress. Let's keep going. We still seem to be on the main path. I'm hoping there's another door on the far side of the room. Maybe we can get into the actual castle from there."

"Hey, you two," a big middle-aged man called out to us. He'd been doing something with a pallet of boxes on one of the racks and we hadn't seen him until he shouted at us. Clearly annoyed, he walked up to where we were standing. He wasn't casino security, more like one of the warehouse workers. He had a huge beer belly and a five-day old beard. He was wearing dark blue work pants and a light blue button-down shirt. The sleeves had been ripped off to show his hairy muscular arms, complete with several faded tattoos. "What are you doing down here?" he asked in a gruff two-pack-a-day voice.

"Um, we're doing the quarterly safety audit," I said. "Everyone was assigned an area. We're supposed to come down here and see how clean and orderly your area is. We're also supposed to make a note of anyone working in an unsafe manner."

As I was talking, Susan pretended to notice something across the room and made a note of it on her clipboard.

"They didn't tell me anyone was coming down today," the man growled. "It's so freaking typical." He looked us over. "Where're your badges?"

"They don't make us wear them in the office anymore," Susan said. "They haven't for a couple of months now."

"Shit," the man said. "They never tell us anything down here. They treat us like we're the freaking asshole of the entire God damned castle."

"But your area looks great," I said. "We've been all over the place and haven't found a thing to report."

"Well, that's the first good news I've had today. The main compactor blew a hydraulic line last night and the bins are starting to back up. I called maintenance, but you know how long it always takes for them to show up."

"Um," I said. "Maybe you could help us. This is our first time down here and we've sort of gotten turned around. How do we get back up to the offices?"

The man smiled at us and shook his head, as if we were children who needed to be tutored.

"You ladies were headed in the right direction. Keep going straight, don't veer off, and you'll find yourself back at the junction. Just be careful walking around down here. I wouldn't want you to brush up against anything nasty and mess up your pretty office outfits." He started laughing, like he'd made a hilarious joke.

We laughed along with him and thanked him for his help. He then turned and wandered back to where he'd been working.

Susan looked at me and blew out a breath. I knew what she was thinking; we'd narrowly dodged a bullet. Even though we were okay for the moment, I didn't think the clipboard disguise would hold out much longer.

We continued along the main path until we found the next pedestrian door. We went through, then continued walking in the direction that would hopefully lead us up into the main part of the casino.

~~~~

We managed to make it through the next two rooms without encountering any more problems. So far, everywhere had either been empty or the people working there didn't mind us being there. Maybe the clipboard thing was still working or maybe security wasn't high on their list of priorities.

Going through the next door on the main path led us to an area the size of a living room. The room was empty except for three doors. The main path led directly to a shiny white door with a keypad next to it. A large yellow and black sign on the door read: "Security Level Five. Authorized Personnel Only."

Susan looked at me with a touch of panic in her eyes. "This must be the junction the man was talking about. What are we supposed to do now? We can't go any further on the main path."

"Well, one of the other doors must lead up to the casino or at least to the offices. I doubt everyone who works down here has a level five security clearance and they'd have to be able to get up to the main casino, at least occasionally."

"Yeah, I get that, but which one?"

Next to each door was a sign. The one to the right of the white security door said: "To GF1 – GF3", the one to the left said: "To TG2, GR3 – GR5".

We looked at the signs for several minutes, trying to make some sense out of them.

"Well," Susan said. "Maybe GF stands for gaming floor? That would be promising."

"Maybe, and maybe GR stands for guest rooms. That would work too."

"We're supposed to be heading to the executive offices in the Tower of the Guard, maybe that's what TG stands for?"

"I think the man on the boat was right," I said. "We're going to need a map."

My phone started buzzing in my back pocket. I pulled it out and saw it was Sophie.

"Hey," I said in a quiet voice. "I can't talk long. Were you able to get my car back into town?"

"Yes, but you aren't going to like it."

"What?" I asked as my heart sank. This sounded like it was going to be expensive. "Was there engine damage? When I popped the hood the engine still looked okay. Was it something internal?"

"That's not what I mean."

"Okay, then what?"

"I went over to the garage as soon as they brought your car in. I knew you'd want to know about it right away. The thing that caused the damage wasn't a blown water hose, it was a bomb. The mechanic found the detonator mounted to the underside of your engine. It was wired to your battery, but in a very sneaky way so you wouldn't notice."

"A bomb? You're serious?"

"Serious as a positive pregnancy test. The detonator had an antenna attached to it, but the mechanic couldn't tell if a radio signal set the bomb off or if it was on some sort of internal timer. He wanted to call the police, but I talked him out of it."

"If it was a bomb, it wasn't a very big one, all it did was blow up a couple of hoses and a fan belt."

"That's what I told the mechanic. He said from what he could tell, the explosive charge was only meant to disable your car. It looks like someone knew you'd be driving through the desert and wanted to strand you out there. Have you pissed anyone off lately?"

"No more than usual. It could've been a lot of people, but I don't see how any of them could've known I'd be in the desert today."

"Well, be careful. Someone doesn't like you."

~~~~

After spending another two minutes debating which door would be better, we heard the faint sounds of people talking and footsteps echoing.

"Shit," I said. "Someone's coming."

"Yeah," Susan said. "The footsteps sound like they're getting closer." Her eyes opened wide with concern. I'm sure mine had done the same thing.

"They're coming, but from which door?" I pointed at the door to the right. "You listen at that one. I'll take the left one."

We each put our ears to our doors. I held my breath so I could better hear the faint noises. Unfortunately, all I could hear was my thumping heart.

After about thirty seconds, the sounds of people walking and softly talking began to clearly come through my door.

"It's this one," I said. "The door to the left."

"So, we take the door to the right?"

"Good idea," I said, as I pulled open the door and we hurried through.

~~~~

The corridor we'd entered was an improvement over the warehousing areas we'd just come through. Instead of bare concrete, the hallway floor had a shiny enamel-looking coating. The lighting had changed from open fluorescent tubes to a softer overhead illumination. The area had a feeling of disuse, but I still listened intently for sounds of anyone who might be working here.

We passed by several wooden doors. Each had a large glass panel so we could see inside. The rooms seemed to be long-term storage for items that didn't belong in a warehouse. We passed by several rooms full of file cabinets, a room with metal shelves full of notebooks, and even a couple of rooms full of old coin-operated slot machines.

~~~~

After walking through the area for about five minutes, it became obvious we were in a separate building that didn't seem to connect with anywhere else. We did find an emergency exit door with a small window in it, but it was alarmed and seemed to only lead outside. We decided to make our way back to the main junction when we came across a door that was different than the others. It wasn't white, but it seemed to be similar to the security door back in the junction. The only sign on it read: "No Entry. Authorized Personnel Only." We looked, but the door didn't have a security keypad.

"It's probably locked," I said, "but you never know."

"I hope this isn't the door that leads back to the warehouses," Susan said.

"Me too," I echoed. "But with all the backtracking we've done, it certainly could be." Mentally crossing my fingers, I pulled on the handle. To my surprise, it opened. Also, to my surprise, there was some sort of metal panel blocking our way through the opening.

"What in the world is that?" Susan asked.

"I don't know," I said, as I put my hand against it. It was flexible and gave slightly as I pushed on it. "It's some sort of metal sheet."

"Can we move it out of the way?"

"I don't know. Let me try."

I pushed on the sheet and after a few seconds, one side started to pull away from the wall. After a harder shove, I was able to stick my head through the opening to see there was another passageway on the other side. This one was gleaming white.

"Is it the gaming floor?" Susan asked after I'd pulled my head back in.

"No, it's another hallway. It seems to be empty."

"Well, that sounds better than this. We're in a dead end here. You've got the panel about halfway detached from the wall. If we push it open a little more, we could probably squeeze through to the other side."

"I agree, we're getting nowhere in this building. Let's give it a try."

Together we pushed on the panel and it slowly pulled away from the brackets holding it against the wall. After another two or three shoves, it had opened enough for both of us to slip through.

~~~~

"Do you get the feeling we're not supposed to be here?" Susan whispered.

"Yeah," I whispered back. "I think you're right."

We were in a gleaming corridor with white metal paneling on the walls, a shiny white floor, and a white metal mesh ceiling. On either side of the passageway were rows of identical rooms, each about eight feet by ten. The doors to the rooms looked like doors to old-fashioned prison cells, with thick bars made of shining stainless steel.

In the center of each room was a pallet covered with paper money. There were wrapped piles of tens, twenties, fifties, and hundred-dollar bills. Each bundle of money had a colorful paper strap holding it together. The currency had all been neatly stacked in tight piles on the pallets.

"I've never seen this much money before in my life," Susan whispered as we walked by the fourth or fifth room. "The bills must be stacked two feet thick and they completely cover the pallets. I can only guess, but there must be five or ten million dollars in each room. There's at least a dozen rooms down here and they all seem to have a pallet of cash."

"This isn't good," I said. "We need to get out before someone notices we're here."

"No shit," Susan shot back, panic in her voice again. "But we don't even know how we got in. Listen, I don't want to fumble around anymore looking for the door to the gaming floor. Let's just go back the way we came. We can even leave the casino if we need to. I bet the guy in the boat would give us a lift back across the river."

"Yeah," I said. "That's probably a good idea."

We turned and began to retrace our steps, but after we'd gone about twenty yards, the corridor split into a Y-junction.

"Do you remember being here?" I asked.

"No, but I wasn't looking behind us when we came through. We must have walked right past this."

"Great, so either one could be the right way."

"Well, crap," Susan said. "You go ahead and choose, my luck's been terrible today."

I didn't want to argue over whose luck had been worse, so I chose the left-hand corridor. After we'd gone about thirty feet, I stopped short as we both looked around. "Shit, we're definitely going the wrong way now."

The passageway was like the one we'd just been down, but in the rooms behind the bars here were pallets of plastic wrapped bundles of what appeared to be white powder. Each bundle was about the size of a bag of sugar.

Shit, shit, shit.

"I think we're in their level five security area," I said.

"I've seen enough drug bust videos to know what's on those pallets," Susan moaned. "Let's go back out the other way, please?"

We turned and halfway ran back down the corridor. We went down the other passageway and quickly found where one of the white metal panels had been pushed away from the wall.

"No wonder they didn't know about this door," Susan said. "It looks like the wall panel's been covering it up for years."

"Let's go through and see if we can pull it back into place," I said. "I don't want anyone to know we've been in here."

We squeezed ourselves under the paneling and slipped back through the door. Once we'd returned to the storage area, we pulled the white metal panel back into place the best we could.

"That won't fool anyone if they examine it," I said. "But it shouldn't be too noticeable if they aren't looking for it."

~~~~

We walked around the storage hallways until we found the door that led back to the junction.

"Well," Susan said. "The door on the right was a complete bust."

"We already know what's behind the middle security door. Do you want to go back to the river or should we go on?"

Susan sighed. "No, let's go on. If I don't do it now, I never will."

"Alright, we take the door on the left then?"

Susan nodded, resigned to whatever happened next.

We opened the new door and went through. This passageway went on for a short way then ended at a flight of stairs. We climbed up three flights, then the stairway ended at a metal door. We opened it and found ourselves in a corridor filled with people.

~~~~

"This looks promising," Susan said as we walked into the brightly lit hallway. The walls were painted a friendly blue and there was dark blue industrial carpet on the floor.

We walked past several doors that seemed to be administrative offices. We turned a corner and found a large employee breakroom that was about a third-full of people. Everyone seemed to be eating, reading newspapers, or watching the news on a television that was bolted to the wall.

Past the breakroom, we heard the sound of several hundred slot machines being played at once and knew we were close to our goal. After walking down the hallway for another ten or fifteen yards, the slot-machine sound was more distinct.

"Look," Susan said, pointing to a door. "We've found the way out."

The door she pointed to had a carved wooden plaque with "East Gaming Floor" written on it in gothic style lettering.

"It's about freaking time," I said.

"Hold it," came a deep but emotionless voice directly behind us. I immediately recognized the tone. It was the voice of a professional doing his job.

We both turned to see two casino security guards, one older, one younger. The older guard had the look of someone who was a veteran. The younger one seemed to be the rookie. Neither one looked happy to see us.

"Guests aren't allowed in this area," the younger one said.

"Really?" I asked, using my best innocent tone. "I'm sorry, we were looking for the powder room and must have gotten turned around."

"Ladies," the veteran guard said, still with the cop-voice, "this is a secured area that requires a badge to access. Plus, we watched you come in through the door that leads down to the basement levels. I'm not sure how you got in, or what you were doing down there, but we're going to need to go to the security office to discuss this."

As he was talking, I noticed he wore both a stun gun and a collapsible tactical baton on his belt. Susan and I looked at each other. She was clearly frightened, her breathing slightly fast and raspy. My mind raced through possible ways to get out of this, unfortunately none of the ways seemed like they would work.

"Ladies," the older guard said in his firm steady voice. "Let's do this the friendly way. Shall we?"

Chapter Ten

The guards led us back through several hallways to a security office. They made copies of our driver's licenses, catalogued the contents of our bags, then led us to an interview room. I'd been in enough police stations over the years to see this one was overly comfortable, with a leather couch and a shiny wooden table, but still very much a holding area.

They left us alone, but I assumed the door was locked. Glancing up, I noted the room had two very visible security cameras pointed down at us. Susan followed my gaze, understood the meaning of the cameras, and didn't say anything. She looked terrible. It was obvious she wasn't used to this sort of ordeal.

~~~~

Twenty minutes later, the door opened and the veteran security guard walked in, along with someone wearing a tie who appeared to be a security manager. The new man was in his late thirties and was good-looking in a rugged, sporty sort of way.

Where do they get all these handsome men?

We'd been sitting on the couch and he invited us over to the table. We got up and sat together on one side. The security guard stood next to us while the good-looking supervisor sat on the opposite side.

"Ladies," the manager said as he flipped through pages in a file folder he'd brought in with him. "We've run your ID's so we know who you are. We know you tried to get over the bridge earlier today and were appropriately turned away. You were caught a few minutes ago leaving a level three security area, somewhere you shouldn't have been able to get into without an authorized badge. Now, the sergeant here thinks we should turn you over to the Clark County Sheriff's office, have both of you charged with trespassing and burglary, and be rid of you. But I don't want anything like that showing up on your permanent records. Criminal charges will ruin your credit score and might even stop you from ever getting a decent job. I'd be willing to wipe the slate clean and let you go. All I'm asking for is your cooperation in giving me the details of how you got in, what you were doing in a level three security area, and why you seemed so interested in going out to the gaming floor."

"Um, well," I said. "We sort of inherited a bag of casino chips and we came here to cash them in."

"Yeah," Susan said. "We knew we couldn't qualify for a membership so we didn't even apply."

"We have thirty thousand dollars' worth of chips," I said, using my most sincere voice. "All we're trying to do is find a way through the casino to get to the cashier's window."

The security guard grunted with disgust, but the manager held up a hand to stop him. "You have a bag of Black Castle chips?" he asked, a hint of disbelief in his voice. He then flipped a couple of pages in the file folder to where the contents of our purses were listed.

"It seems you're correct," he said. "You do have a large quantity of casino chips. May I see them?"

Susan searched through her purse and pulled out the bag. The security manager held out his hand and Susan gave it to him. He pulled out a purple chip and closely examined it. He made a notation of the chip's serial number on a paper in the folder. He then eyed the remaining chips in the bag, and I could see him doing a quick mental calculation of their value.

"These chips are very old," he said, half to himself. "They're from the first year or two of the casino's opening."

"They've been sitting in a safe for the last twenty-five years," I told him truthfully.

After a moment, he laughed and shook his head. "You went through the trouble of breaking into the Black Castle just to turn in some twenty-five-year-old chips? Don't you know you could have done that through the mail? People are always taking chips home with them then mailing them back for cash."

"Oh," Susan said. "We didn't know you could do that."

"And besides," I said, "what guarantee would we have that you would pay out their actual value, if we mailed them to you?"

"Alright," the manager said. His manner shifted to that of a bureaucrat whose task was done, except for finishing up some required paperwork. "We're reviewing the surveillance videos to see exactly how you got in. It seems we have a hole in our security system that needs to be fixed. We'll need you to describe all your movements within the casino, who you talked to, and who helped you. If your story checks out, we'll let you cash in your chips, then you'll be escorted off the property."

Susan's eyes opened wide and she looked at me. I knew she was thinking the same thing as I was.

Reviewing the surveillance videos? Shit.

I knew all casinos had camera's everywhere, but I'd hoped to be in and out before we caught anyone's attention on a security video. If they saw we'd been in their level five area, the chances we would be allowed to leave would drop to zero.

~~~~

Ten minutes later, the door to our room opened and a man in a suit appeared. He had a look of panic on his face that told me our movements had been traced. He motioned the manager out into the hallway and we could hear them yelling at each other for almost two minutes.

Things went quiet and I began to get very nervous as the implications of our situation started to sink in. The door to the room opened and the manager stepped back in. His face had gone pale and he looked terrible. In the hallway were four uniformed security guards.

"Ladies," he said quietly. All traces of friendly persuasion had left his voice. "I'm afraid this situation is now out of my hands. They're going to take you down to some holding rooms in the basement to wait for the head of security." He seemed to think about it for a second then bent close to us. His voice changed to the tone of a concerned friend. "Look, I'm not sure what your involvement is in this, but you're both in serious trouble. The head of security may seem friendly enough, but he isn't a nice guy, remember that. For your sakes, I hope you have some good answers for him."

~~~~

We were escorted by the four guards to an elevator, which took us down four or five floors to another security area. From the bare rock floors of the corridor, I assumed we were somewhere in the lowest level of the castle. Pipes and ductwork crisscrossed the ceiling and water seeped from between some of the large stones that made up the walls. The place smelled of mildew and I saw more than one cockroach scurry out of our way as we were led through the passageways.

The guards led us to a dead-end corridor containing three rooms, each with a thick wooden door. Each door had a small window with iron bars and a heavy sliding bolt.

"I'll need you to remove any belts or shoelaces," the lead guard said. Susan's dress had a slim black belt that she unfastened and handed to the guard. He set it on a table on the far side of the room, along with our bags. They then locked us in the middle room. Hearing the bolt slide home filled me with dread.

~~~~

"Well, this sucks," Susan said for the third time during the hour we'd been locked in the cell.

We each sat on a green army-style canvas cot, the only furniture in the otherwise bare room. The floor and walls of the cell were made of black stone. There wasn't any light except for what came through the barred window in the door from the brightly lit hallway. The cell had the strong odor of a roadside public toilet.

"I came here to find my father," she said, "not to be locked up in some sort of freaking medieval dungeon. The only decent thing that's happened is we got some cool jewelry. What do you think's going to happen to us?"

"I don't know," I said. "We'll need to convince them that we didn't mean to go inside their security area. That'll be the easy part."

"What's the hard part?"

"We'll also need to convince them that we'll keep quiet about everything we saw."

"This really sucks. Damn, I'd give a lot for that cheeseburger we fed the dog. If we ever get out of here, I want another one. First thing I want to do is see if that freaking bar's still open. I want another cheeseburger, only with bacon this time. I also want a double order of those fries and a beer. A big beer."

~~~~

Another hour passed in the dark cell. We didn't have our phones and there wasn't a way to tell the time, but I guessed it must have been around four or five in the afternoon. Even though the place smelled like an outhouse, I was also starting to get hungry. What was worse, I really had to go to the bathroom.

When we'd first walked in, I'd noticed a ceramic pot on the floor, the size of a bucket, with a piece of wood laying across the top of it. After being in here for a couple of hours, I was starting to get the idea they expected us to use this as a chamber pot. I knew there was no way I was going to squat down on a bucket, especially in front of somebody else. Unfortunately, I was starting to get to the point where there might not be any other option.

Susan saw me eyeing the chamber pot. "I was thinking the same thing," she said. "I understand them wanting to keep us locked up while they figure out what to do with us, but the idea of peeing in a bucket is too gross."

"Let's see if there's somebody out there. I'm hoping they won't object to letting us use a real bathroom."

I went to the door and called out the small window for someone to come to our cell. I yelled for two or three minutes but no one came. From what I could see, the corridor was empty. Apparently, they thought we were secure and there was no need for anyone to be nearby to guard our cell.

I went back and sat on my cot, now seriously fighting the urge to go. I was about to say "screw it" and squat down on the pot, when I heard a voice in the distance.

"Susan? Laura?" someone called out in the corridor. The voice sounded vaguely familiar.

We went to the door and both tried to look out the window at the same time. "We're in here!" we called out. Thirty seconds later we heard footsteps and Jonathan's head appeared in the window.

"Hello," he said in his bright cheery voice. "What are you two doing in there?"

He slid open the bolt and our door swung open. We both stepped out and blinked at the brightness of the corridor.

"Let's get you out of here," he said. He pointed to the table where Susan's belt and our purses sat. "Are those yours?"

"Thanks," I said as we grabbed our things. "Is there a bathroom down here?"

"I passed one in the last hallway, but it looked kind of nasty."

"Doesn't matter," Susan said. "It'll be better than a bucket."

~~~~

After a quick stop at the bathroom, we were hurrying down the passageway with Jonathan in the lead. He seemed to be in a good mood at his feat of releasing two desperate criminals. I noticed he'd shaved off his beard. Under the fluorescent lighting, his skin seemed much paler than it had looked when he'd picked us up earlier in the day. He'd also pulled his hair back into a tight ponytail with a rubber band. It somehow made him look older and somewhat less attractive.

"There's been a rumor going around about two pretty women who tried to sneak in and were caught," he said. "They were supposedly locked in the dungeons. I figured it was you two. I know how this place works and I thought you might need a helping hand."

"That's the second time you've rescued us," I said. "We really owe you. How'd you find us?"

"Everybody knows about the dungeons," he laughed. "They were originally storage rooms from back when the castle was first built as a tuberculosis sanitarium. Now they use them as holding cells, mainly to scare people who try to cheat at blackjack. I figured if you two were anywhere, you'd be here. I've never been down here before but I had a vague idea where the dungeons must be. I'd been walking around down here for about five minutes when I heard you call out. I just followed your voice."

"Thanks," Susan said. "But won't you get in trouble for helping us?"

"Look around," he said. "Most of these lower levels don't have security cameras. They're probably worried about having a record of who they put in the holding cells. They won't have a clue what happened. Whatever did you do to get yourselves locked up down here?"

"It's a long story," I said. "You've already guessed we don't have memberships. We tried to get in by showing the guards at the bridge a bag of casino chips. When that didn't work, we snuck in. We were trying to find a way up to the executive offices and accidently ended up somewhere we weren't supposed to be. That's what's gotten them so riled up."

"I was wondering why they had you locked up. They normally just kick people out who aren't members after they sneak in. Why the executive offices?"

Susan and I looked at each other. I shrugged my shoulders. At this point, we could use all the allies we could get. "I'm looking for Michael McKinsey, the owner," she said. "I need to talk with him."

"You went through a lot of trouble to talk with the owner. Wouldn't it have been simpler to make an appointment?"

"I need to talk with him about something personal," Susan said. "It's not something I can discuss with his admin first."

"Did he get you pregnant?"

"No, jeeze, why does everyone ask me that?"

"Sorry," Jonathan said as he led us down a corridor leading an elevator. "Okay," he said. "This is where you need to decide what to do. Leave the casino or go to the executive offices? This elevator goes up to the Tower of the Guard, that's where the offices are located. On the other hand, if you go along this passageway, it will lead you to some storage warehouses. I'm assuming that's the way you were able to sneak in, maybe you could sneak back out the same way. Tell me what you want to do and I'll lead."

I knew we should get out of here as fast as we could. Several emotions crossed Susan's face. I could tell she knew we should go and go quickly. But she also knew this would be the one chance she'd get to find her father.

Susan looked at me and I could tell she'd made up her mind. Her eyes were pleading for me to agree to do something foolish.

Well, you wanted an adventure and to help someone. Here's your chance to do both.

"Okay," I said to Susan. "Let's do it."

"I want to find the owner," she said.

~~~~

We stepped into the elevator and I pushed the uppermost button labeled "Executive Offices". When the button didn't light up, I looked at Jonathan. He smiled and pulled out a card from his pocket and held it against a black sensor pad. There was a soft ding, the button lit up, and the doors closed silently.

"How do you have access to the executive offices?" I asked.

"I'm a casino escort," he said. "I sometimes have to go to some pretty weird places for my job. I'm authorized for any security area in the castle up to level three."

"What are the offices?" Susan asked.

"Level three," he said. "You've topped out my security privileges."

~~~~

The elevator doors opened onto a wide hallway with thick blue carpet and dark wood paneling. Several oil paintings hung on the walls, mostly landscapes of the southwest desert, or cowboy and Indian scenes. Jonathan led us out and we walked down the corridor, trying to look like we belonged there.

"I think the owner's office is at the end of the hallway," Jonathan said. "The one with the big double doors."

Susan grabbed my hand and squeezed it tight. I could feel the tension in her as she realized she was about to meet her father for the first time. Of course, walking in unannounced like this would probably raise some questions, but hopefully we'd manage.

We walked past several nice-looking offices, each with a nameplate on the door identifying who the person was and what they did. Almost everyone who worked in these offices was a vice president of something. About half of the offices had somebody sitting behind a desk, working on their computers.

We'd gone about halfway down the hallway, when Jonathan turned to look at us.

"Okay," he said. "This is far enough." All friendliness had dropped from his voice. In fact, he sounded a little upset. Maybe it was only the unflattering light of the office hallway, but his face seemed to have grown even paler and acquired a slightly skeletal look.

"What?" Susan asked. "Isn't the owner's office at the end of the hall? You just said it was."

"Yes, but I'm afraid we're going to need to have a little chat first. Follow me." He opened the door of one of the offices and went in. As he did, I read the nameplate on the door – Jonathan LaRose, Vice President, Security.

What? Jonathan's the head of security? Shit, this is not good.

Susan gasped. She must have read the nameplate at the same time as I did. We both stood there, unmoving, trying to take in what we'd just seen. How could Jonathan be vice president of security? Up until now he'd been both our friend and our guide.

Without thinking, we both began to back up. From the surrounding offices, four uniformed security officers stepped out and blocked our way. They looked like the same four that had originally taken us down to the dungeons.

"I said follow me," Jonathan barked out at us.

The security guards herded us into his office then closed the door.

"Take a seat," he commanded as he sat in a black leather chair behind a massive wooden desk. "You know, I've heard some piss-poor excuses for people wanting to break into the castle over the years, but yours are probably the most pathetic. What's worse, you keep changing the reason why you wanted to break in. With the guard on the bridge, you implied you were only here to gamble away the chips you had. You told the security officer you wanted to break in to cash in a bag of old casino chips. Now you've told me you broke in to talk with the owner. Well, which one's the real reason?"

He looked at us, as if expecting an answer. When we didn't say anything, he continued.

"Once I found out about you trying to break in, I thought it would be a good test of our security systems. I honestly didn't think you'd be able to do it. I don't know how you got across the river and through the locked gate, but I'm guessing it was Hobbs, the ferryman. All these years, I've thought he wasn't a security risk. I've even sent men down to try to pay him for rides across the river, but he's never taken the bait. So, either he's now open to bribery or maybe you two offered him something my men couldn't. Something a little more personal perhaps?" He leered at our exposed legs and snickered lewdly. "Either way, it looks like we'll need to set up some new patrols and install cameras on the garbage docks and in the warehouses."

Susan and I sat without saying anything. I knew our situation had gotten worse, even more so than it had been while we were locked away in the dungeon. Our silence seemed to upset him further and he started yelling at us.

"You know, the thing that really pisses me off is that you broke into our vault and now you know all about the little side business we have going on here. It troubles me because you seemed to know exactly how to do it. After we reviewed the security videos of you coming through the wall, like a superhero with some weird ability to go through solid rock, the first thing I did was to pull up the old blueprints of the castle. The door you went through doesn't show up on the original prints, so I'm guessing it was added during one of the many rebuilds over the years. You can imagine my surprise when you found a new way into what I thought was a very secure vault. And you say it was all an accident. Well, is there anything either of you want to add to your story? You might say I'm a little curious at this point."

Susan and I looked at each other and we each shook our heads. I wasn't sure what we could say to get out of this. Even the truth would sound ridiculous after the stories we'd already told him.

"Well, you can either tell me now or go back to your cell in the dungeon for a couple of days. Maybe hunger and thirst will loosen your tongues. Although this time, nobody will let you out for bathroom breaks. It's interesting that the lack of a proper toilet was what troubled you the most about being locked up. I'll have to remember that the next time we lock up a woman. Normally, we only have men in the cells, and they don't seem to care one way or another. Sometimes they don't even use the chamber pot and just go against the wall, like they're in a back-alley somewhere."

Susan looked at me and I could see she was terrified at the thought of being locked up again. Although my main concern was what would happen to us after the talking was over, it seemed like they were going to get the truth from us one way or another. I didn't want them to resort to starvation, abuse, or even outright torture for them to get the information.

"Might as well tell him the truth," I told Susan. "I think he intends to get the story from us, one way or another."

Susan nodded and I could see she was thinking the same thing. Jonathan leaned across his desk to better hear what she was about to tell him. His leering face had an almost hungry look to it.

"We came here because I believe Michael McKinsey is my father. I wanted to let him know who I was and maybe ask him to give my mom a call, to let her know he's alright."

Jonathan didn't say anything for several seconds, then he broke out laughing. It seemed genuine, like it was the funniest thing he'd heard in days. "That's your new story?" he said taking a breath. "You should have stuck with the cashing in the chips version. I maybe could have believed that one."

"It's true," Susan said. "My mom has a photo album with pictures of her and Michael McKinsey together right up until the time I was born."

"I have files on everyone of any importance who works at the casino," Jonathan said. "I even have a file on the owner. He's never been married and doesn't have any children. Over the last five years I've known him, he doesn't even date, other than the occasional cocktail waitress or showgirl. You're going to need to come up with a better story than that."

"Susan," I said. "Show it to him."

Susan reached into her bag and found the marker. She pulled it out and set it on the edge of the desk. Even in the flat illumination of the office, it sparkled as though it glowed with an inner light.

Jonathan's laughter stopped as he reached out to pick up the gold coin. He tested its weight as he turned it over a couple of times.

"Where'd you get an owner's marker?" he growled out at Susan.

"It doesn't matter where I got it," she said, with a surprising amount of grit in her voice. "I was told having an owner's marker would allow me to get to my father. Supposedly without interference."

"Yeah," he said. "That's supposed to be the rule with these things. Not a lot of people use markers anymore so it's rare to see one. But it certainly feels like a real marker."

"So, now you know I have an owner's marker and wish to present it to him, are you going to help me or interfere?"

Jonathan seemed troubled as he held the coin, as if he were having an inner debate. After almost a minute, he put the coin back on the desk in front of Susan. He then got up and quickly walked to the door.

"Don't try to leave," he said. "There are four men out there and they've been instructed not to be gentle if you try to escape." He then disappeared into the hallway.

As soon as the door closed, I had a thought. I quickly went through my bag and pulled out my phone. I was surprised they hadn't confiscated it.

I hit the speed dial and the phone on the other end began to ring. "Come on, answer," I muttered to myself. I held my breath as it rang four times, before flipping to Max's voicemail.

Damn it.

I waited impatiently as Max's message played, until I heard the beep. "Um, remember how I said I was going off to have an adventure at the Black Castle Casino?" I told the voicemail. "Well, it might've gotten a little out of hand. I'm with a client named Susan Monroe. We're being detained by casino security. They had us locked in a dungeon cell in the basement but now we're up in the executive offices. We accidently ended up seeing some things we shouldn't have seen, drug and money laundering related things, and now they're deciding what to do with us. Honestly, it doesn't look good."

I was about to describe the dungeons and the executive offices when I heard Jonathan talking with someone directly outside the door.

"Shit, gotta go," I said as I disconnected and shoved the phone back in my purse. I assumed a casual look of indifference as the door opened and Jonathan stepped in. Following him was a tall handsome man. He had a touch of gray in his otherwise dark hair and I pegged him at about sixty years old.

Susan stood and stared at the man. Her eyes had already started to tear up as she mentally compared photos she'd long memorized to the man standing before her. "You're Michael McKinsey," she said, her voice trembling with emotion. "I'm Susan Monroe. I'm your daughter."

She took a tentative step towards him. Her arms half-lifted in a purely instinctive gesture. Her body began to shudder as she readied herself for his long-awaited embrace. Realizing what she was doing, she dipped her arms slightly. Unsure what his response would be but hopeful he would acknowledge her as his daughter.

"Cut the act," he said with a dismissive wave. "Jonathan already told me your story. I'm not your father. Why are you really here? You snuck into our vault? Are you both cops or maybe with the DEA?"

Susan's face fell and her arms dropped. She backed up and collapsed into her chair. She started gulping air as if she'd been punched in the stomach.

"But I have pictures," Susan said, almost pleading. "You and my mom were together for months before I was born."

"Who's your mother?" he asked.

"Olivia Monroe."

"Liv Monroe? Sure, we dated, probably for four or five months. I hate to tell you, but she was pregnant before I started seeing her."

"Why'd you leave her? You broke my mother's heart."

"You want the truth? I was only looking for someone to date. She was looking for a husband. I didn't want to stick around and play daddy, so I broke it off. If you're looking for your father, find out who she was dating before I came into the picture. Didn't she ever tell you that?"

"No," Susan said, tears sliding down her face. "She never came out and said you were my father. I guess I made a bad assumption."

"Jonathan says you have one of my markers. Show it to me."

Susan picked up the marker and handed it to Michael. He took it and turned it over. "This isn't mine, it's Kathleen's. Did she put you up to this? You know, for the last several years, I've had the feeling she was going to try something to get back at me for buying out her half of the casino. Jonathan's been monitoring her activities for years, but even after he told me Kathleen was sending two women up here to run a scam, I only halfway believed him. What's your plan? Make me believe you're my daughter so maybe I'd give you partial ownership of the casino? Then what? You'd give it to Kathleen? Was that it?"

"No," Susan said quietly. "I only wanted to find my father. Kathleen gave me some chips and a marker to help me get into the casino so we could see you."

I turned to Jonathan. "Wait a minute," I said. "You knew we were coming up here?"

"I've been monitoring Kathleen Alastor for several years. I still consider her a security threat. Yes, we monitored the conversation you had with her in her office. The recording was somewhat distorted, but we heard enough to know you were coming up here to try to run some sort of scam. I never believed the find-my-father story. I thought it was only a way for Kathleen to start to cash in some of her stockpiled chips, but now I see the scam ran deeper than that."

Hearing him talk, I was struck by a revelation. "You put the bomb in my car. You wanted us to become stranded in the middle of the desert."

"Clever girl," he said. "It was simple. After I reviewed the audio file of your conversation the other day, I paid the security company at Kathleen's office to give me the record of who'd gone in and out of her office. I found your address from your driver's license and had my men plant the bomb and a tracking device in your car. I followed you out to the desert, then used a remote to disable your car next to the only parking lot within ten miles. Then I just drove by and 'rescued' you. I was curious to see what you would tell me about why you wanted to come up here."

"Is that why you made up that lame story about being an escort?" I asked.

"It wasn't a story. I started out at the casino as an escort. But honestly, having sex with rich old women does get old after a while. I find security to be more stimulating."

Michael turned the marker over one more time, then slipped it into his pocket. "I'll keep this, if you don't mind. Markers shouldn't be given away lightly and Kathleen needs to be reminded of that. Maybe next time she won't be so eager to interfere."

"You know," Jonathan said to Michael, his voice a sneering accusation. "Marcus isn't going to be happy when he learns about this. He's always given you a free hand to do as you please, but that was on the condition you kept out of trouble." Jonathan pointed in our direction. "People coming to the castle, then disappearing, is going to eventually cause a stink. If this is the sort of thing we can expect to keep happening, I'll need to advise Marcus to replace you as head of the casino."

"And you'd also advise him that you should have the job instead?"

"Why not? I at least know how to follow his orders."

"Keep in mind I'm still listed as the owner of this casino and it's my name on the gaming license. I might advise him to get rid of you."

"Paperwork can be changed. Marcus knows I'm loyal to him. He's not so sure about you. If you want my advice, I'd start to keep a lower profile if you don't want to end up in a hole in the desert yourself."

"What are we going to do with these two?" Michael asked.

"They've seen the operations in the vault. We really don't have a choice."

"Fine, put them back in the dungeon and I'll discuss it with Marcus. Keep in mind they were only able to get into the vault because you wanted to see if they could sneak into the castle through your security system. I'll make sure Marcus knows that as well. He'll be back tomorrow morning. I'm sure he'll want to talk with them before he makes the final decision."

~~~~

The four guards escorted us back down to the prison cells in the basement. What surprised me was that no one working even looked up at us as we passed. I could only guess the sight of security officers leading women in dresses around the offices was a common occurrence here.

When we reached the cells, the guards again took our bags, along with Susan's belt, and set everything on a table against a far wall. Neither of us went in voluntarily and they had to physically shove us into the cell. As they closed the door and slid home the bolt, I felt all hope vanish.

~~~~

We sat on our cots and talked to pass the time. Several hours went by like this but conversation eventually stopped. Neither of us had eaten or drank anything since lunch back at the burger place. My mouth was getting dry and I was having a hard time swallowing.

"Next time we do this," Susan said, "let's wear pants. I feel a little exposed sitting in a prison cell in a dress."

"Pants would be nice," I said. "It's cold in here. Even a blanket would help."

~~~~

Another hour or two slowly went by and it must have been about midnight when Susan finally fell asleep. I eventually did the same.

~~~~

When I woke up, it felt like I'd been asleep for maybe two or three hours. I slowly sat up and stretched. The hard canvas cot had made me hurt all over. Susan was sitting on her makeshift bed with her back against the wall. She looked terrible. My throat had dried to the point where it felt sticky and swallowing was painful.

"The only good thing about not having anything to drink," Susan croaked out at me as she laughed to herself, "is you can't cry, and you don't have to pee in the bucket."

~~~~

Another hour or two passed. I was getting lightheaded and had gotten a killer headache, probably from lack of water. I was hoping sleep would help with that. I lay back down and after another half-hour or so, I again fell asleep.

Chapter Eleven

"Susan, are you in there?" a voice whispered into the cell.

As I woke up, my thoughts tried to come together. Someone was at the door to our cell. From the way I felt, I'd been asleep for at least an hour, maybe two. My headache had eased up, but my throat had become even drier.

"We're in here," Susan croaked out. Her voice sounded worse than before.

The bolt slid back and the door opened wide. From the dark cell, all we could see was the silhouette of a man. I remembered Jonathan had said we were going to talk with someone named Marcus before they killed us. I guessed that was what was happening now.

As the man stepped into the cell, I saw instead that it was Michael McKinsey. He left the door open and I could see that there were no guards in the passageway.

"What?" Susan began to ask.

Michael held a finger to his lips. "Talk very quietly," he whispered. "Jonathan doesn't have cameras down here, but I wouldn't be surprised if he had microphones."

He was carrying a reusable canvas grocery bag and set it on the floor. He pulled out two bottles of water and handed one to each of us. I grabbed my bottle and downed half of it in one long gulp. Susan did the same. My stomach spent a few seconds trying to decide if it was happy, but then I felt a rush of relief as I was able to swallow properly again.

"Here," he said as he pulled out two turkey and cheese sandwiches on white bread, each sealed in a plastic container. "They aren't much. I got them from a vending machine. I didn't want to raise suspicions by going to the deli."

We each ripped the plastic film off the containers and began to shove the sandwiches into our mouths. Honestly, it'd been a while since I'd had anything that tasted so good. After we'd eaten the food, and each had a second bottle of water, we were ready to learn what was going on.

"What the hell are you doing here?" Michael asked Susan. Even though he'd just helped us, he sounded pissed.

"I came to find you," Susan said. "I thought you'd at least be interested in knowing about me, in case I really was your daughter. Plus, mom's sick. I thought you'd want to know about that before the end."

"I'm sorry to hear about Liv, but yes, I know who you are. I've spent the last twenty-five years making sure nobody associated with the casino knew you existed. And here you come, breaking into the vault, and telling everyone you're my daughter. You have no idea how much danger that puts you in."

"I don't understand."

"It may seem like I run the place, but I only handle the day-to-day operations. The casino is actually controlled by a group of vicious criminals, led by a man named Marcus. They're ruthless and would think nothing of killing you, me, or anyone they thought posed a threat."

"Okay," Susan said. "So, why are you still working with them? If they're as terrible as you say, why don't you leave?"

"I can't. Nobody leaves an organization like this, ever."

"But you seem to come and go as you please."

"That's only because they didn't have any real leverage over me. I'm listed as the owner of the casino. Due to some legal and political issues, it would be almost impossible for them to change the title. That gave me a certain amount of leeway in what I could get away with. But now that they know you exist, they'll make your safety conditional on my complete cooperation."

"But you told Jonathan you didn't believe my story," Susan said.

"It doesn't matter. I don't think he believed your story when he first reviewed the audio files of you in Kathleen's office. He only thought you were trying to run some sort of scam against me. That's one of the reasons he encouraged you to come up here. But now that he's heard your claim again, he'll likely go back to Scottsdale and do a complete investigation. Jonathan's thorough that way. I wouldn't be surprised if they ransack your house to look for evidence. If he thinks of it, he'll also extract some of your DNA and check that way."

"I don't understand," Susan said, clearly frustrated. "You knew they were criminals, even back then, and you still left mom and went with them anyway? Why would you do that?"

Michael was clearly in a hurry, but when he saw the look in Susan's eyes, he paused. It was obvious she wanted to know what had happened to tear her family apart all those years ago.

"Okay," Michael said. "Here's the short version. Back when we started the casino, Kathleen was the brains and I handled the financing. Our main loans came from a group out of Las Vegas. The group was headed by a guy named Marcus, who, as I told you, has the backing of some pretty bad men. Once the casino started to take off, it became clear the criminals were going to take over, through violence if necessary. I resisted as long as I could, but when your mom got pregnant, I knew if they found out about you, they'd be able to use it as leverage. The only way I knew to protect everyone was to cut all ties with you and your mother. I was able to keep Kathleen out of this mess by having her kicked out. Like I said, both of our names are on the gaming license and Marcus only needed one of us. The criminals keep me here to run the place, mainly as the public figurehead."

"You're saying you left my mom and took over Kathleen's half of the casino to protect them?"

"Well, that's the really short version, but yes. Unfortunately, we don't have time to talk. I need to get back to the office before anyone notices I'm down here. Hopefully we'll get a chance to catch up soon."

"You're leaving us in here?" I asked.

"It can't be helped. Jonathan's set up new patrols in the warehouses and around the garbage dock. There isn't any way I can sneak you out."

"Do you at least have a plan?"

"I'm working on one. Unfortunately, I don't think I can avoid Marcus meeting with you. He'll be here in a couple of hours."

"According to Jonathan, Marcus will order us to be killed," Susan said.

"I'm working to keep that from happening. Hopefully after that we can get out of here."

"What?" Susan asked. "We?"

"I can't stay here, not now. Knowing that you exist, Jonathan would put me under an unofficial house arrest and I'd never be able to leave the casino. I'm not sure how, but I'll need to figure out a way to quit the organization without becoming a target, then leave along with you."

Susan stepped forward and wrapped her arms around her father. After a second of hesitation, he hugged her back. "Okay," she said. "I trust you. Figure out something that'll get us out of this dungeon and away from this horrible place."

Michael quickly gathered up the empty bottles and the food wrappers then put everything into his bag. When he closed the door to the cell and slid the bolt home, I felt my stomach start to knot up again. Michael's promises aside, we were still trapped in a prison cell and it looked like we were soon going to meet someone who would likely order us to be killed.

~~~~

An hour went by, then another. We alternated between sitting on our cots and pacing in our cell.

"I know I shouldn't complain," Susan said. "Being so thirsty was terrible and I'm grateful for Michael bringing us the water and food. But now, um…"

"Yeah," I said. "Me too. After drinking a quart of water I'm starting to think about the bucket again."

"It's just so gross. I mean, how hard is it to put a toilet in a prison cell? You'd think that would've been the first requirement in finding a place to keep people. Come on, how hard is it? Everybody pees."

~~~~

Twenty minutes later, we heard a group of people coming down the hall. When the door opened, the four security guards were there indicating we should exit the cell. We walked out and blinked in the light of the bright hallway. Our purses and the belt were still on the table and the guards handed them back to us.

One guard holding a billy club led the group, while we each had a guard holding us by the arm, with the veteran guard trailing behind. He had his taser out of its holster, not exactly pointed at either of us, but the implication was clear.

When we walked by the bathroom we'd used the night before, I asked if we could stop. The senior guard wasn't happy, but Susan assured him that we either had to stop or he could explain why we'd both had an accident in the elevator on the way up. Fortunately, the guard saw the logic behind this.

After our stop, they walked us through the musty passageways and we eventually arrived at the elevator that led up to the Tower of the Guard. When the elevator stopped at the top floor, the guards led us straight to Jonathan's office.

Since it was midway through Tuesday morning, many of the same people who'd been working the day before were again in their offices. No one seemed to notice anything wrong with four security guards leading two women down the hallway, even though we were wearing the same dresses we'd had on the day before. It made our walk down the hallway seem even more creepy.

Jonathan was seated behind his desk, a smug smile on his face. His hair was still tightly pulled back into a ponytail, again giving his face that slightly skeletal look. His eyes, which had seemed so beautiful and vibrant the day before, were dull and lifeless, even soulless, now. From my years of watching Shark Week, they reminded me of the unemotional eyes of a Great White.

Sitting front-and-center on the desk was a clear pitcher of ice water along with three tall tumbler glasses. Jonathan would've assumed we'd had nothing to drink since the day before and we'd be parched. Seeing the water pissed me off. I knew he would want to tease us with it.

What a jerk.

The guards led us to the chairs in front of Jonathan's desk, then left the room. As we sat, he stared at us, still with the arrogant smirk. It was the kind of smile that made me want to grab him by the ponytail and slam his face on the desk three or four times. I knew one slam wouldn't be enough. It would take several slams to get my point across. I hadn't felt that way about anyone since back when I'd first met Amber, and that was months ago.

"I trust you ladies had a pleasant night," he said. "I hope the accommodations were to your liking."

Not wanting to tip our hand, I stared at the water pitcher. Out of the corner of my eye, I saw Susan doing the same. This seemed to please Jonathan and the wide sadistic grin that appeared on his face did nothing to improve his skeletal look. With deliberate pleasure, he took the pitcher and slowly poured a glass of water. Several ice cubes fell into the glass with small splashes.

Jonathan picked up the tumbler, then paused and held it out. He looked at each of us in turn, as if deciding who'd get the water first. He then slowly raised the glass to his lips and took a long swallow.

"*Aaahhh,*" he said. "That's good. The ice makes it really cold."

It wasn't hard to guess what he was looking for. "Could we have some water?" I asked, trying to make my voice sound as dry and raspy as possible.

"Please?" Susan asked. "We're both really thirsty." There was a genuine pleading tone to her voice. She'd obviously caught on to what was happening and was also making herself sound as dry and weak as possible.

"Oh?" Jonathan asked in mock surprise. "You're thirsty? I'm sorry." He then paused, as if he'd been practicing his speech for maximum effect. "Well, I'd like to give you both some of this water. I really would. I hate to see you ladies suffer like this. But let's be honest, neither of you has earned any water yet. All you've done so far is lie to me."

He then picked up the half-full glass and slowly drank the rest of the water. He was purposefully sloppy about it, so he had to wipe off his wet lips with his hand.

"*Aaaahhh,*" he said again as he set the empty glass on his desk. He looked back at us, as if he'd almost forgotten we were there. "Now, I don't want you to think I'm a heartless monster. I'll make a deal with you. You're both going to meet a man named Marcus in a few minutes. If you're both gracious during our conversation with him, you'll each get a glass of this nice cold water. If you're not polite, well…"

He shrugged his shoulders, as if to show how little he would care about us if we didn't behave. "So, you see," he continued, "in this case, it'll pay for you both to be on your best behavior."

Jonathan stood up and looked down at us. His face was a mix of loathing and disgust. "Get up. We're going to take a walk down the hall."

He opened the door and the four guards came in. We stood up and followed him into the hall. The four security guards silently fell in behind us as we made our way down to the big double doors at the end of the corridor.

Jonathan knocked twice, then opened the door. The brass nameplate on the door read: Michael McKinsey, President and CEO. Susan reached up and lightly rested her fingers on her father's name. She then smiled to herself.

Jonathan went in first and we followed behind. The guards stayed in the hallway.

Michael's office was bigger than I'd expected. A massive wooden desk took up much of the space on the thick blue carpeting, and several oil paintings hung on the walls. There was a small conference table off to one side, next to a huge picture window that looked down over the bridge and the Colorado River.

The parking lot where we'd been the day before was about three-quarters full of cars and the strip mall where we'd gotten our cheeseburgers was crowded with people. Arizona stretched out as far as the eye could see. The tops of some storm clouds were visible, probably fifty or seventy-five miles away. Michael stood at the window gazing down at the waterway where the security patrol boat was slowly making its way upstream.

Against the wall there was a black oversized high-backed chair. It was occupied by a man dressed in loose black clothing, long sleeves covering his arms. His hands were casually resting on the armrests. I had to assume this was Marcus, the head of the five-member board that controlled the casino. He was in his seventies, had pale skin, dark bags under his eyes, and a head of short, gray hair. The man wasn't very big, but his bright blue eyes radiated the confidence of someone who always got what he wanted.

Standing on either side of Marcus were two huge men, both in their thirties. They each looked like former football players. The bodyguards both wore black suits with black shirts and blood red ties.

We were directed to stand in front of the man in the chair. He looked us both over, only pausing long enough to stare at Susan's boobs exposed by her low-cut dress. He chuckled to himself.

"Jonathan," the man said in a raspy voice. "Introduce me to these charming young ladies." He had an unusual way of talking. He spoke very slowly but went to great pains to enunciate each word. The effect was more than a little creepy.

"Marcus," Jonathan said, "This is Susan Monroe and Laura Black, both from Scottsdale. They're the ones we discussed earlier." All the bluster was now gone from Jonathan's voice. It was now the voice of a servant talking to his master.

"Yes," Marcus said as he continued to look us up and down. "I have been told of your remarkable exploits. You both managed to sneak into our castle, then you broke into our vault. However, you do not seem to be thieves. I was told you did not attempt to take anything from our treasury. Now, I ask myself, why would two attractive young women want to break into the most secured area of our entire business, then merely observe what we were doing there?"

"We didn't mean to go there," Susan said. "We got there by mistake."

"Mistake?" Marcus asked. "How could somebody accidently break into a locked vault? You will need to explain this interesting concept to me in detail."

"We were lost in a building that had a lot of storage rooms in it," I said. "We were trying to find our way out and up to the gaming floor. We saw a door that looked different so we tried it. But when we opened it, it was blocked by some metal paneling. We pushed it away from the wall and were able to slip through. Once we saw it didn't lead to the gaming floor, we left as quickly as possible."

"That's exactly what happened." Susan said.

"Jonathan?" Marcus asked. "Could their account be correct? Did these women just walk into your vault? As I recall, at your recommendation, we spent four hundred thousand dollars on security for that area."

Jonathan had turned pale while he was being rebuked, but now his face was flushed from embarrassment and anger.

"I've been looking into it," Michael said calmly as he turned back from the window. "When we did the security upgrades six years ago, that doorway was to be bricked over. Because of that, it doesn't show up on the new blueprints. For some reason, the work order to seal the door never happened. The opening was paneled over, so you couldn't see it from the vault side. The door has several warning labels on it, so no one would have gone through it from the storage-building side. Well, nobody until these two. That it happened to be unlocked was just another oversight."

As Michael was explaining what had happened, Jonathan glared at us, his look full of anger and hatred. I knew he wasn't going to offer either of us a glass of ice-water after this.

"Jonathan?" Marcus asked again. "Could this be true? Have these women uncovered a major weakness in your security system?"

"Yes, Marcus," Jonathan said. "They did." His head was lowered and you could tell he was trying to sound as calm and as businesslike as possible, even though he was angry to the point of wanting to blow up.

"I see," Marcus mused. "It is clear to me now. You are both very clever women and, by exposing the flaws in our security, you have done our organization a favor." He looked over at Jonathan. "I trust the error is being corrected immediately?"

"They're bricking over the door as we speak," Jonathan said.

"Very good," Marcus said. "Now, all that remains is to decide what to do with you two. Tell me, are either of you associated with law enforcement or are you members of the press?"

Susan and I looked at each other, then back to Marcus. "No," we both said at the same time.

"Jonathan's looked into their background," Michael said. "They aren't with any government agency or newspaper. It seems they were coming up here to run a scam, on me. Something about Susan here being my long-lost daughter. Fortunately, Jonathan uncovered their scheme in time to prevent anything from happening."

"Actually," Jonathan said, "since yesterday, I've been looking deeper into her story." His confident smile had returned. Something about that creepy smile set off warning bells in my head. "It seems that Michael did indeed date a woman in Scottsdale who gave birth to Susan. I think there's a good possibility that Michael is in fact her father. It's my suggestion we hold onto her while we run a DNA test to determine the truth. If she's Michael's daughter, I suggest she stay here, under our protection. Maybe we could even find some work for her to do."

"How interesting," Marcus said. "Michael, it seems you may have found a daughter. One that you had been previously unaware of. But Jonathan is correct, it is a good idea to hold her here. We certainly cannot risk letting her go after seeing the vault."

Michael visibly deflated. With Jonathan holding his daughter, he'd be forced to do anything Jonathan instructed. Susan's safety would always hang in the balance if he didn't eagerly comply to any instruction given to him.

Jonathan looked at Marcus, then at me. "What should we do with her?"

Marcus paused as he again looked me up and down.

"My dear," he said to me. "You are a very fascinating woman. It is a shame we will not have more time to get to know one another better. You see, we have some rather strict rules about what must happen in these cases. You know too much about our operation and the risk is too great."

Oh no.

When I heard this, I realized Susan would be safe, at least for a while, but nothing I could say or do would stop them from doing something horrible to me.

Why now?

How could they threaten me just as things seemed to be coming together? My rent was being paid for, my job seemed fairly stable, and I had a fabulous romance starting up with Max. Ending up in a hole in the desert wasn't something that would fit into my happy new life.

Marcus looked at me, expecting some sort of outburst. But I kept my dignity and didn't even try to beg for my life.

Marcus looked at me and slowly shook his head. "You are indeed interesting," he said. "Nevertheless, Jonathan, I have an unpleasant task for you to do."

Jonathan raised his head and the smirk was back on his lips. Marcus had apparently forgiven his security lapses, plus he'd been given instructions to imprison Susan and get rid of me. I only hoped he'd be quick about it and he wouldn't put me through too much abuse first.

Oh, who am I kidding?

As I thought about it, I knew I was fooling myself. Jonathan would take great pleasure in making me suffer as much pain and humiliation as he could inflict on me before I disappeared.

"Well, look here," said a woman's voice. "If it isn't Marcus and his trained dogs."

We all looked over at the doorway to see Kathleen Alastor just stroll in as though it were her office. She had a rather satisfied look on her face.

"Kathleen?" Michael asked.

"How the hell did you get in here?" Jonathan growled.

"How did I get in? Did you forget I'm still listed, along with Michael, as the owner of the place? I have membership card number one and several million dollars' worth of casino chips. Why would anyone want to keep me out? In fact, security escorted me up here."

"Kathleen," Marcus said. "I heard you might be stopping by today. Unfortunately, you will have to excuse us for a few minutes. We are in the middle of some rather important business."

"Oh, I know all about your business. In fact, that's partially why I'm here."

"Oh really?" Marcus asked. "Please explain yourself."

"The woman standing in front of you came to my office a couple of days ago with a story about her and Michael. I don't know if it's true or not, but it sounded close enough to the truth to be a major problem for Michael. I knew when she came up here with her claims, you'd have Michael trapped like a rat in a cage. He wouldn't be of any value to you as head of the casino anymore. In fact, he'd probably bolt with the girl as soon as he got the chance. The four members of the board know how I got your marker and what you owe me. I've already let each of them know I was coming here today to collect on it and that my favor would be to take Michael's place and for you to release Michael and these two women."

"That is extremely bold of you," Marcus said. "Early this morning, I received a message from each of the four board members. They all informed me that you were coming here to call in your favor. I assumed your request would be to merely replace Michael as head of the casino. I did not realize that releasing these two girls would also be part of your demands."

"No," Jonathan fumed. "We can't simply let them go. They've seen the vault. There can be no exceptions."

"Yes, Jonathan," Marcus said. "That is indeed our policy. But you know I cannot go back on the marker." He then looked at Kathleen. "Are those all of your demands of me?"

"I'll make it clear. Release Michael and the women. I'll take Michael's place and run the casino for you, but not as your slave. I'll come back in as an equal partner in the business. As I recall, we discussed something like this twenty-six years ago. You chose Michael over me back then. I hope you'll see the wisdom of bringing me back to run the place again."

"Kathleen hasn't run a casino in twenty-five years," Jonathan said to Marcus. "It's a little late to make a change now."

"Jonathan," Marcus said. "I have no objections to Kathleen and I have the full support of two of the four board members. That makes it a majority decision. I have been closely following her career, as have you. After she left us, she started a successful enterprise that now supplies half the casinos in Las Vegas. She knows the business side of hotels and gaming as well as any of us."

"I'm completely opposed to this," Jonathan angrily blurted out. "What if they talk? Marker or no marker, the risks to the organization are too great to allow them to go free. Plus, this woman knows nothing about what we do here, yet you want her to take over?"

"Jonathan," Marcus calmly said. "It is not your place to approve or disapprove of my actions. Remember that, if you do not want to find yourself in more trouble than you can handle."

Jonathan's face was red with anger, but he somehow managed to hold his tongue.

"As you can see," Marcus said to Susan and me, "this situation puts me in a rather delicate position. However, Jonathan is correct. If either of you breathe a word of what you know about our operations here, you will be killed. Marker or no marker, I don't think any of the board members would have a problem with that."

Marcus stared at his head of security, who glared back at him.

"Very well," Marcus said to Kathleen. "I grant your request. You will take over from Michael as the co-owner and operational head of the casino. We will also open a seat on the board for you to come in as a partner. I release Michael from service to our organization, along with these two girls."

"Thank you, Marcus," Kathleen said. She reached into a pocket and extracted the shiny platinum marker she'd showed us in her house, four days before. She walked over and laid it on the conference table. It made a loud *clunk* as she set it down.

"Michael," Marcus said. "This is a parting of the ways for us. However, if this girl is indeed your daughter, perhaps leaving is a good outcome for you. You did a good job for us over these many years and I thank you for your service to the casino. You will be welcome to return, from time to time, but remember, even though you are still listed as an owner, Kathleen will be the head of the casino."

I somehow expected some sort of outburst from Michael. After all, he'd just been fired from his longtime job. Instead, he seemed to consider his options as he looked at Susan. "Alright, Marcus," he said. "Maybe I do need a change. Maybe it's time for me to explore a new direction in my life."

"Jonathan," Marcus said. "Escort Michael and these two girls off the property. See that no harm comes to them."

Jonathan glared at Marcus, but didn't say a word. Instead he opened the office door and walked out. Michael went next, and then Susan and I followed. Everything had happened so quickly; I was still trying to sort it all out in my head. Marcus had handed me a death sentence, but Kathleen had come in and rescued me.

Maybe it will work out alright after all?

Jonathan led us down the hallway but stopped when we reached the elevator. At his gesture, the four security officers stepped into the corridor.

"What is this?" Michael asked angrily. "I know the way out."

"No," Jonathan growled. "You aren't going anywhere except to the dungeons. You know too much to be allowed to leave. All of you do."

"Marcus said we could go," Michael shot back. "Why are you interfering?"

"Well, it looks like there's going to be one more change in management today. Marcus isn't the only one who's gotten messages from the board. It seems the decision to have an outsider run the operations is not unanimous, even if she is an original owner. I've been instructed by the two dissenting members to remove Kathleen from the equation. After I make sure the three of you are locked safely away in your cells, I'll go back up and deal with her, directly."

"You still have visions of taking over, don't you?" Michael asked. "I know you have two friends on the board, but they're still a minority. If you try something like this, Marcus and the rest of the board will come down hard on you."

"Well," Jonathan said, half to himself. "Marcus and the other two board members are about to find out their situation has just changed."

He made a gesture and the guards approached us. One held out some thick plastic zip-ties to bind our hands. I tensed at the sight of the manacles. I then decided I'd had enough. They weren't going to put them on me, at least not without a fight.

The guards must have sensed my intent. Two of them flicked open their collapsible batons and the veteran guard pulled out his taser. This time he wasn't even trying to be subtle about pointing it at my chest. He looked into my eyes with calm assurance. "Well?" he asked. "Are we going to need to do this the hard way?"

Deflated by the aggressive show of force, I didn't fight them as they attached the plastic cuffs. Within seconds, our hands were securely bound behind our backs and Jonathan was leading us into the elevator.

~~~~

We quickly descended to the sub-basement level. When the doors slid open, Jonathan led us out into the empty corridor. A guard took each of us by the arm and led us towards the cells. The veteran guard trailed several yards behind, the taser still in his hand.

I was beginning to know the way around the corridors leading to the dungeons. We moved past some empty rooms, then turned down the hallway toward where the cells were.

Behind us came the sound of something crunching. I couldn't immediately place the sound, but it somehow felt deeply wrong. Everyone turned to investigate.

Gabriella stood calmly in the middle of the corridor, smiling with her hand raised, wiggling her fingers in a friendly greeting. One glance told me she was ready for combat. The veteran guard was already crumpled at her feet.

From there, time seemed to move in slow motion. At first, everyone simply stood there, trying to figure out who the beautiful woman was and what had happened to the guard.

I nudged Susan with my shoulder and forced her to take a few steps back. I knew what was about to happen and wanted us to keep well out of the way. Michael also seemed to understand what was happening and had also stepped back.

Fortunately, both Jonathan and the remaining guards were a little slower on the uptake. All they saw was a tall, beautiful woman wearing a black-leather jumpsuit with blood-red trim. They definitely noticed the front of her outfit was open down to her navel and her boobs were all but falling out. Maybe they noticed she was wearing combat boots and that there was a large black bag sitting on the ground behind her. If they'd looked closer, they would've seen her long black hair was pulled back into a ponytail and her face was flushed pink. Her breathing was fast and uneven, even though she didn't look tired. If they had the time, they might even have been puzzled by the expression on her face. It was a look both of anticipation and of growing arousal.

But, even if they had seen all these things, it wouldn't have mattered. In an almost casual manner, Gabriella took a step towards the nearest guard and kicked him solidly in the chest. He flew backwards and landed with a hard thump against the wall. His eyes rolled up in his head and he went limp. The next guard tried to hit her with a roundhouse swing of his baton, but she easily dodged the blow and drove a knee into his guts. He also fell to the floor and did not move.

The last guard lifted his club above his head and rushed towards her. He gave what I could only assume was a battle cry as he ran. Gabriella looked up and pivoted around to plant a boot squarely in the guard's face. He dropped the baton, fell to the floor, and began to roll around in pain.

As all this was happening, I turned to keep my eye on Jonathan. From behind his back, he pulled out a semi-automatic pistol. He raised the gun and tried to get a bead on the swirling woman.

Without thinking about the wisdom of what I was doing, I put my head down and tried to tackle him. I collided with his shoulder at the same instant he fired. There was the deafening sound of the pistol firing in close quarters and my ears immediately began to ring.

Gabriella flew past me and was on him in an instant. Apparently, Jonathan also had some martial arts training in his background. He and Gabriella traded several fast punches and kicks. Both were doing damage, but neither one was able to land a finishing blow. Michael and I stood by and tried to figure out how we could help. With our hands cuffed behind our backs, we wouldn't be able to do more than look for an opportunity to knock Jonathan off balance.

After the fifth or sixth time they'd traded punches and kicks, they both went down to the ground and began to wrestle. Gabriella quickly had Jonathan's head pinned between her powerful legs as he lay on his back, trying to reach his arm around her head. I was still looking for a way to assist, when Gabriella looked down and smiled.

Jonathan was still on his back and his legs were spread; all his focus was on trying to attack his opponent. She'd noticed his vulnerable situation a second before he realized his danger. She lifted her arm above her head, then drove her elbow down, directly onto his groin.

Jonathan's face turned red as he screamed in pain and his entire body began to spasm and shudder. Gabriella's face was flushed red and had a glow; she had started to tremble as well. She cried out along with Jonathan, but in her case, it was more orgasmic sounding.

Again, and again, her elbow smashed down into Jonathan's sensitive flesh. With each blow, he cried out in fresh agony. Each time, she moaned and shuddered with pleasure.

After almost two minutes of enduring this punishment, Jonathan went limp, finally passing out from the pain. Gabriella had also briefly collapsed from the effort.

I did what I could to help her untangle herself from the unconscious but still twitching man. Jonathan must have caught her with a fist as they were trading blows. A bright red mark marred the side of her face and her lip was split and oozing blood. But even then, she had a big smile on her face and her body still shuddered periodically with aftershocks. She stood in the hallway, hands on her knees, panting and trying to catch her breath.

She pointed to her bag and I used my foot to slide it to her. She then bent down and pulled out a big military knife. "Turn around," she told me between breaths.

I did so and she cut my plastic handcuffs free. I then took the knife and released Susan and Michael.

Now that Gabriella had started to recover, she took a moment to fix her hair. Most of it had come lose from her ponytail during the fight with Jonathan and was hanging in her face. She pulled it back and quickly retied everything. As she did, she looked down at the crumpled men sprawled out on the floor and smiled with satisfaction.

For a moment, she'd lost the look of a jungle predator and had become merely a beautiful woman. Granted, one who needed to hurt men to achieve happiness, but a beautiful woman nevertheless.

The guard who'd been kicked in the face started trying to get up. Gabriella casually walked over and gave him a hard kick to the stomach. He rolled over and again went limp.

It was then I noticed the wound. On Gabriella's left side, slightly above her hip bone, was a small hole in her leather jumpsuit. It was wet with blood.

"Oh my God," I said. "Gabriella, you've been shot."

Gabriella put a hand over the wound. "Yes. He was going for my head, but you made him miss. It's okay. I've been shot there before. It will bleed, but is not too bad. We must go."

I gathered up Jonathan's pistol while Susan and Michael each grabbed a baton.

"Where's Max?" I asked Gabriella as we hurried down the passageway. I knew if she was here, Max couldn't be far away.

"He's waiting on the river for us," she said.

"He sent you in alone?"

"Oh, no. You know Max. He want to do everything himself, but I no let him come in. I knew this would be no problem for me, but if

Max come into Nevada territory on business, it would be big problem and cause war. He's upset about it, and he almost come in anyway, but he knows I'm right. We already have problems in Arizona without needing to fight all of Nevada too."

"I'm glad you came for us. We were in a bad situation."

"We're not out of danger yet. I come down from the main part of the casino. We can't go back that way. We still need to find a way out."

"I think I know the way," I said. "I'm starting to know my way around down here."

With me leading, and Gabriella covering us from the rear, we started down the next hallway, hopefully in the direction of the garbage dock.

~~~~

Less than ten minutes from when we'd come down the elevator, we found ourselves back at the junction. Seeing the white door that led to the level five security vault made me shudder. I turned and opened the door that I knew led into the first warehouse.

When we entered the first massive room, I saw an out-of-the-way space and made Gabriella stop. She was starting to turn a little pale and didn't object. Susan and I searched through our bags and came up with some supplies to help control the bleeding. As Susan helped Gabriella with the first aid, I talked with Michael.

"You said there're guards patrolling the warehouses. Do you know specifically where Jonathan has them stationed?"

"No. All I know is Jonathan ordered additional security down here, especially for the garbage dock. It's likely they'll be armed. We'll need to watch out for them."

Chapter Twelve

We made it through the first two warehouses without incident. At the last one, we ran into a problem. A group of four guards were clustered at the far end, holding some kind of discussion. Fortunately, we saw them first and were able to pull back into one of the side aisles.

Knowing four guards would be a challenge, we all turned to Gabriella. Unfortunately, she was looking a little worse. More color had drained from her face and she was visibly weaker.

"I'm okay," she said. "I take care of them." She took a step forward on wobbly legs and almost collapsed. Susan rushed over to prop her up.

"Michael," I said. "Do you know of another way out?"

"No," he said. "That's the only way from here. Everything else leads up into the castle. We'd need to go back to where the dungeons are to find another exit that leads down to the river." He looked at us and our poor assortment of weapons. "We only have Jonathan's pistol and two tactical batons," Michael said, doubt in his voice. "I don't know if it'll be enough to get through all four of the guards."

"At least one guard has a pistol hanging on his belt," I said. "I don't think we're going to be able to shoot our way out of this. We might need to go back and find another way out."

"I think it's already too late for that," Michael said. "Jonathan and the guards have probably regained consciousness by now. He'll raise an alarm soon, if he hasn't done so already. Every guard in the castle will converge on us down here. You all need to get out, now."

"Yes, but how?"

"I'm still the owner of the casino. I can order the guards back up to the main part of the castle. I'll go with them so it doesn't look so suspicious."

Susan looked up at him. "No, Dad, you need to come with us. Otherwise they'll know you were in on our escape."

"I'll be fine," he said. "The only one who'll care about your escape is Jonathan. Marcus already ordered our release." He pointed to Gabriella. I'll tell them the warrior woman here only wanted to rescue the two of you. I'll say she threatened me unless I helped you both to escape. Besides, you heard what Jonathan said. He's been ordered to kill Kathleen. I need to alert both her and Marcus. Because of the marker, Kathleen's still under his protection, for at least the next couple of months."

"We need to stay together," Susan said to her father, pleading in her voice. "I just found you. I can't lose you so soon."

"You won't ever lose me. The secret's out and there's no use pretending any longer. We still have a lot of catching up to do. But first, you'll need to get away from here. Jonathan's going to be pissed and he'll kill you if he can get his hands on you."

Susan stood for a moment, helplessness on her face. At last she nodded. "Okay, she said. "I know you're right. But we need to get together as soon as possible. I need to know my father and my mom needs to know you're alright. She's been worried about you for the last twenty-five years. It would be best if she heard it directly from you."

"Your mom's still interested in me? I know she never married, but I figured after all this time she'd have moved on."

"No, she never found anyone after you. Apparently, you made an impression on her."

"Okay. Well, let me figure a way out of this mess, then I'll see about a visit. Deal?"

Susan wrapped her arms around her father and we could all see it was indeed a deal.

After a moment, Susan released him and we began to plan. "I'll get the guards," he said. "But the only way back is the door we just came through. You'll need to hide as we walk by."

"There's another problem," I said. "Look."

Everyone looked to where I was pointing; there was a drop of wet blood on the floor.

"We stopped her from dripping for the last two warehouses," I said, "but it's starting up again. I imagine there'll be blood in the passageway leading to the junction."

"I'll try to distract the guards," he said. "The floors there are pretty dark so hopefully none of them will notice."

"Good luck," I said.

"Be careful," Susan said, "Remember your promise to come to Scottsdale. You were right. We still have twenty-five years of catching up to do."

"Thanks," he said. "And I will."

He turned and strode down the main aisle in the direction of the four guards. We helped Gabriella to a corner where we all could hide behind a stack of boxes. As long as no one noticed the blood trail, we would be okay.

We stood in our hiding place, waiting to see what would happen next. My thoughts drifted to Max and I wondered what he was doing. Gabriella said he was somewhere out on the river. I only hoped he wouldn't be too pissed that I'd caused yet another problem for him.

We could hear Michael talking with the guards at the far end of the room. Apparently, he successfully persuaded them to abandon their posts, because the sound of their voices slowly grew louder.

The more I thought about it, I realized Michael had likely been right. Even though Marcus had ordered our release, if Jonathan got ahold of us again, he'd probably still try to kill us. Well, I had the pistol and Susan was still holding the tactical baton. We could at least make a fight of it.

I looked over at Gabriella. She looked terrible. All color had drained from her face and the leg on the side she'd been shot had started to tremble. She was rummaging in her bag, and I was about to ask her about it, when she pulled out her Uzi.

Shit.

"Max say no shoot inside the casino building," Gabriella said weakly, then she smiled. "Plans may need to change."

The voices grew louder, then they were at the door to the next warehouse, not more than twenty feet from us. I held my breath and readied myself for whatever would happen next. Gabriella slowly pulled back a lever on her Uzi. I heard a click that meant the submachine gun was ready to unleash its fury into whoever happened to be stupid enough to stick his head around the corner.

The group of guards had stopped at the doorway and there was some sort of loud discussion. I heard the word "blood" and I knew our trail had been seen. Gabriella and I looked at each other. She was smiling and I was beginning to recognize the look. Even in her weakened condition, she was still hoping for a fight.

Michael's voice raised above the others. They continued arguing for a few more seconds, then we heard the pedestrian door open. The voices faded as the door closed behind them.

"Come on," I said. "We'll need to hurry. They could still change their minds and come back this way."

Susan and I each took an arm and we half-carried, half-dragged Gabriella through the warehouse. We made it safely to the garbage dock, unfortunately it wasn't empty. The man who we'd talked to the day before was working at the desk. He turned to look at us, surprise in his eyes.

"The safety audit ladies," he said in his gruff voice. "Come back for another look?" He looked closer at Gabriella. "What happened to her? Is she alright?"

He then saw the pistol in my hand and the Uzi in Gabriella's. "Shit," he said. "I shoulda guessed you were the ones they was looking for. But don't worry about me, I didn't see a thing. Make sure you're careful when you go outside. I think there's an armed security patrol out there somewhere."

Susan thanked him and we hurried out the metal door that led outside. We stopped to look for the patrol, but they were nowhere in sight. We went down the stairs and onto the concrete ramp that led down to the iron gate.

Gabriella tried to search through her bag again. I asked what she needed. "Radio," she said. I looked through the bag and pulled out something that looked like a military version of a walkie-talkie. Gabriella took it, adjusted two of the knobs, then held it to her lips. "Boat dock," she said. "Three minutes. All is well."

Someone was receiving our message because there were two quick clicks from the speaker.

Still holding Gabriella between us, we made our way down the concrete ramp, then finally to the gate separating us from the river and the dock. I was hoping there'd be a latch to unlock it from the inside and allow us to escape. Unfortunately, there was nothing but a key slot. I pulled on the gate to see if it was unlocked but it didn't budge.

Through the gate, I saw Milo piloting a small military-style Zodiac assault boat. He slid it smoothly against the side of the dock. Max climbed up and began to tie-off the boat to one of the cleats.

Both Milo and Max wore black outfits with bulletproof vests. I'd never seen Max like this, but I could now imagine how he had looked back when he worked for the government. My heart sped up at the sight of him coming to rescue me.

"Look out," Susan yelled.

I turned to see what was happening. Three new guards had burst through the metal door from the garbage dock and were hurrying down the stairs. Two of them had pistols drawn.

I looked at the lock on the gate and at Max beyond it. I then looked back at the guards. They'd gotten about halfway down the concrete ramp and they looked pissed.

Shit, we're trapped.

I brought up the pistol I'd taken from Jonathan, determined to make a final stand. Susan appeared next to me, the baton in her hand.

From beside us came the deafening *burrrrrrr* sound of a dozen bullets spraying out of the Uzi. The bullets landed at the guards' feet and a slug might have hit one in the foot. This was enough action for the guards. They turned and ran as fast as they could, back toward the door at the garbage dock.

"I didn't think you were supposed to fire your gun," I said.

"Max said not shoot inside castle. But we not inside now."

"You missed the guards."

"Max said not shoot anyone unless I have to." As she said this, she looked surprisingly sad. "Well, it doesn't matter now. We make so much noise the cat is now out of bag. Everyone know we're here now."

We turned back to the immediate problem. "The lock in the gate," Gabriella said. "We need to step back. Then hold me steady."

Susan and I each grabbed a shoulder and we all got into position. Gabriella lifted the Uzi and tried to sight it at the gate. Unfortunately, she'd become so woozy she couldn't hold the gun steady enough to aim at the lock.

Without thinking, I took the Uzi from her hands and sighted it on the lock. Gabriella didn't object. The gun was heavier than I had imagined it would be and it felt strange in my hands. Before I could even start to worry about flying metal or ricocheting bullets, I pulled the trigger. With a deafening noise, fifteen or twenty rounds flew from the submachine gun, emptying the clip. The lock exploded and the massive iron gate slowly swung open.

Gabriella was weak but still conscious. "Get a new clip," she said. "In my bag."

As we stumbled toward the gate, I fished around in her big black bag. Ignoring something that looked suspiciously like a hand grenade, I found a fresh clip. I gave it to Gabriella, along with the Uzi. Even in her weakened condition, she switched the old and new clips with a speed that could only come from years of practice.

The sound of the submachine gun must have alerted the patrol. Three new guards came around a corner on the far side of the garbage dock and began running towards us.

Gabriella took a step forward, then collapsed. All energy seemed to have drained out of her. We each grabbed and arm and pulled her to her feet. Susan and I were both charged on adrenaline and we easily dragged her the final fifteen feet.

We passed through the gate as quickly as we could and made it onto the dock. Max was there to help us into the boat. Susan went first and Max looked her over in a quick but very specific manor as she came on board. I could only guess this was from some sort of military training to assess soldiers coming off the battlefield. He managed to thoroughly inspect my entire body with two swift glances. Satisfied I was uninjured, he gave me a quick kiss as I climbed aboard. He winced with concern as he looked Gabriella over and saw her wound.

"How bad is it?" he asked as he helped her onto the boat.

"I can fight," she said weakly.

Max nodded approval then looked over at Susan and me. "Get down and stay down," he said. "This is going to get bouncy."

Looking back through the gate, we saw that the guards were almost to the dock. Max flicked out a knife and cut the rope holding the boat to the mooring.

"Go!" he shouted as Milo gunned the engines.

The guards ran onto the dock as our boat leapt forward. One guard raised a pistol, but as he did, Gabriella raised her Uzi and pointed it in the general direction of the dock. The guard saw it wouldn't be a fair fight and slowly lowered his gun.

"Look out," Susan shouted to Milo. Everyone looked to see where she was pointing. Downriver, under the bridge, the casino patrol boat was charging up the river at full speed. They must have been alerted to our escape and had been ordered to prevent it.

"Damn," Milo yelled. "That's a fast boat. Boss, I'm not sure we'll make it across before they catch us."

"Give it everything you've got," Max shouted back. "Try to outrun them."

"Another problem," Susan yelled out. This time, she was pointing across to the far bank. The garbage ferry was churning across the river, also coming to intercept us. The old man, Hobbs, Jonathan had called him, was at the helm. Chopper stood at the prow, his stubby tail standing up, wagging back and forth.

"They're going to block us both ways," Milo shouted.

Max opened a tool box and pulled out a submachine gun, similar to Gabriella's Uzi.

"Stay down," he shouted. "We might need to fight our way out of this."

The patrol boat was less than a hundred yards away and closing fast. There were three guards on the boat. One had a pistol drawn and one had a rifle. Fortunately, with their boat going so fast, aiming accurately would be almost impossible for either of them.

The garbage ferry was moving slower, but it was almost upon us. It wasn't slowing down and it was obvious it was intent on ramming our small boat. Chopper started barking and was now hopping up and down with excitement.

"We may have to jump," Max shouted. "Try to get across to the Arizona side, if you can. Johnny's waiting about half a mile upriver."

Milo still had the Zodiac running full out, but the patrol boat had almost caught us and had even started to slow. The garbage ferry was still coming at us at top speed. I tried to imagine how we were going to survive being run over by the big ferry. I knew we needed to jump before it hit us, but I didn't know if I should try to jump upriver or down. Either way was risky.

The five of us watched helplessly as the garbage ferry closed in, now only twenty or thirty yards away. The pilot on the patrol boat saw what was about to happen and he cut his engines. The three guards stood, each with a grin, eager to watch the fun.

Chopper was still barking and hopping, when the garbage ferry suddenly turned hard to the left. It was still coming fast, but no longer pointed towards us. Instead, it slid past us, our small boat bouncing hard against the side of the fast-moving ferry. I felt myself being tossed toward the side of our little boat, but fortunately managed to grab a hand-hold in time to keep from being pitched over the side.

Time seemed to slow down as the garbage ferry headed directly towards the patrol boat. But then everything happened too quickly for the security crew to take any sort of evasive action. Instead, all of the guards jumped overboard a second before the ferry hit the patrol boat directly amidships. Max began to shout orders to Milo. There was a loud splintering and grinding noise as the ferry ploughed through the black boat.

Chopper ran to the back of the ferry and looked down at us, still barking and hopping with excitement. Hobbs, the ferryman, was shouting something to us and was pointing at the river, maybe twenty or thirty yards back from where we were. I saw he was rapidly turning the wheel on his boat to bring it around to where we were.

Puzzled, I looked around. Susan wasn't on the boat. It was then I realized what Max had been shouting. Susan must have gone overboard when we'd collided with the ferry and Max was telling Milo to turn around.

I looked in the river where Hobbs had been pointing. About thirty yards downriver, I saw Susan. It looked like she was trying to tread water but there was clearly something wrong. Her face had turned white and there was blood covering her forehead. She made a couple of weak attempts to stay afloat, then slowly sank below the surface.

It only took Milo a few seconds to get to where we'd seen her go down, but she hadn't yet come up again. Milo quickly cut the motor and we began to float down with the current. Hobbs had also brought his boat to a stop and was staring down at the river.

I leaned over the side of the boat, peering into the murky water. As I was scanning the water, I tossed my purse to the deck and kicked off my shoes. Milo and Gabriella were searching from the other side of the boat and I felt Max slip in to look beside me.

We stared intently down into the water for another twenty or thirty seconds, but there was nothing visible. The river had become smooth and as peaceful as it ever had been. Water gently splashed against the side of our little boat. The faint shouts and curses from the men swimming to the other shore were the only other sounds we could hear. Even chopper had stopped barking as we all searched for Susan.

"Do you see her?" Max called out as he quickly went from one side of the boat to the other. "She's out there somewhere. Keep searching."

As the seconds slowly ticked by, my chest tightened and I began to feel sick to my stomach. Everything had happened so quickly. How could Susan be safe on the boat one moment and be gone the next? My emotions took over and my entire body started to shake. The river blurred as tears filled my eyes. This only made me angry and I wiped the tears away, determined not to give up on my friend.

I looked at the water next to the boat, then farther downriver. I tried to guess where she'd be floating if she were unconscious. Searching the river, about twenty yards from the boat, I thought I saw what looked like a hand, bobbing just below the surface. About two feet from the hand, I thought I saw something that looked like a mass of hair. Chopper must have seen it at the same time as I did. He jumped off the boat and landed in the water with a loud splash.

Without pausing to think, I stood up on the side of the little boat and also dove in. The water was frigid and it took my breath away. I opened my eyes underwater but couldn't see a foot ahead of me. I took five or six strokes toward where I'd seen Susan's hand. I desperately began to search, swimming down into the cloudy water, reaching my hands out as wide as possible, hoping for something to grab onto. I stayed under for as long as I could, then resurfaced. I took a quick breath, then dove under again.

I stayed under and searched the murky water until my lungs began to burn. As I was starting back to the surface, my fingers brushed against something solid. I reached out and in desperation grabbed onto something that felt like human flesh. My head was spinning from lack of air, but I didn't let go as I tried to pull the lifeless form to the surface.

The dead weight of Susan's body slowed my progress and I actually felt like I was being dragged back down. I looked up toward the light of the sun and I didn't think I was going to make it. In my mind I knew if I let go, I could probably survive, but something inside of me refused to abandon my friend. I just closed my eyes and kept kicking my legs.

After two or three kicks, my efforts had grown feeble and I'd started to black out. I felt something grab ahold of my dress and pull both Susan and me up to the surface.

When I got back to the air and the light, I saw that I still had hold of Susan's wrist and Chopper had me by the top part of my dress. He let go and I focused on Susan. I quickly found her hair and pulled her face above the water. As I did, I knew the worst had happened.

Oh no.

Her eyes were halfway open and her mouth was parted in a way that told me she was already dead. I gulped in some air as I tried to keep her head above the surface. I then felt someone next to me in the water. Max had already taken Susan by the shoulders and was pulling her body back towards the boat, making sure to keep her face out of the river.

I heard the sound of a motor as Milo brought the boat next to where we floated. He bent over the side and lifted Susan up by her shoulders and laid her on the deck. Max climbed in next while Milo quickly pulled me in.

"Keep going upriver," Max yelled to Milo. "We're not done yet."

As the boat surged forward, Max crouched next to Susan. He felt her neck for a pulse, then rolled her on her side to let the water drain from her mouth. When the flow more or less stopped, Max rolled her onto her back.

When it was obvious she still wasn't breathing, I dropped to my knees and positioned her head as I remembered from my high school health class. I pinched her nose and began to breathe into her mouth. As I did, I heard the gurgling sound of air mixing with the water in her lungs. I gave her four deep breaths, then Max rolled her onto her side again. This time, even more water poured from her mouth. We rolled her on her back and Max performed thirty chest compressions. Each time he pushed, more water came out of her mouth.

Damn it.

Losing all hope, I bent down, positioned her head, pinched her nose, and breathed another deep breath into her lungs. As I did, Susan's body spasmed violently.

That can't be good.

I sat up and looked at her chest. Nothing happened for a second, then a quart of water shot from her mouth as she gave out a long wheeze. Susan's eyes opened in panic as she took in a deep rasping breath. She then started to cough violently. Between each cough, she gasped in a deep breath. Each time she coughed, more water came out of her mouth.

Oh my God. She's alive.

Susan coughed for almost a minute before she began to calm down. Her coughing and near drowning had left her exhausted and she weakly tried to roll over. Max helped her to all fours. Susan stayed in this position, panting and still trying to breathe. Every time she tried to take a deep breath, she ended up coughing and spitting up more water. But the coughs were becoming less violent and each time she spit out a little less.

Susan's purse was still hanging over her shoulder by its strap and had gotten tangled up in her hair. I undid the strap and unwound it from her wet tresses. I unzipped it and allowed the water to pour out.

As Susan gradually recovered, I looked back to see the results of the collision. The patrol boat had been cut in two, both pieces were floating downriver with the current and had almost made it to the bridge. All three guards seemed to have escaped unharmed and were climbing up onto the bank on the Nevada side.

Hobbs had apparently decided not to be on the same side of the river as the three angry guards. He was slowly bringing the ferry back over to the Arizona side. Chopper was already on the shore and was barking at the big boat as it came in. We then went around a bend in the river and I lost all sight of the bridge, the castle, and the guards.

In the excitement, we'd travelled another half-mile upriver. Milo smoothly pulled the boat into a landing on the Arizona side. Two men in black polos pulled the boat onto the shore then helped everyone out.

Three black SUV's were parked close to the river; Johnny Scarpazzi standing next to the open door of the closest vehicle. When he saw the blood on Gabriella's jumpsuit, he ran down and easily scooped her up. He then carefully carried her to the middle SUV and placed her gently on the back seat. As I hurried to keep up with him, Milo picked up Susan and carried her to the same SUV.

I climbed in next to Gabriella and Milo sat Susan next to me. Max took shotgun in the front. One SUV pulled out of the parking lot first, we went next with Johnny driving, and a third followed us. There was a pickup truck with a trailer in the parking lot. The two men in black polos were already pulling the Zodiac onto it.

Still dripping with river water, Max handed a well-stocked first-aid kit back to me. "How is she?" he asked as he eyed Susan.

Susan was looking better than she had been. She was breathing more-or-less normally and her color had mostly returned.

"She's dazed," I said. "But other than that, she seems alright. Her name's Susan, by the way. There's a nasty bump on her forehead that must've happened when the boats collided. The bleeding's mostly stopped and I think that part's okay. But we'll still need to get her to a hospital and get her checked out. We don't know what kind of damage she has from being under that long. At the very least, she probably has a concussion."

"I'm okay," Susan said weakly. "My head hurts and my lungs are burning. I remember going under the water and not being able to breathe. I also remember thinking I was going to die. It was the most terrifying thing that's ever happened to me."

"I'm glad you came back to us," Max said. "It was touch and go for a few minutes."

Max looked at Susan with some concern. "Right," he said as he looked back at me. "We're going to head down to our clinic in Scottsdale. The trip will take about three hours, but I know she'll get the best care possible and no one will ask any questions. I'll need you to watch her closely. If her condition changes, let me know. I'd rather not stop at a hospital along the way, but we'll do whatever's needed to make sure she's alright."

Max turned to look at Gabriella. "How bad is it?" he asked. The tone in his voice was one I'd never heard before. There was deep concern and tenderness in his voice. It made me realize how much history Max and Gabriella had together. I also realized there was a lot I still didn't know about him.

"It's not too bad," she said weakly. "Medium caliber bullet, probably nine-millimeter, but solid core. He shot me in the same place as in Zagreb. I think it went in and out through the old scars. I will bleed, but I'll be okay until we get to the clinic."

Max hunted around in the glove compartment for a moment then took out a black zippered case. He opened it and pulled out a small syringe. "Gabby?" he asked, holding it up so she could see. "Do you need this?"

She saw the syringe and visibly relaxed. "Oh yes. Now would be a good time for that."

Max passed it back and Gabriella gave herself an injection in the leg. I opened the first aid kit and pulled out some pads to control the bleeding for both Susan and Gabriella. Within a couple of minutes, everything was in place.

"Thank you," I said to Gabriella. "If you hadn't shown up, I don't think we would have made it out of there."

"It's no problem. I have fun. Remember, we talked, I needed an adventure too."

Max was still turned to face us and I put my hand on his shoulder. "I guess you got my message. Thanks for coming to rescue us. It looks like I owe you again."

"Yes," Susan said, her voice still a little spacey. "I'm not sure what all is happening, and maybe I don't want to know, but thank you. After we stumbled onto everything in the castle, I was pretty sure they were going to kill us. Then I almost died in the river. You know, it's been a really shitty couple of days."

"It's not a problem," Max said. "Hostage rescue was one of the things Gabriella and I did back when we worked together in Europe. We thought it'd be fun to try it again." Max then looked at me and his voice dropped. "I hope you know I wanted to come in and get you out of there myself, but unfortunately, with the current situation, that was impossible."

"I understand," I said, my hand still on his shoulder. "Gabriella already told me that if you personally went into Nevada territory, it would've started a war. Besides, all we needed was her. That woman's a force of nature."

"That's true," Max said, looking over at her. "She's amazing."

I turned back to Gabriella. Whatever had been in the syringe was already working. Her color had improved and she seemed to be more alert.

"Why weren't you wearing your bulletproof vest?" I asked. "You were almost killed."

"Look at outfit," Gabriella said as she passed her hand over the open front of the jumpsuit. "Where I put vest?"

"You could've worn a looser outfit with the vest underneath. You did that a couple of months ago."

"I like this outfit. I can't move properly wearing vest."

"How'd you sneak in an Uzi and the other stuff? When we tried to get in over the bridge, they checked our purses."

"Bag has false bottom, like bag with diamonds. The security guard only look at my boobs and no pay attention to bag. It was easy, no problem."

"Looks like you've found another hole in the security system. After Jonathan recovers, I guess he'll need to install an x-ray machine on the bridge."

"After this," Max said, looking at me, "maybe you'll reconsider letting me put a location tracker in your car and in your purse. It would have saved us a lot of problems."

"Um, maybe," I said. "I'll think about it."

~~~~

We'd been driving for about thirty minutes and were almost to Kingman, when I had a thought.

"Damn," I said.

"What?" Max asked.

"Our bags, I completely forgot about them. They're at the coat check in the building at the Black Castle parking lot, right across the river from the casino."

"Do you really need them now?" Max asked.

"The clothes don't matter so much, but my Baby Glock's in there. I probably shouldn't leave it like that."

Max made a sound. I was unsure if it was amusement or frustration. He pulled out his phone and hit a button. Someone took the call and Max relayed what we needed. I found my claim ticket, then fished out Susan's from her waterlogged bag and gave them both to Max.

All three SUV's pulled off on the side of the road. Max gave the tickets to Milo, who was driving the rear vehicle. Milo then made a U-turn and drove back toward Bullhead City.

~~~~

We arrived at the clinic off of Frank Lloyd Wright Boulevard in Scottsdale a little after six o'clock. They ushered both Gabriella and Susan back to the examination rooms. Max went into one of the offices and began making phone calls. From what little I could overhear, at least one of them was to Tony. I sat out in the waiting area with Johnny and Milo arrived with our bags about an hour later.

~~~~

By nine o'clock, the doctors reported back on both of Susan and Gabriella. Despite being shot, they said Gabriella's wound was the lesser of the two. As she'd already guessed, the bullet had gone cleanly through and nothing major had been damaged. They cleaned the wound and gave her several shots to prevent infection and promote rapid healing.

Susan was apparently going to be fine, but they were going to hold her overnight for observation. They ran some tests on her brain and fortunately there seemed to be no permanent damage. The bump on her head was only a bump, the impact wasn't hard enough to have caused a concussion. As it turned out, their main concern was possible pneumonia, infection, or even heart failure caused by the river water in her lungs. They were hopeful the antibiotics and other medicines they'd given her would prevent the worst of it.

At the doctor's insistence, she also looked me over. She asked a lot of questions, especially about my time in the river and how much water I'd swallowed. In the end, she said I looked okay, but to come back right away if I developed cramping, chills, or a fever anytime over the next two weeks.

~~~~

My car was still in the shop, but they'd already fixed it. It turned out not to be as bad as I'd feared. They had to replace all of the belts and hoses, but the engine itself hadn't suffered any damage.

Max said he'd be happy to drive me home and I took him up on his offer. When we arrived back at my building, I was so tired that I briefly nodded off as we rode up the elevator. We went into my apartment and I dropped on the couch, Max sitting close beside me.

"You were wonderful today," I said as I wrapped my arms around him. "You can have me if you want to. But honestly, it's been a shitty couple of days. I mainly just want you to hold me."

Chapter Thirteen

When I woke up, I had a brief vision that I was back in the prison cell in the basement of the Black Castle Casino. As I more fully came to consciousness, the cell faded and I was back in my own room. I laid in my bed for another ten minutes, enjoying the softness of the sheets and the feeling of security.

I remembered spending time with Max the night before. After we'd cuddled on the couch for a few moments, I think I fell asleep. I vaguely remember Max helping me into my bedroom. Judging by the few clothes I still had on, he must have helped me get undressed and put me to bed.

As I got up to make the coffee, I realized I hurt all over. I shuffled into the bathroom and looked at myself in the mirror. I could see several obvious bruises and a few other discolorations that were either dirt or a deeper bruise.

I tried to think back to how I'd gotten all of them. I could place a couple of them from sleeping on the hard cot, but, looking back, most of them were probably from being battered around on the boat when Hobbs and Chopper sideswiped us. I'd probably also gotten a few from trying to intervene when Gabriella was fighting with Jonathan.

I found where I'd left my phone and called Sophie. I asked if she had any time to drive me to the repair shop to pick up my car.

"Oh sure," she said. "It's been pretty quiet here so far and I don't see that changing any time soon. When do you want me over there?"

"I just woke up and I'll need to get some coffee in me first."

"Okay, I'll swing by in an hour. Does that work?"

"Perfectly."

~~~~

An hour later, there was a knock on my door. Sophie came in, sat on the couch, and started petting and playing with Marlowe. By this point, I'd made the coffee, taken a shower, pulled on some clothes, and fed my starving cat.

~~~~

The ride over to the repair shop was pleasant, almost like a mini-road trip. Sophie knew me well enough not to bug me too much about the details of what'd happened. She knew she'd eventually get a full download and didn't push it.

"I forgot about Lenny's date last night," I said. "I was sort of busy with the assignment. How'd it go?"

"It was a nightmare," Sophie said. "Lenny kept group texting us, asking how he should handle different situations. Gina eventually stopped replying, but I felt like I sorta had to. It was like having someone text me in the middle of a car crash."

"Yeah, I saw all of the texts when I looked this morning. What did he say about it when he came in?"

"That's the part that really has me worried. He called first thing this morning and asked if he had any appointments scheduled. When I told him no, he said he wouldn't be in."

"Do you think the date went that badly?"

"I don't know, but if it did, it'll be worse than ever around here."

~~~~

When we reached the shop, Sophie waited in her car while I went in. As with most of my recent repairs, when they told me the total for the bill, it was uncomfortably high, but not so high that it would have made more sense to scrap the car and instead use the money as a down payment for something new, or at least newer. I thought again about selling the gold nugget Professor Mindy had given me. That in itself would be enough to get me a decent used vehicle.

When I walked outside to get my car, I found Sophie standing next to it. She looked down at the hood, then up at me as I walked closer. The day before, the shop had asked if I wanted a new hood or if they should try to bend the old one back into shape. They said the bend would still be noticeable, but my hood would be functional. After telling me the price for a new hood, I told them the bend back the old one.

Stopping next to my car, I saw what Sophie had been looking at. There was a big crack in the paint where the hood had bent. I knew the cracked paint would eventually start to chip, then it would completely flake off revealing the crease in the metal underneath. I inwardly sighed as I thought about driving my car around with yet another blemish.

~~~~

I returned to the clinic around ten o'clock. When I walked in her room, Susan was sitting up in bed, eating breakfast, and watching TV. A woman who I assumed was Susan's mother, Olivia, sat next to her.

"Hey," I said, as I walked in and introduced myself. "How are you feeling today?"

"I'm doing good. They've been in to check on me, once an hour or so, and nobody seems worried. The last time I saw the doctor, he said I could go home this afternoon."

"That's great."

I didn't stay too long. Susan's aunt showed up a few minutes after I arrived and the room suddenly felt very crowded. I told Susan to call me if she wanted to talk and I let her know she had a standing lunch invitation with everyone at the office.

~~~~

I stopped by Ski Pro and picked up some socks and a balaclava. I looked around until I found the same brand of jacket and ski pants as I'd picked up at the thrift store. Although the one's they had here were the current year's style, buying everything new would have cost over seven hundred dollars. It made the outfit I'd bought the weekend before seem all the more special.

~~~~

After a casual dinner, I got back to my apartment house about seven o'clock. I thought I should check in with Grandma and see how she was doing.

When she answered her door, she seemed like she was back to her old self. Marlowe was asleep on his afghan and looked as happy as ever.

"Well, Laura, come on in. Let me get you a caffeine-free Diet Pepsi. How was your trip? You said you were going to a casino somewhere?"

"Thanks," I said as I sat on the couch. "It was for work and honestly, it wasn't a lot of fun."

"I'm sorry to hear that," Grandma said as she came out of the kitchen and handed me a bottle. "The last time I went to Casino Scottsdale I won two hundred dollars."

"What's happening with you and Grandpa Bob? Is the engagement still on?"

"I think so. We've come to a compromise on the ring."

"That's great. What are you going to do?"

"Well, we're going to take the diamonds from his mother's ring and make a new ring. We'll use some diamonds and gold from my mother's old jewelry. That way, I can still have his mother's diamonds, but I won't need to wear his dead wife's ring."

"What's he going to do with the old ring?"

"He can throw it in the trash, as far as I'm concerned. But I think he's going to take the gold and make it into a tie-tack or something like that."

"I'm glad you were able to work something out. Have you set the date yet?"

"No, although honestly, the thought of eloping to Las Vegas is sounding better. I've started asking everyone in the family what dates would work for them and there doesn't seem to be a time when everyone can make it. Our kids have work schedules to get around and the grandkids have school and sports. My daughter said she'd help, but all she wants to do is make it bigger and more expensive."

"Like how?"

"Well, I was thinking about going to a chapel, saying the vows, then maybe all of us could go to a nice restaurant for drinks and dinner. Meghan says we need to rent a hall, set up a menu, order flowers, get a band, use a limousine, and the list keeps growing longer every day. Then there's the dress."

"What about the dress?"

"I was thinking about wearing a cream-colored evening dress I already have. It seems foolish to spend money on a new dress that I'll only wear once. But Meghan wants to go dress shopping with me to pick out a formal wedding gown. One with a veil and a long train. She says she wants me to have a 'bridal moment' when I get 'jacked-up' and then 'say yes to the dress'. Honestly, I don't know what she's talking about. But I'm starting to feel like the wedding's taking on a life of its own."

"I won't try to compete with your daughter, but let me know how I can help."

"Thank you, dear. I'll keep you up to date. I might end up needing you to come to my rescue."

Great.

~~~~

I woke up late and spent twenty minutes relaxing in bed. Since it was only Thursday and I wasn't leaving for Vail until Friday, that gave me the day to pick up anything last minute and finish packing.

I put on a pot of coffee and got ready for the day. I called Sophie to find out what was going on and see if her and Gina wanted to do lunch.

"Lunch would be great. It's only ten o'clock and I'm already starving."

"Did Lenny come into the office today?"

"Yeah, he's back, but he's worse than ever. I've been too afraid to bring up the date, but I don't think things went very well."

~~~~

I got to the office about eleven thirty. Walking through the back offices, I saw Gina in her cube, working on a report.

"How did everything go?" she asked. "I know you had some problems. I was worried when I didn't hear from you Monday night and I debated on going up to Nevada. If you hadn't called and said you were on your way back to Scottsdale, I would have driven up on Tuesday afternoon."

"I appreciate you looking out for me. Yeah, it was touch and go for a while. But everything seemed to work out alright."

"How's Susan? You said she was in the hospital for observation?"

"They released her yesterday afternoon and her mom took her home. I was going to give her a call after lunch and see how she's doing."

Gina followed me to the front and we each grabbed a chair at Sophie's desk. I knew both of them would want the full download on what'd happened. I'd been debating how much to tell Gina about Max and Gabriella's part in the rescue. I imagined that Sophie might have heard some of it already from Milo, but I didn't think she would have told Gina about that part of the rescue yet. I also knew I'd need to steer clear of the drugs and the money. It wasn't only that I had promised not to say anything about it, but if Gina heard about illegal activities, she might be compelled to make some phone calls. I didn't think that would work out well for anybody.

"Do you want to head down the street for tacos?" I asked. "I'll tell you about our visit to the Black Castle."

"Damn straight," Sophie said. "I appreciate you calling me on Tuesday to tell me you and Susan were alive and everything, but I want the details."

"So do I," Gina said. "You said they held you both in a prison cell overnight?"

"Yeah, well. It was an adventure."

"Speaking of adventures," Sophie said with a grin. "Gina went out with Jet again last night."

"Oh, really?" I asked. "How'd it go?"

Gina flushed red and ducked her head down with embarrassment.

"Oh my God," I said. "You did it this time, didn't you?"

"Yes," Gina squealed out, a happy smile on her face. "He's an amazing man."

"Fine," I said. "I'll give you details about what happened to Susan and me, but you'll need to give us details about you and Jet."

Lenny came out of his office, holding a couple of folders. He looked at the three of us, then walked to Sophie's desk and handed her the files.

"Gina," he said, clearly irritated. "I need those revisions on my desk. I know I said two o'clock would work, but I need them right away."

He stopped and looked around the office, as if he hadn't really seen it before. "Sophie, I know you're still upset that I never hired another admin, but I want these files cleaned up. The place is starting to look like a recycling center."

He then looked down at me. "Are you working on something or are you still expecting the rest of the week off? It seems to me that if you aren't currently working a case, you could help Sophie around the office."

He looked at us like he was waiting for someone to complain. When nobody said anything, he turned to go back to his office. He'd taken two or three steps, when his cell phone rang. He pulled it out of his pocket and answered.

"Hey, baby," he said in a voice I'd never heard Lenny use before. It was a tone someone in high school would use. "Nothing, what are you doing?"

Sophie, Gina, and I looked at each other.

"I've been thinking about you too," he said, still with the high-school voice. "Tonight? Well, I think I can break myself free and come over." He stood there grinning as he listened to someone, who I could only assume was Elle, on the phone. "You can make me anything you want," he said. "You're so delicious, I'm sure your cooking is delicious too." Then he giggled. It was a sound I'd never heard Lenny make and it was a little creepy. "Alright, see you at seven. I'll bring the wine. Bye, beautiful."

Lenny disconnected the phone and stared off into space for a moment. He seemed to gradually come out of it, then looked back at us. From the look on his face, pissy Lenny had returned.

"Well," he said. "I don't pay you people to sit around and talk, do I?" He then turned and walked back into his office, closing the door.

"Oh shit," Gina said.

"What was that?" I asked.

"Elle likes him?" Sophie said in disbelief.

"Dear God," Gina said, also with a tone of disbelief. "What did we do?"

"Going on a date was supposed to make him better," I said. "But I think we've just made everything worse."

As we stood around Sophie's desk in an uncomfortable silence, my phone rang. I saw it was Susan.

"Could you come over to my Mom's house?" she asked. "Something's come up and I need to talk to you about it."

There was something off with her voice, but I couldn't put my finger on it. "Susan, is everything alright?"

"Everything's fine. But I really need to talk with you, right away."

"Sure," I said. "Where do you live?"

I punched the address into my phone as she gave it to me. It seemed to be a house off of Granite Reef and Thomas, a little north of the neighborhood where I'd grown up. "Okay," I said. "I'll be there in fifteen or twenty minutes."

I disconnected and stared into space for a moment.

"What's wrong," Gina asked.

"I'm not sure," I said. "Susan want's me to stop by but something seems off."

"Do you want some back up?" she asked. "Just in case?"

"I should be good. But do me a favor, keep your phone on in case something comes up."

~~~~

I drove to the neighborhood where Susan and her mom lived. It was filled with houses that were smaller than the more expensive areas further north, but everybody kept their house well maintained and it seemed like a pleasant place to live.

As I approached Susan's street, I became more convinced that something was wrong. I decided to park a few houses down and look around for anything amiss. The house seemed to have a living room in the front, with windows looking out to the street and on the side. I kept more or less out of view of the house as I approached the side window. I bent low and peered in.

Susan and her mother were both sitting on the couch. I watched them for almost a minute, looking for signs of trouble, but they only seemed to be quietly watching TV. The room around them seemed peaceful as well. I did notice there were several oil paintings on the walls and many pieces of art on the shelves.

Feeling somewhat better, I walked to the front entrance and knocked. After a moment, Olivia pulled it open. I took a step in and she gave a halfhearted push on the door to shut it. It only closed partway before it stopped, still two or three inches short of latching.

Without speaking, she turned and walked back to the couch. Now more confused than ever, I looked at Susan. Her eyes were red, as if she'd been crying. Red warning bells were starting to clamor in my head. Susan looked up at me. "I'm so sorry."

I opened my purse to get the Baby Glock as I saw movement across the room. I looked up to see Jonathan standing in the hallway. He held a large caliber semi-automatic pistol in his hands. Unfortunately, I knew my gun was buried underneath my wallet, keys, and a packet of tissues. With his pistol already pointed at me, if I went for my Glock, it wouldn't even be a contest.

Shit. Not again.

I slowly pulled my hand out of my bag and looked at him. His lips were twisted into a sneer which I took for his version of happy. His face also bore a couple of red and purple areas from bruises that had only just started to heal.

"Laura Black," he said. "I'm so glad you could join our little party. I've been scouting things out and I decided it would be more private here than in your apartment. There're too many people coming and going at your building, plus I'm not sure your elevator is all that safe. I'm surprised you'd trust your life to that thing."

"What do you want?" I asked.

"You two are coming back with me to the Castle," he snarled, looking at both Susan and me. "Some people on the board aren't satisfied with how things went the other day. They want to talk to you directly and learn exactly how much you know about our operation. After that, of course, you'll be free to leave."

From his nasty tone and the way his eyes sparkled, it was obvious things wouldn't stop at talking and we wouldn't ever be allowed to leave. If we went with him, we'd end up dead. First, we'd be put through whatever kinds of sick abuse he wanted, then we'd end up in holes in the desert like he'd already threatened to put us in.

Susan glanced at me. From her scared but determined look, I could tell she was also aware of how dangerous our situation was.

"My car's parked out back," Jonathan said. "They have a little alley there. I'm going to put cuffs on the both of you and we're all going to quietly walk out to the car. If one of you tries to yell or run, I'll shoot the other one in the middle of her back, right through her heart. I'm not sure how fond you are of each other, but you'll be signing the other one's death warrant if either of you try anything."

I started looking around the room, trying to think of a way out of this. Unfortunately, nothing clever or useful jumped out at me. I still had my Baby Glock in my purse, but with Jonathan's gun trained on me, it would be useless to reach for it. If Gina were here, she'd be able to smoothly kick the gun out of his hand, then she'd slam his head against the wall a couple of times for good measure.

Unfortunately, I knew if I tried it and missed, it would end up getting everyone in the room shot.

"I'll go with you," Susan said. "I'll tell you anything you want to know. But you have to promise not to hurt my mom."

Olivia began to protest. I looked at Susan in surprise, but Jonathan was suddenly very happy. "Of course," he said. "I don't want to hurt your mom. But I'm sure you'll understand that I have to make sure she doesn't alert anyone to where we're going."

"I promise, I won't say a word." Olivia said.

"Nice try," Jonathan sneered. "But I have a better idea. I'm going to tie you up and gag you. After we get to our destination and I finish with your daughter, I'll call someone to come over here and let you go."

"No," Susan said. "That could be a day or two. I'm not going to leave my mother tied up that long. She'll promise not to say or do anything."

"I'll be fine," Olivia said, fright clearly in her voice. "I'm not sure what this is all about, but it's obvious we have to do what he says."

A sturdy wooden chair sat in the corner of the living room. Jonathan moved it to the center of the space. "This will do nicely." He looked over at Susan. "Find me something to tie her up with. Rope, string, maybe an electrical extension cord. But don't leave my sight or attempt to escape. If you try anything, ka-pow, your mother will die, right here. I have a lot of bullets and I'm sorta in the mood to shoot someone."

Susan went into the kitchen area and hunted through the drawers and cabinets, eventually coming back with several pieces of rope and a coil of thick string.

"This will do nicely." He looked around again and saw a pair of red socks curled up on the floor in front of the couch. "And give me one of those nasty looking socks. I'll roll it up and stuff it in your mom's mouth so she can't make any noise."

Susan picked up the dirty sock, shook it out the best she could, then delivered it to his outstretched hand.

Jonathan waved his gun back and forth between Susan and me. "You two, on the couch over there. If either of you move, I'll shoot you both, right here. Do you understand?"

We both nodded, then sat. My purse with the Baby Glock was close enough to be tempting and I was now seriously considering it. Everything would depend on how distracted Jonathan would be while he was tying up Olivia.

As I watched him start to wrap the first piece of rope around Olivia's wrists, I noticed movement in the side window. It was the same window I'd looked into, ten minutes earlier. It was Michael, peering into the house.

I made an effort not to look directly at the window, in case Jonathan were to glance my way. Through the corner of my eye, I saw Michael watch as Jonathan finished up with the knots on the rope binding Olivia's hands.

Thoughts began to race through my mind. What was Michael doing out there? How had he found out where we were? Would he be able to help us?

Still looking scared, Olivia remained quietly in the chair while Jonathan started to wrap a new piece of rope around her. As he bent down to tie the first set of knots, the door to the street slowly swung open. Michael, also with a semi-automatic pistol in his hand, quietly took a step into the room.

Susan and I both looked at him, but he held his finger to his lips for us to remain silent. He took two more quiet steps toward Jonathan, who was still bent over, tying a complicated knot in the rope. On the third step, the floor underneath Michael creaked. Jonathan turned to look, just as the barrel of Michael's gun smashed down on the side of his skull. There was a wet thud and Jonathan collapsed in a heap.

Susan ran to untie her mother. Fumbling with the ropes seemed to be Susan's emotional tipping point and tears started running down her cheeks.

"He won't be out for long," Michael said, half to himself. "What are we going to do with him?"

"He thought tying up my mom was a great idea," Susan said. "Let's tie him to the chair until we can figure out what to do with him."

It took all three of us to lift Jonathan's limp body and keep him in position as Michael firmly secured him with the ropes. When he was done with the last knot, he stood up. "We'll also need to keep him quiet. Get me something soft to stick in his mouth as a gag."

"He wanted to use a dirty sock on my mother," Susan said. "It'll be good enough for him."

She walked to the couch, picked up the sock she hadn't shaken out, rolled it into a ball, then shoved it into Jonathan's mouth. Olivia used a piece of rope to complete the gag.

With the excitement over, at least for the moment. We stood in a group, looking down at Jonathan's unmoving body. There was an awkward silence when nobody said anything for several moments.

Jonathan began to stir, then quickly regained consciousness. He blinked his eyes for almost a minute, waiting for everything to come back into focus, then he looked at us all with fury. He began to struggle against the ropes and tried to yell at us. The gag we'd used was effective and we couldn't make out the actual words, but it was obvious he wasn't happy.

Michael had pulled out his pistol and was about to give him another blow to his head, when Susan held up her hand to stop him. With a look of determination, she walked to a bookshelf and picked up a plaster bust of a stern looking man. She then looked over at her mother. "Do you mind if I use the Renault?"

"Go ahead," Olivia said. "It's not the best representation of his work."

Susan walked up to Jonathan with the statue in her hand. As she did, Jonathan's eyes glared at her. His shouts got louder and he struggled harder against the ropes.

"Shut up, jerk," Susan said, as she lifted the bust then brought it down on the top of Jonathan's head. The plaster bust shattered into a dozen pieces and Jonathan again went limp.

"What are we going to do with him?" Susan asked. "We can't keep smashing things against his skull. It'll eventually cause some permanent brain damage. Although, I'm not sure how you could tell with him."

"This is going to be a problem," Michael said. "Arizona isn't our territory and for me to even be here is sort of a violation of the rules, even if it was only to stop Jonathan. I had a tracker on his car so I knew where he was heading. But I guess I didn't think this part out very well."

I looked down at Jonathan's unmoving body. I knew what I had to do, even though having to ask for help pissed me off. I also knew that asking for help would only pull me tighter into Tony's world.

"Um," I said to Michael. "I might know someone. I'm always telling him I don't need his help, but maybe this time I do."

I pulled out my phone and called Max.

Shit, after all my protesting how I don't need anyone's help, I'm never going to hear the end of this.

"Hey," I said when he answered. "I've got an interesting story for you." I spent several minutes describing what had happened. When he realized that the same man who'd shot Gabriella had come to Scottsdale for Susan and me, he became quite concerned. He calmed down a little when I described how we'd secured him to a chair and that he was being closely watched by the four of us.

"Hang tight," he said. "Don't take any chances with him. From what Gabriella says, he's a trained killer. I'll send Milo and a couple of guys over there to get him. We'll hold him while we figure out what to do. I can't imagine Nevada sanctioning his entering Arizona on business, but if they did, this could get sticky."

I let everyone know what was happening and that we'd need to watch him for a little while longer. We again stood in a loose circle around Jonathan's limp body in an uncomfortable silence.

"Um, hi, Liv," Michael said, finally looking at Olivia. "It's been a long time."

"You're right," she said with a slight smile. "It's been a *very* long time. But it sounds like you've been keeping yourself busy." She glanced over at Jonathan's limp body. "It looks like you've been leading an interesting life. Susan tells me Bill Southard isn't your real name."

"No, it's Michael, Michael McKinsey. It's the name I was born with. I'm sorry I deceived you. I created the William Southard identity back when I didn't want anyone to know about my connection to the Black Castle Casino. I think I knew, even back then, that my association with it would lead to trouble. I hope you'll forgive me for that."

"From what Susan's told me, it makes sense. I always suspected you had a past you weren't proud of. At the time, I even suspected you were part of something criminal. But for some reason, it only made you more attractive. I guess I've always had a thing for bad boys." Olivia smiled shyly at him.

Michael looked over at Susan. "I guess the secret about me being Susan's dad has been blown."

"Well, I kept to our agreement and tried to keep her out of it," Olivia said. "But the girl has a mind of her own. Sort of like her father. What have you been doing the last twenty-five years? I hear you're the head of the Black Castle Casino. That must be exciting."

She again looked at Jonathan. "Does he have anything to do with that?"

"Well," Michael continued, "I was head of the casino and Jonathan there was part of it too, but now that's over. It's time for me to find something new to do. Maybe I'll travel."

"But you won't have a job." Susan said. "How will you afford it? Traveling's an expensive hobby."

Michael started to laugh. "Money's not an issue. I've been the owner of a very successful business for many years and have had nothing to spend my fortune on. You could say I'm pretty much set for life." He looked over at Olivia and Susan. "Actually, all of us are set for life."

He then walked over and took Olivia's hand. "I hear you have some health problems. Let's have the best doctors in the country see what they can do."

"You're being very sweet," Olivia said as she continued to hold his hand. "But I don't know if there's anything they can do at this point."

"Well, if that's the case, we'll go down fighting together. I'd like to try to make up for the years I've been gone. What do you say?"

Olivia smiled and nodded her head. "I'd like that. It'd be good to get to know each other again. I've missed you."

"I've missed you too."

By mutual agreement, they both took a step closer and wrapped their arms around each other in a long embrace.

Michael looked over at me. "Actually, I'm glad you're here. I need to talk with you. First, I wanted to thank you for everything you did to get Susan into the castle and then to get her out again. It was very brave of you, and because of it, I got to meet my daughter."

"It's no problem," I said. "Susan wanted to find her father and I was happy to help."

"Now, the second thing," Michael said, looking at both Susan and me. "This part is serious. I need you both to remember, mum's the word on the things you saw while you were visiting the casino."

Olivia looked at Michael with a puzzled look, but he continued.

"It's not only Jonathan here who's nervous. Everyone's still quite concerned that you both know all of our, um, trade secrets, and that you might want to eventually tell someone about them. Kathleen and I intervened and let everyone know you'll both be able to keep the secrets of the casino. Unfortunately, two of the board members were unconvinced and I believe they were the ones who ordered Jonathan to kidnap you. These are the same two members that caused the problems the other day. Marcus was forced to take direct action last night and he's removed them from the board."

"Um, removed them?" Susan asked.

"Removed them."

"Oh."

Michael looked directly at the two of us. "However, even with them gone, telling anyone about what you saw wouldn't be looked at kindly and there'd be a general feeling of betrayal. Trust me. That wouldn't be a good thing, for anyone. Will that be a problem for either of you?"

"I know how to keep a secret," I said.

"So do I," Susan said. "The less I think about your secrets, the happier I'll be."

"Good," Michael said. "I'll relay your feelings on the matter back to Marcus. He's still obligated to protect you both as a part of Kathleen's favor. I think he'll help to sway any remaining skeptics." He cleared his throat and again glanced at Olivia.

"Oh, you don't need to be coy," Olivia said. "I have a pretty good idea what's going on. You talked about the Black Castle enough times when we were together that I figured you had some sort of connection with it. About three years ago, one of the Laughlin papers had a picture of the owner of the casino and I was pretty sure it was you, even with the different name. Since then, I've been keeping an ear open to learn what actually goes on up there. It seems like a pretty lively place that only barely manages to fly under the police radar. Your real name's been mentioned a time or two in connection with the shenanigans up there."

Michael looked at her and shrugged his shoulders, but he didn't say anything.

"What happened to Hobbs?" I asked. "I've been worried about him. He risked his life for us out on the river the other day. I imagine Jonathan and the security guards weren't very happy with him after he used his ferry barge to smash into their patrol boat."

Olivia raised her eyebrows, but tactfully didn't say anything.

"Yes, that caused quite a problem," Michael said. "Almost as big of a problem as you two breaking into our level-five security area. Fortunately, both Kathleen and I found out what happened and we were able to convince Marcus and the board that it was all due to a communication error. We put out a story that, in the confusion of the escape, Hobbs was radioed and was told the patrol boat was the problem and to take it out. We let Hobbs know what we were doing and he went along with it."

"And everyone believed that?" Susan asked.

"Johnathan didn't, of course. Neither did the two problem board members. But Marcus and the rest of the board only wanted the entire incident to be behind them as quickly as possible. From what I understand, there's never been any love lost between Hobbs and the guards on the river. It's also not the first time he's run over a patrol boat. He'll have to watch his back for a while, but I suspect he's pretty good at that."

"Michael," I asked. "There's one thing that's been bugging me about what happened at the casino. How did Kathleen know to show up when she did?"

"That's no mystery," Michael said. "I called her. Once everyone learned the truth about Susan being my daughter, I knew I couldn't stay there. But I also knew they needed an original owner to run the place. The casino deed and the unrestricted gaming license are still in both of our names. There's no way the Nevada Gaming Control Board would ever let the casino reassign the license to the current ownership group. There's been a lot of bad blood between them over the years and they'd use it as an excuse to shut the place down. I know Kathleen's been upset for the last twenty-five years because she wasn't running the casino. I also knew she still had one of Marcus's markers and she could use her favor to force him to appoint her as the new head of the casino. I thought it would be a way for everyone to get what they wanted."

"Everyone but Jonathan," I said. As we looked over at him, we saw he was starting to come around again.

"Well, I never did like him," Michael said. "He made it clear from the start that he wanted to run the place. I was only an obstacle in his quest. He's been a pain in my ass ever since they brought him into the security group. Personally, I thought we should have kept him as an escort."

Jonathan was now fully awake, although his eyes still seemed a bit unfocused. After a moment, he finally seemed to realize where he was and what was happening to him. He started cursing us through the gag and was again struggling to escape.

Fortunately, there was a knock at the front door and we looked out to see Milo, along with two other big men. I opened the door and let them in. Milo looked at the struggling man in the chair and then over at me. He cracked a small smile and shook his head.

"Ma'am?" Milo asked Olivia. "Do you possibly have a bed sheet we could use?"

Olivia brought Milo a sheet and he draped it over Jonathan. The two men then walked over and picked up the chair with Jonathan still tied to it. They'd backed a van onto the driveway and Milo went out first to open the rear doors. Within a few seconds, they had Jonathan secured in the van and we all breathed a sigh of relief.

~~~~

By six o'clock, I'd made it back to my apartment. I was mentally drained and had forgotten to get anything for dinner. I pulled out a random frozen thing from the freezer and popped it into the microwave. As it cooked, I opened a Corona, sat on the couch, and turned on the TV.

The microwave dinged but I was comfortable where I was. After a few minutes of dinging, the microwave gave up and stopped making noise. As I drank down my beer, the phone rang. When I looked at the screen, I saw it was Tony DiCenzo. Normally, this would send a jolt of apprehension through me, but today there was nothing.

"Laura Black," he said as I answered the phone. "Max tells me you've had quite an adventure over the past few days. I might have mentioned this before, but your exploits remind me of some of the situations I found myself in, back in my youth. I also heard some complications arose."

"Yeah," I said. "About those complications."

"Well, put your mind at ease, I took care of that little problem for you."

"Tony, are you saying what I think you're saying?"

"No, nothing like that. All I did was make a few phone calls. I'm having my guys drive him back to Nevada. Matter of fact, when we made our initial inquiries into the matter, they seemed rather eager to get their hands on him. Apparently, he was already in some hot water and coming into our territory on business only made his situation worse. Honestly, it doesn't seem too good for him. I don't think we'll ever hear from him again.

I felt a rush of relief. I hadn't realized I'd been so worried about Jonathan coming back for me. "Thank you for doing that."

"Don't think about it too much. We transgressed by going into their territory, they transgressed by coming into ours. Fortunately, neither side wants a conflict and I think we can stop it here. I was only doing what needed to be done. You've made yourself some powerful enemies in Nevada. For your safety, you needed to show them you have equally powerful friends in Arizona."

"Thanks Tony. I really appreciate it. I'm always telling you and Max that I don't need anyone's help, but in this case, I wasn't sure who else to turn to."

"Not a problem. It's what I'm here for. Matter of fact, I've been looking for ways to say thank you for everything you've been doing for me over the last year."

"You already gave me your beautiful car. And I didn't even have it two months before I destroyed it."

Tony chuckled, as if the thought of his Mercedes convertible blowing up amused him. "As I recall, one of your enemies did that. Besides, it was only a car, and not even a new one at that. You've pulled me out of a couple of tough scrapes. I'm glad, for once, I could do something for you."

Chapter Fourteen

I got up early and finished packing for the trip. Max was coming for me at eleven o'clock and I wanted to have everything ready.

Surprisingly, I'd stopped feeling nervous about learning to ski. I guess having your life threatened made things like skiing seem rather mundane by comparison.

At about nine, Susan called and said she needed to talk.

"Not another problem, I hope."

"Nothing like that, but some things are still bugging me. On the positive side, I also have some good news."

"I'm taking off from my apartment at eleven, but you can have me until about ten thirty."

"It won't take that long. Can I meet you at your office about ten o'clock? I'd like to do this face-to-face."

~~~~

I got to the office at nine thirty and walked through to the front. Sophie was typing away on her computer while the radio on her desk blared out some upbeat song in Spanish.

"Hey," I said. "How's Lenny been? Has he gotten any better yet?"

Sophie turned down the radio. "Nope, he's still being an ass. He got in late today and barely had time to pick up his stack of documents before heading down to court. He wasn't here a total of five minutes, but he still managed to piss off both Gina and me. If this doesn't stop soon, I'm thinking we might need to break up the happy couple."

"I'm sorry I ever mentioned setting Lenny up with Elle. I was thinking he'd get better if he had some sort of outlet. But it looks like it's only put his issues into sharper focus."

"Well, he seems happy, at least with Elle. Let's give it a week or two. If he's still being an ass, we'll break them up and maybe find someone who has a better effect on him. Hey, you never did get a chance to tell us the details of what went on in Nevada. From what little you've told me so far, it sounds like it sorta sucked."

"It did. There was a time when I didn't know what would happen to us. If Max, Gabriella, and Milo hadn't shown up when they did, I don't think we would have gotten out of there."

"Well," Sophie said. "You wanted an adventure. It sounds like you had one."

"Yeah, but I think I've had all the adventure I can handle for a while. Actually, hiding in a closet and taking videos of people having sex doesn't seem as bad as it did two weeks ago."

"Lenny'll be happy to hear that." She opened her desk drawer, pulled out a folder, and slid it across to me. "Like I said before, be careful what you wish for."

Great.

"Don't worry about your weekend," she said. "I told Lenny you caught a cold while you were in Nevada and were sick in bed today. He said you can start on this one next week."

I held the folder to my chest as I looked down at Sophie. "Thank you."

The door to the street opened and Susan walked in. She was dressed in a smart looking outfit that seemed to be new. When she saw us, she broke out in a confident smile.

"Hey, Laura. Hey, Sophie," she said as she walked over to Sophie's desk.

"Hi, Susan," I said. "How's everything going? Is Michael still in town?"

Susan let out a laugh. "He hasn't left mom's side since he came over yesterday. It's weird, but they seemed to pick up exactly where they left off twenty-five years ago."

"And your mom's good with that?"

"She's the one who insisted Michael spend the night. He tried to say he didn't have his stuff with him, but mom didn't care. She said she'd been waiting twenty-five years for him to show up again and she didn't care if he'd brought his toothbrush or not."

"That's great, how's she feeling?"

"I think I told you, but she hasn't had a lot of energy for the past couple of months. We found out it's partially from all the medicines they've been giving her. But all last night, she acted like she's a teenager again. It's really great to see her laughing and in a good mood. Last night, Michael and my mom started doing research on medical specialists around the country. They're going to the first one next week."

"I hope they can help her," Sophie said.

"So do I," Susan said. "But having my mom happy again will probably help as much as whatever the doctors do. I've never seen her smile as much as she did last night."

"With them gone," Sophie said, "you'll have the place to yourself. What are you going to do to keep busy?"

"After the week we've just had, I'm looking forward to the quiet. I've already told my boss that I'm quitting. Michael wants mom to reopen her art gallery somewhere here in Old Town and I'll help her run it. I have an appointment at two with a realtor to start looking at some available storefronts."

"You found a father and your mom's getting back into the art business?" I asked. "That's not a bad outcome from our adventure."

"A lot of it was terrifying, but overall, it's been a great experience. I'm glad we decided to go through with it. I wanted to thank you for all your help."

"Um, I hate to put a damper on your happiness," Sophie said. "But I just finished up your final invoice. Even after the big retainer you put down, you're still going to owe Lenny a couple of thousand dollars."

I expected the news to come as a shock, but Susan only laughed. "That's not a problem. Send me the invoice and I'll give you my card number." She looked at me. "Actually, that's part of why I came over today. I talked to Kathleen last night."

"Really?" I asked. "How's she doing?"

"Apparently pretty well. Her and my dad talked about the business side of the casino for about forty-five minutes, then he handed the phone to me."

"What'd she say?"

"Well, she thanked me and wanted to thank you too. I guess my dad was right. She's been upset for twenty-five years that she wasn't running the casino. Now that she is, I think she wants to make some changes. Dad was telling her how to get things done through Marcus and the board. With the two problem members gone, dad thinks it will start to go a lot smoother there."

"I hope it works out well for her. Was that it?"

"No, I'm just coming to the best part. Now that she's in charge of the casino, Kathleen said she's going to slowly put all of those chips she has back into circulation. Apparently, the casino's had them on the books as an outstanding liability for the last twenty-five years. She said with her bleeding the chips back in, the casino side of the business should stay solidly in the black, for at least the next three or four years."

"That's great," I said. "But what does that have to do with us?"

Susan opened her purse and pulled out the sandwich bag full of casino chips, the ones Kathleen had given us to start our adventure. Looking at them, it seemed like a long time ago that we were in Kathleen's house, even though it hadn't even been a week.

"This is what it has to do with us. When Kathleen started talking about casino chips, I remembered these and asked her how I should get them back to her. She only laughed and said we could keep them. She said to consider it a thank-you present."

Damn.

"You're serious?"

Susan opened the bag and fished out ten of the purple chips, then ten of the orange ones. She made a stack of each on Sophie's desk.

"There," she said. "That's fifteen thousand dollars for each of us."

"Damn," Sophie said as she picked up one of the purple ones. "So, you're saying this little piece of plastic is worth five hundred dollars?"

"Yup," Susan said. "And the orange ones are worth a thousand."

"And Kathleen just gave them to you?" Sophie asked. "Nice, she must be doing pretty well up there."

"I can't take these," I said. "You're the client here and Kathleen gave the chips to you. You should use them for a down payment on a house or something."

Susan broke into a beautiful smile and she laughed happily. "No, Kathleen said they were for both of us. Besides, Michael's been as good as his word. This morning, he paid off all of mom's bills as well as mine. We're debt free for the first time in years. As for somewhere to live, it turns out he owns a big house in Paradise Valley. It's actually not too far from Kathleen's. He hasn't lived in it for years, but he's apparently been paying to have it kept up. He said he'd always planned on moving back to Arizona after he retired. We're all moving into it next week. We went over there this morning and oh my God, you should see the view from my bedroom. It even has a private balcony."

Feeling a little less guilty about accepting the gift, I walked over and looked at the chips sitting on Sophie's desk. I lifted the purple chips about an inch, then let them fall back into a stack. They made a very pleasant clinking noise. "Well, if you're sure."

"I'm positive," Susan said. "You risked your life for me and we've become friends. It'd make me feel better if you also got something nice out of it."

"I'd do it if I was you," Sophie said. "Who knows when that cranky cheap-ass boss of ours will give us another bonus."

"Okay," I said. "But if you ever talk to Kathleen again, tell her thank you from me."

"What are you going to do with those chips?" Sophie asked. "They may be worth a lot, but right now they're just pieces of plastic."

"Kathleen talked about that," Susan said. "She said we could mail them to her and she'd cash them in for us. We'd get a check in about a week." Susan then dropped her voice. "She also said if we preferred, she'd give us each a full membership and we could go up to the casino and gamble with them."

At the thought of returning to the casino, I got a cold shiver and a bad case of the heebie-jeebies. "Um," I said, "if I can help it, I'm not getting to within ten miles of that place. Like ever."

"God, no. Me either. I didn't want to hurt Kathleen's feelings, but there's no way I'd ever go back there. I was just going to mail mine in. Do you want me to turn yours in as well?"

"I know how much you like to collect souvenirs," Sophie said.

"But I don't think reminiscing about the Black Castle will give you warm and fuzzy feelings. I'd turn them in."

I looked at the two piles, lifted the orange ones slightly, then let the chips fall back into the stack, just to hear the clinking sound one more time.

"You're right," I said. "Go ahead. Turn them in. I'm starting to dump things on my credit card again. This will help pay everything off."

But as Susan reached for them, I stopped her. "Hold on," I said. I then took a chip off of each stack. I bounced them together in my hand a few times and they made the friendly clinking sound. "Okay, go ahead and turn the rest in. I'll keep these two. You're right about not wanting to think too much about the Black Castle. But we got to know each other as friends during our time together and I'd like something to remind me of that."

"Great minds," Susan said with a laugh. "I'm doing the same thing. I'm keeping two of the chips and turning the rest in. I sort of feel like we've earned these souvenirs."

"Hey," Sophie said. "Laura needs to take off soon. She has a ski date in Colorado. But Gina will be here in a few minutes. Why don't you come to lunch with us? You can tell us all about your escapade."

"Um, sure," Susan said, some hesitation in her voice. "I'd like that." She then looked at me. "Can I talk with you for a minute before you go?"

"Sure, I said. "Come back to my office."

I led Susan through the polished wooden door that leads to the back. We went to the breakroom and each took a chair next to the long table.

"I didn't want to ask in front of Sophie," Susan said, "but what about Jonathan? Those three scary looking men came over yesterday and took him away. That solved the problem for the short term. But what about six months from now? I'm worried he'll hold a grudge and come after us again. Michael's been on the phone a lot, well, when him and mom aren't in the bedroom, and I think a couple of the phone calls were about Jonathan. But when I asked him about it, Michael only told me not to worry about him. I thought you might know something."

"Well, I don't know anything for sure, but unofficially I heard a rumor that Jonathan won't ever bother anyone again."

Susan paused to let it sink in. "That matches with what Michael hinted at. I know I should feel terrible about it, but I can't. Jonathan threatened to kill us more than once and I don't doubt he would've kept trying until he succeeded. Thanks for letting me know."

She seemed to think about it. "Um, all of this will be our secret, won't it? The drug vaults, that scary woman taking out the guards, the shootings, and especially Jonathan. That's the part that's been keeping me awake for the past few nights. I'm the one who started all of this and I'm pretty much responsible for what ended up happening. I'm not so much worried from a legal standpoint, since everything we did was to protect ourselves. But if word of this gets out, if people learn what we did, I don't know who they'll send after us next."

I was going to tell her that none of this was her fault, but I got the feeling that wasn't what she was looking for. I think she was satisfied with the adventure and the outcome, but she didn't want anyone else to know her part in it. In thinking about it, it was a valid concern. I did the only thing I could think of to reassure her of my silence.

I held up my little finger.

"Pinky promise?" I asked.

Susan smiled and I knew this was what she'd been looking for. She held up her finger and we intertwined them.

"Pinky promise," she said.

"Keeping secrets?" Gina asked from across the room. In the concentration of wrapping our fingers around each other, I hadn't heard the back door opening.

We quickly released each other's finger. Susan and I looked at Gina, then back at each other. I put on my best innocent face as I looked back at Gina. "Secrets? Who? Us? No, never."

~~~~

Max and Gabriella showed up at my place right at eleven. She discreetly waited in the hallway, while he came into the apartment.

My two bags and the carry-on were packed and sitting by the door. I'd hoped to be able to put everything into one bag, but the ski outfit and my snow boots took up almost an entire bag by themselves.

After a minute or two of soft passionate kisses, I stepped back to take a good look at Max. He looked different. Instead of wearing his traditional suit or a loose-fitting golf shirt, he was wearing a tight black turtleneck that perfectly showed off his great body.

He caught me looking at him and smiled. He then held up his arms to better show off the shirt. "I know," he said. "It's seventy degrees here in Scottsdale, a little warm perhaps for a turtleneck, but by tonight it'll be in the teens, maybe even the single digits."

"Single digits still sound like something from a science fiction movie, but not to worry, I've come prepared. I even bought a balaclava."

"I'm surprised you know what a balaclava is," he said. "You being from Scottsdale and all. Not much of a call for such things in the desert."

"I guess there's a lot you still don't know about me."

"Oh yeah?" he said with a smile. "Well then, why don't you spend the entire weekend letting me explore you? Maybe I can start to find out some of your secrets."

"That sounds like a good idea," I croaked out. I was finding it somewhat hard to talk with all the hormones bouncing around in me. "I'd really like it if you explored all of my secrets. Although, it might take you more than a weekend, well, if you want to do a good job."

Max leaned over and gave me another kiss. It was soft and our lips barely touched, but I felt my body quiver all the way down to my toes.

"That's okay," he said with a smile. "I'll take my time. I want to do a very good job."

Yes!

About the Author

Halfway through a successful career in technical writing, marketing, and sales, along with having four beautiful children, author B A Trimmer veered into fiction. Combining a love of the desert, derived from many years of living in Arizona, with an appreciation of the modern romantic detective story, the Laura Black Scottsdale Series was born.

Comments and questions are always welcome.
Email the author at: LauraBlackScottsdale@gmail.com

Made in the USA
San Bernardino, CA
26 May 2019